TOR

JENNIE LYNN ROBERTS

First paperback edition November 2021

Editor: O. Ventura at Hot Tree Editing
Cover design by Damonza.com

ISBN 978-1-8383389-6-1 (paperback)
ISBN 978-1-8383389-7-8 (e-book)

www.jennielynnroberts.com

For Frank

"Home is people. Not a place."

Robin Hobb

Acknowledgments

Thank you to everyone who has read and enjoyed these stories! Readers bring a story to life and I'm so grateful to everyone following this adventure with me.

A special thank you goes to Olivia Ventura for her insightful editing wizardry as well as to Donna Pemberton and the rest of the team at Hot Tree for keeping such a close eye on my book-baby. Thank you also to Charlotte Polland at Proof It Plus for her skilled proofreading and generous support, as well as to the awesome design team at Damonza.com for this gorgeous cover.

Thank you to all the amazing people in my life who have supported and encouraged me in pursuing my dream of being a writer. And most importantly, thank you, always, to Mark, Alethea and Michael.

Prologue

*AUGUST – **Night of the Ravenstone Meadow Massacre***

THERE WAS blood under his nails. Dark red, almost black, now that it had dried.

It wasn't the first time his hands had been covered in blood, certainly, but this was the king's blood. Geraint's blood.

Gods. The king's blood was still on his hands, on his torn tunic, even on his boots.

One of the arrows had caught him on his cheek, and the long cut burned relentlessly. More blood. Streaked across his face where he'd tried to wipe it off.

Just a few steps away, through the luxurious suite, was a bathing room with a huge marble bath, creamy soap, and hot water. Water that would soak away the blood and sweat and grime. Fresh linen towels. A fire to ease the chill seeping through his bones like frost spreading over glass.

A bathing room his parents had not invited him to use, and given the tension in the room, weren't about to.

"Tor! Are you even listening to me?" Pellin's lip twitched up, almost into a sneer.

He looked into his father's face. A face so like his own: olive skin, full lips, dimple in his chin, and eyes the color of midnight. Eyes that were now boring into him as if they could see all the way down to the cold in his bones.

"Tor!" Pellin repeated loudly, his voice thick with displeasure and frustration.

Tor shoved his hands behind his back where he didn't have to see the blood. "Sorry, what?"

His father brushed a big hand, heavy with rings, down the pristine fall of his tunic and then folded his arms over his wide chest, red-and-black tattoos rippling as he leaned back to glare at Tor. "How could you do this to us? Just look at your mother."

Tor twisted to look at the elegant woman collapsed on a plush settee. Her dress was deep red velvet—perfectly matched to the tattoos twining around her forearms—offsetting her dark eyes and artfully curled black hair. She was holding a crystal flask of smelling salts loosely in one hand and occasionally dabbing gracefully at her eyes with a lace handkerchief held in the other… although he couldn't see any evidence of actual tears.

Could either of his parents truly be suffering so badly? Really? Here in their lush apartments. Safe and warm in the bosom of the city they never left.

They certainly never scrubbed blood from under their nails. Neither Pellin nor Revna would dream of walking through mud, let alone a battlefield. Or trying to survive the horror that had been Ravenstone.

Tor closed his eyes, remembering the screams, trying—but failing—to push away the images of men falling and dying. Whistled commands breaking through the roar of battle. Carrying the king with Tristan as arrows fell in relentless waves. The king's page staggering as he took an arrow to the chest, and how slowly the boy fell, choking and drowning in his own blood. The horrifying realization that the king was dead, and then the desperate, frantic flight to Kaerlud bearing Geraint's body— and the incriminating Verturian arrows—back to the palace.

They'd not even been back for half an hour when Tristan stormed into the barracks, coming straight from his audience with the new king and bringing news. Their friend —former friend—Lanval had been conspiring with the Verturian princess. Together, Val and Alanna had planned the massacre of Ravenstone.

Val, a man Tor had trusted, had been having an affair with the princess, and now he'd betrayed them all. Gods.

The Hawks had not only failed Geraint, but the new king, Ballanor, had also declared them guilty of treachery by association. They were all demoted. Banned from the palace. Sent down to an obscure cavalry division. Posted far away and leaving within the hour. Lucky not to be thrown into a cell with Val.

Tor had to pack. Get clean. Saddle Perseus. Poor Perseus, already exhausted from the full day's ride to Ravenstone and back, the horror of battle, the long, hard gallop coming home.

But first, before any of that, he'd rushed up to see his parents. He'd wanted to speak to them before he left. Wanted... what? Some kind of reassurance. Wanted the people who cared for him to tell him that all was not lost. That he would be back again someday, and that they would fight to repeal this decision while he was gone. That they would work to get him back.

He didn't expect forgiveness for his failure or even any declarations of their love—they were not that kind of family —but they had power, and they could use it to help their oldest child.

All his life Tor had been the perfect son. He had worked staggeringly hard, excelled at all tests, joined the army as instructed, and climbed the ranks quickly and surely. He'd been everything they wanted: strategically brilliant, known for his iron self-control, and promoted to the Blues—the highest level a soldier could hope to reach. Only twice had he failed them. Once, when he chose to stay with the Hawks. And now.

Somehow, he had believed that all those years of proving himself would count for something. They had pushed him, demanded more from him, but that was how they showed their love. Wasn't it? He had done everything they ever asked. And now, for the first time, he needed something in return.

Pellin was a senior in the Royal Brythorian Council; he could help. Perhaps intercede on the Hawks' behalf. Speak to Ballanor about keeping the squad at the palace. Revna knew everyone of importance. She could help too.... Couldn't she? At the very least, they could offer him their regard. Send him away with their good wishes. Some reassurance that he hadn't lost his entire life on the blood-soaked meadow of Ravenstone.

But, instead, he found himself standing alone in the center of the room, weighed down by their oppressive hostility.

Tor let out a slow breath, struggling to find the right words to answer his father's indignant question. Struggling to understand the anger and resentment churning through his parents—the anger and resentment directed at him.

He was exhausted, too much had been lost, and words did not come easily to him at the best of times. "What exactly did I do to you?" he asked eventually.

"You should have protected the king," his father hissed. "You were the one who insisted on staying with the Hawks even when we told you there were better opportunities. You were the one who said the Hawks were the true king's guards.... And now Geraint is dead."

There was no suitable response. Yes, the king had died in front of him. In his arms, even. Yes, he would gladly have given his life for the king. Yes, he had failed in his duty. He would live with that guilt—that awareness of his failure—every day for the rest of his life.

But he had also been at war for years. Fighting in the desperate campaigns on the bleak northern border and joining the raiding parties creeping through the high mountain passes as their enemies gathered on all sides. He had accepted long ago that people died in battle. Even kings.

The Hawks had been betrayed by the northern princess and her lover, Val. Their secret location handed to their enemies and their strategies revealed by the man who should have been their closest ally.

Gods. A man he had trusted and relied on had deceived them all. Tor had lost his friend, his king, his home, and the position he had worked so hard for. And it was quickly becoming clear that his parents would do nothing to help.

He had known that Pellin and Revna would be thrown into turmoil by the loss of the king. Their noble family had been staunch supporters of the royal line, their lives deeply entrenched in the politics of the council, and their powerful position at court had been intrinsically linked with their allegiance to Geraint. Now the old king was gone, and they would need to quickly switch allegiance to Ballanor, the son Geraint had never respected—the prince that the council, too, had disregarded—or Pellin's position might be threatened.

Stupidly, even knowing that their status at court would be threatened by the loss of Geraint, Tor had not imagined that they would choose to blame him for their precarious politics.

He should have known better. Failure had never been acceptable. Not when he was a child, and certainly not now.

Tor flexed his fingers, fighting the urge to crack his knuckles, knowing how much his mother hated it. "I'm as sorry as you are that Geraint is dead, but there is nothing I can do to change it."

Revna surged to her feet in a flurry of perfume and red velvet. "Yes, there is. You can leave the Hawks and throw yourself on the mercy of King Ballanor. You can support us in keeping this family in its rightful position. Not drag us down with you."

Tor shook his head slowly. "Mother, your position here at court has nothing to do with me. The council will need to—"

"Your behavior reflects on us, Tor," Pellin interrupted. "You are a failure, a risk to this kingdom, and we will be seen in the same light."

Tor held his hands rigidly at his sides, working to keep his voice smooth and polite as he disagreed. "What happened at Ravenstone has no bearing on Ballanor's relationship with the council. Any difficulties you might have with the new king are because of the way the council treated him."

His mother sniffed. "The council supported Geraint. *You* let Geraint die. *You* put us in this position."

Gods. She was determined not to understand. "No, Mother—"

She cut him off. "Your father and I are trying to fix this. If you use this opportunity to prove to Ballanor that you support him, it will reflect well on all of us. Perhaps you know something about the Hawks that you could share? Something that would gain his favor?"

He flinched. Was she genuinely suggesting that he stab his squad in the back in some desperate attempt to curry favor with Ballanor?

He shook his head. "Mother, the Hawks did nothing wrong. You must know that it won't help anything if I go to Ballanor now. The new king has exiled us, trying to force myself into his circle will only make things worse."

Pellin looked at his wife. His lip remained curled, his arms folded over his chest, but otherwise, his emotions were as unreadable as always. Unsurprisingly. The men of their family did not show their feelings. Not ever.

"I told you they were exiled," Pellin muttered toward his wife. "Ballanor wants them gone."

Tor blinked. "You already knew? That we were being demoted?"

"Yes, we already knew." Pellin's nostrils flared. "Everybody knows. The entire court is talking about it. About how you've dishonored our family and shamed us, risked our position here, your brothers' future—"

Tor folded his arms across his chest, mirroring his father. He had failed. And he had brought dishonor to the family. That was true. And yet…. "I was betrayed; we all were. I can't change it, any more than you can change the fact that you voted with Geraint and against Ballanor on the many occasions that the king disagreed with the prince."

Pellin looked Tor up and down, his face blank except for that tiny sneer. "You're right; I can't change that I stood against Ballanor in the past, but I can certainly show him that we stand with him now. I—we—can demonstrate to Ballanor that we do support him, that we have recognized his authority. We can save our position here."

Revna nodded slowly. "You can still fix this, Tor. I accept that you can't go to Ballanor, but you can take up the offer to join the Wraiths. They are Ballanor's men; they'll get you closer to the king. You turned them down before, but that was a mistake. Even you must see that now."

Even him. What did that mean?

He might have asked, but she was still speaking. "Apologize, Tor. Publicly. Ask for a place among the men who have never wavered in their support of our new king. Show them, and Ballanor, where your true loyalty lies. Where *our* loyalty lies."

Tor let his head hang down for a moment before raising his chin tiredly and meeting her eyes. He had never wanted to be a part of the Wraiths. Never wanted the status or the riches enough to justify the politics or the ruthless maneuvering that they excelled at.

Yes, the Hawks were never rewarded as richly or given the status that the Wraiths had—but in the end, it was still the Hawks the king had trusted as his personal guard. Precisely because they couldn't be bought. And now it was too late anyway. "Mother, the Wraiths are gone. None of them returned from the massacre at Ravenstone."

Revna waved his words away. "That can't—"

Tor interrupted her. "Men died today, Mother. Many of

them. I've seen the squads returning, and the Wraiths were not among them. Changing allegiance is not an option."

Pellin looked at his wife. "Do you see now, Revna? There is only one choice if we are to save our position here at court. We have to purge the shame, swiftly and cleanly. We have to take immediate action, provide our new king with a strong, tangible demonstration so there is no doubt where our loyalties lie."

Revna stepped up beside her husband, hands clasped tightly in front of her. She looked at Tor for a moment, her eyes almost black in her pale face, and then she looked back at Pellin.

She was quiet for a long moment, but then she dipped her chin firmly. "Yes, husband. You're right, there's nothing else to be done. The Hawks are responsible for the death of King Geraint, and Ballanor blames Tor and his squad. I didn't want to accept it... but there really is only one option left."

Gods, he was tired. Tor ran a dirty hand around the back of his neck and gripped the tight muscles as he tried to understand the sudden change in the conversation. "What is our only option?" he asked.

Pellin and Revna stood side by side, staring back at him.

The silence stretched painfully as they watched each other—Tor on one side, still covered in the king's blood; his parents on the other, pristine in their lavish court costumes. The room was so quiet that he could hear his own ragged breathing, even the sound of his heart thudding.

Pellin cleared his throat and then turned away, so that his back was to Tor, and took Revna's hands. "Wife, I'm sorry to tell you that Tor, son of Pellin, son of Bar-Ulf, died this day in the massacre of Ravenstone Meadow."

What?

"What are you saying?" Tor asked slowly. But no one answered.

His mother sniffled and leaned against his father. "My son is dead. Gods. My oldest son." A genuine sob rocked her body.

It was as if a vise had clamped over his lungs, squeezing his ribs with a malevolent grip that drove the air from his body. He had obviously misheard. Obviously. They wouldn't renounce him like this. Would they? Surely their position at court wasn't so valuable to them that they would... what? Disown him? They weren't even looking at him, for fuck's sake.

He had to force his words past the blockage in his throat. "I don't understand."

Neither of them answered him.

"Mother—" He fought for the right words. How could he possibly convince them that his life had value? That he was worthy of their protection. Their love. That this failure shouldn't mean his death in their eyes.

He had heard of other noble families where the children had been cast out for bringing shame on their parents. But he had never, not even in his worst nightmares, imagined that it could happen to him.

Pellin wrapped an arm around Revna, holding her close as he spoke into the room. "Our son is dead, and we may grieve his loss. The new king will reward this huge sacrifice made in his name. And then, when we have mourned, we will bring our remaining sons back to court and present them to King Ballanor as his servants."

"No. Gods. I'm standing right here!"

Pellin ignored him completely, but Revna glanced at him through her tears. She was genuinely upset. Surely, she would do something. Anything. She could change Pellin's mind. Couldn't she? If she wanted to?

His mother's voice was muffled and watery. "Ballanor will see what our family has lost. You're right, husband; he will understand this sacrifice."

This sacrifice? Who was making this sacrifice? Not them. *Him.* Gods. He had to stop this. Had to show them, somehow.

Tor stepped forward, reaching toward his parents. His family. The foundation of who he was in the world. The people who were supposed to stand beside him. He supported them, and they supported him. Didn't they? "Don't do this. Please."

His mother flinched back, body arching as she avoided his touch and turned her face away, and he froze, hand still hanging in the air.

"Mam?" His voice broke on the word, the desperate plea that tore out from deep inside him, taking him back to a time when he was a little boy and she was his mama. But she still didn't look at him.

"Father, I—"

Pellin cut him off. "We don't want strangers in our rooms. Can't you see that you're upsetting my wife? If you don't leave, we'll call the guards."

Tor clasped his hands in front of his belly, trying to hold himself together. "The guards? I'm your son!"

Pellin shook his head. "My sons are in the country with their tutor. You are no one to me."

The words buzzed in his ears as the need to retch forced its way up his throat. "*I* am your son. You can't do this."

Pellin spun toward the door, face set cold and hard. "Guards!"

"No—"

"Guards! Help!"

Help? Who would the guards choose to help? The dirty soldier still covered in the blood of Ravenstone or the respected councilor and his sobbing wife? Gods. There was no doubt; the guards would arrest him. And prison would be even worse than this nightmare. Finding himself in a cell beside Val, that would be worse. Wouldn't it?

He took a deep breath, reaching for his last reserves. Trying to find the clarity of battle. That place where he locked his feelings deep in ice. He needed that sharpness. Needed to remove all emotion if he was to move. To act.

He could do this. He could keep himself together and walk away. He pulled on every ounce of the self-control he was known for and took a step. And then another.

They had really done it. They had seen his failure and cut him from their lives as if amputating a gangrenous limb.

Tor forced himself out of his parents' rooms, hardly noticing where he was going, barely aware of his mother sobbing while his father closed and locked the door behind him.

He had thought he had lost his king, his friend, and his position in the palace. In reality, he had also lost his family, his heritage, and his entire understanding of the world. All in one day.

He was adrift in a ruthless, treacherous ocean with no oars and no land to rest on. He was of so little value that he could be thrown away again and again.

Nothing made sense. It might never make sense again. But if he didn't think about it—if he didn't let himself feel it —he would be okay.

That was the key. He had to make sure that he didn't feel.

He let a cold numbness sweep over him and settle down

his spine. It allowed him to walk that long corridor, down the stairs, and into the barracks. It allowed him to gather his things and ride out with the Hawks. To keep his eyes forward and his head down. It allowed him to leave the place he'd thought of as home and never once look back.

Chapter One

SEPTEMBER—THE palace at Kaerlud—King Ballanor's banquet

THE BEAT of bass drums thudded hard against Tor's breastbone, the accompanying vielle and high soprano providing an eerie, melancholy counterpoint that scratched at his nerves like a blade down glass.

Tor tugged at the collar of his new tunic. So new that the blue dye still gave off a bitter reek that burned the back of his throat and caught in his lungs. He wanted to strip it off his body and fling it into the frothing waters of the fountain that dominated the palace courtyard…. Along with the extra tunic gripped too tightly in his fist.

Instead, he forced himself to stand still, swathed in shadows beside the wall. Keeping himself, and his thoughts, tightly controlled.

Walking out the palace with his parents' words still

ringing in his ears, he hadn't imagined he would ever be back. He definitely hadn't imagined that he would be back like this. Wearing the Blue. Spare tunic in his hand. About to finally, irrevocably, blow up his life.

Those long weeks that the Hawks had spent living in exile, scratching out an existence in a bleak corner of the kingdom, were already a blur. Those strange, numb days had come to a sudden, brain-jarring end with the arrival of the messengers bringing a new mission—capture Val's sister, Nim, hand her to Lord High Chancellor Grendel for execution, and be pardoned for their role in Ravenstone. One easy mission and they would be welcomed back into the palace. Blue Guards once more.

It had seemed perfect. The first thing in weeks to break him from the chilly impassivity he'd wrapped himself in. The opportunity to take back their place in the Blues and for him to prove to his family that he was worthy. To show them all that he was good enough. To show *himself* that he was good enough.

But it had all been lies. Grendel was a sadistic bastard of the worst kind. And Ballanor, presumably, just the same. The soldiers serving under the new king had been allowed, encouraged even, in the worst cruelties. And he hadn't seen it until Nim forced them all to truly open their eyes.

But now he knew the truth, and he couldn't stomach serving under Ballanor ever again.

Boots ringing on the courtyard cobbles broke into his thoughts, and he pushed himself further back into the shadows as a small unit of the new Blue Guards dragged a woman down the opposite corridor.

He knew her instantly—Keely, the queen's maid. He had seen her in the palace before, even guarded her as part of his duties on occasion, but never paid her any attention. She'd merely been the companion to the difficult, tantrum-prone Verturian princess—the princess everyone had loathed—not someone he needed, or wanted, to know.

But now he was questioning everything. Was any of the gossip about the queen true? Nim was adamant that they had made a terrible mistake in misjudging Alanna and Val. That they had abandoned Val when he needed them most. And now, for the first time, he considered just how awful living at court had been for Alanna. And, also for the first time, he looked properly at Keely.

She was barefoot, wearing only a short, sleeveless muslin shift that showed the green bands of stylized Verturian knots tattooed around her biceps. Her arms and legs were bare, her red-blond hair falling loose down to her waist. Despite her athletic build, she seemed petite and delicate beside the burly guards hemming her in on both sides.

One of her guards carried a chain that led to a brutal ankle shackle. The chain clanked against the cobbles with every step. Gods. She must have been freezing in the chilly wind, nothing between her small feet and the cold, hard stone.

She looked like a sacrifice to the ancient gods, vulnerable and alone. But her chin was high, her shoulders down, and her fists clenched. Utterly defiant. And beautiful. Not with a soft, sweet prettiness, but with the striking beauty of windswept plains and stars over the ocean.

She stared straight ahead as she walked, untamed and uncowed, not looking at anyone or anything except the path ahead of her, and she didn't see him, swathed in shadows beside the wall.

If the first flicker of feeling to break through his icy

numbness had come with the chance for their redemption, this was the second. A spark of admiration flared deep inside him. Admiration—awe, even—for her strength and her fierce beauty.

The thought was swiftly followed by the unsettling realization that as glorious as she was, his family would hate everything about her. Her foreign customs, her red hair and creamy skin, her bare forearms—with no proud red-and-black tattoos to represent her family's heritage—and her green encircled biceps. Even the way she stood up for herself and defied the fate that she'd been handed.

When the messengers had arrived, breaking their exile and offering the Hawks their place back in the palace, he had imagined taking up his blue tunic once more. He'd imagined sauntering into the palace, reveling in the look on his parents' faces when they realized he was back. Imagined what it would feel like to atone for the mistakes he had made and buy himself another chance.

But now those thoughts filled him with a rumbling unease. This entire court was rotten, and that must surely include the people who had given him life.

He gripped the tight muscles at the back of his neck, anchoring himself. He needed to stop thinking about Pellin and Revna. Had to stop imagining their dubious approval. He should have cut them out of his mind as easily as they had cut him out of their lives, but he hadn't, and now he was on the cusp of finally ending any chance he ever had of returning to the palace.

Strategy had always come naturally to him. Planning each step. Predicting the unguarded flank or the unwatched pass. That had been his role in the Hawks—setting the pieces into exactly the right positions so that moving one meant all the others fell into place, one after the other.

Now, standing in the courtyard, the water of the fountain tinkling behind him, he was one final move away. About to set everything in play so that the pieces could fall. And they could fall in either direction—depending on which way he pushed. He could betray Nim in truth and be richly rewarded by Ballanor, promoted back into the Blues, perhaps as captain. Maybe even get his family back, exactly as he'd wished for. Or he could turn his back on everything he'd worked so hard for—accept that he would never again be welcome in his home or family, that he would always be the failure, the child who disgraced their family name and was disowned as a result—and try to save Nim and Val.

Honestly, there was only one possible choice he could make. Only one choice he was ever going to make. No matter what it cost him.

He followed the path Keely had taken and then turned to the side when he reached the open doors to the great hall, to hide in the shadows once more.

Keely had been locked in chains, and yet she had glowed with fire and life. While here he was, watching from the darkness, palms sweating as he gripped the tunic he had worked for years to earn.

Inside the hall, the music faltered and the crowds fell deathly silent, Ballanor's voice rang out clearly in the oppressive hush. "I told you you'd get on your knees for me eventually."

There was only one person Ballanor would be talking to —the woman dragged before him in chains. Keely. Gods.

Seconds later, Queen Alanna was shoved into the hall by her own set of brutal guards. One side of her face was purple and swollen, her lip split. Had the king done that to her? Had she always seemed so exhausted? So alone?

Tor closed his eyes for a moment, but it didn't help the

disgust rising through his belly like vinegar. Disgust at Ballanor. Disgust at Grendel. Disgust at himself and just how much he'd missed.

He opened his eyes again and paced further away from the door, wishing he could escape the horror unfolding inside the hall. Wishing he could be anywhere else in the kingdom. Wishing he was not about to walk into that hall and declare his support for Ballanor.

He was going to look Nim and Tristan in the eye and make them believe it too. Fuck.

He had frightened Nim before, with his anger and his judgments about her brother, Val. Now he was going to convince her that she had been betrayed by the man she loved.

It was going to hurt. But it was the only way to save them.

Keeping his mouth shut in Gatehouse Prison, taking his beating in silence, and meekly following orders—none of it had helped. They had dragged him to the Constable's Tower and he'd been recognized by the guards. Even before Grendel had arrived to interrogate him, the Lord High Chancellor had known exactly who Tor was. There was no way to hide it.

Instead, Tor had spent the time in his cell working on a plan. The only plan he had to save them all. He would have to take on the Blue and convince Tristan to leave Nim with Grendel and Ballanor so that they could come back later and free her. Her and Val. The friend they'd all abandoned. Whose torture the other guards had been only too willing to discuss in all its awful detail. Yet another failure on his record.

Maybe, just maybe, there was a chance. They would free

Nim and her brother, and one day Val would forgive him. Tristan too. One day, Nim might understand that he was doing the best he could to get them out.

He was dead to his parents and his brothers—never to be loved by them again, never to see them ever again. The only family he had left was his squad. And if they sent him away, he had no idea what he would do.

Gods. *Please let this work.*

He had wandered far enough that the words in the hall were muffled by the pouring fountain, and there were long quiet moments when he heard nothing over the water, when he could only imagine someone was speaking too quietly to be heard. Val, perhaps.

Tor groaned. As much as he didn't want to face the nightmare in the hall, he couldn't hide any longer. He had to know what was happening. He stepped up to the door and looked in just as Keely lifted her chin and set her gaze on Ballanor. "Val is *my* lover. We planned the massacre at Ravenstone together. The queen never had anything to do with it."

Alanna tried to stop her, but Keely continued as the court watched in riveted, appalled fascination. "It was me. I hated this kingdom, and I hated this court. I've detested every minute of the time I've spent here."

Keely was magnificent. A true warrior. When the time came to face his own end, he hoped he would have half the conviction, half the bravery that she did. And he couldn't blame her for her bitter hostility; he was starting to hate Ballanor's court himself.

He wished he could have known her before. Wished he had spoken to her, even once, before the world came crashing down.

Then he heard the words he had been dreading—Ballanor's prepared speech. "Traitors die. And their loved ones are purged from the earth. Lovers. Fathers... even sisters. Let this be a lesson to you all."

That was his cue. As agreed with Grendel.

Tor's boots clicked on the marble floor, loud in the silence, as all eyes watched him striding forward. Eyes filled with fear. Hatred. Suspicion. And a few gleaming with jealousy and their own plans for seizing power in this corrupt court.

He couldn't help looking over the crowd until he found them. His parents. They were watching him with stoic faces but an aura of approval. As if they knew what he'd offered the Lord High Chancellor. The bargain he'd made. As if they were glad he would denounce Val and sacrifice Nim. The thought churned through him, filling him with conflicted horror—he had come from that family.

He blanked his face, and strode forward, forcing himself to ignore the expression on Nim's face. It was by far the worst of all. Her eyes were wide and devastated, utterly betrayed, as she spun, looking frantically around her, searching for an escape. There was none.

He shoved away the rioting mass of revulsion that surged through him, reaching for the calm detachment he would need to make it through the next five minutes. He swallowed the rising bile back down his throat, clapped Tristan on the shoulder, and made himself smile. "You did it, brother."

Tristan stared back at him, face shuttered. As stoic and as guarded as Tor hoped he also was. They had to be equally composed. Equally committed. If Tristan disagreed now, they were all lost.

Tor's ears rang, the buzz so loud he could hardly hear Nim calling for Tristan or his own voice as he gripped Tristan's shoulder and leaned down to whisper, "Trust me." And then, too low for even Tristan to hear, he added, "Please."

Chapter Two

KEELY CLUNG to the slick rocks of the moat, buffeted by the freezing waves, trying to keep her head above the water.

Bard. They were out of the palace. The Hawks had arrived and freed her, Nim, and Val. Standing in front of Ballanor, Val chained to the wall behind him, she hadn't imagined it could be possible.

The pounding agony down her arm from where the arrow had struck her shoulder during their flight was making it impossible to get a good grip with that hand, and the cold was leaching the last of her reserves as quickly as the wound had been spilling blood. At least the cold might slow it down.

Nim was doing her best to help, but she was also struggling, and the heavy chain between them dragged and pulled with the current. All Keely could do was cling to the rocks, hold her face out of the water, and focus on sucking in one burning breath at a time.

One of their rescuers—the captain had called him Jos—treaded water, urgently gesturing for Nim to swim toward them and the boat they had brought to escape in. But Nim shook her head, her exhausted shivers rattling down the chain.

"I c-can't let go," Nim whispered. "Keely's hurt. And the ch-chain...."

The biggest of the guards, the Apollyon from the banquet hall, swam closer, joining Jos. "Nim, can you pass Keely to me?"

There was a long, loaded moment as Nim stared at the guard and he stared back. He was the guard they'd thought had betrayed them all. But there must have been more to it —he had returned with the rest of the squad, he had searched the palace for them, fled with them, and found them a way out. He had helped save Nim and Val. And her.

"C-can y-you help me?" Nim whispered through blue lips. "I'm trying, but I c-can't let go."

It was hard to tell in the dim light, but Keely imagined she saw his face soften slightly. In relief, perhaps. As if he'd been afraid that Nim would refuse him.

He swam closer and then reached out to hold her, and suddenly Keely had help. Her face was clear of the water and she could breathe.

The Apollyon pulled her gently into his arms and cradled her against his chest. He was so big and warm that she found herself wanting to curl into him. Wanting to hold on to him. Bard. That was a bad sign.

"I'm Tor," he whispered.

She lifted her head, leaning back so she could look at him properly, and whispered, "Can I trust you, soldier?"

He looked down at her, dark eyes sincere, his grip firm but careful where he held her. "Yes. You can trust me with your life."

Maybe it was the freezing cold burning through her

body to her bones. Maybe it was the throbbing torment in her shoulder—she had snapped the wooden arrow shaft off as close to her shoulder as she could while they stood in the darkness of the tunnel, but the arrowhead still grated, shredding muscle and sinew with every movement. Or maybe it was the conviction in his deep voice. Whatever it was, she found herself believing him.

She had watched him in the great hall as he'd handed the blue tunic to Tristan. Everyone else had been riveted on the drama of Nim calling to Tristan as she was dragged away. None of them had been watching the powerfully built Blue Guard standing quietly to the side. But she had.

She had seen him flinch. Seen how his shoulders had curled over, just a fraction, before he straightened and glared out at the crowd. It was enough for her to recognize the movement. The instinctive need to protect your vulnerable belly as the world disintegrated around you. And the need to fight back.

Oh, his face had been grim and blank, unmoved, but she'd seen blank faces like that before. She'd seen her own in the mirror.

It hadn't meant anything to her at the time. Tor's guilt at his and Tristan's betrayal was irrelevant compared to the horror of their immediate future as she and Nim were dragged to the king's rooms.

It had left her mind completely in the devastating, utterly disastrous moment when Alanna had sacrificed herself so they could escape, and they had been forced to leave her behind.

But then the Hawks had come for them, and despite everything, Nim trusted them. And they trusted Tor. They had followed Tor as he led them safely out and it had suddenly made sense. He had never betrayed them. He had bought his squad access into the palace, and he had paid for it at the cost of his reputation and any chance he might have had for a future in Kaerlud. Bard. An honorable Blue. Who would have thought it was possible?

Keely tucked herself into his chest and tried to help as best she could as he swam them out to the small boat and then lifted her over the side, still chained to Nim.

The movement jarred her shoulder, and she gritted her teeth, forcing herself not to howl. Tor climbed in beside her and gently helped her to move so that she half-lay, half-sat, propped against his legs. Lanval lay unconscious at her feet, Nim beside her in the darkness. The squad piled in around them, all covered by a heavy tarpaulin as they flew through the water.

Long moments passed until the tarpaulin that had shielded them from the archers on the battlements was pushed away and she could breathe. And as she breathed, she whispered half-formed prayers. *Please let Alanna be okay. Please forgive me for leaving her. Please. Bard.*

Guilt and shame swam heavily through her gut. Leaving her friend behind with Ballanor and Grendel was the worst thing she'd ever done. And it hurt even worse than the arrow in her shoulder. It was her only job. Her only role and meaning in the world—protecting Alanna. And she had failed at the worst possible time.

Keely fought against the tears that threatened to clog her throat. She forced herself to focus on the dip and slide of the oars. On Lanval's ragged breathing. On Tor's steady presence. She had no choice other than to leave Alanna behind, but she could choose not to fall apart.

She began to settle into a strangely detached daze. Weeks of terror culminating in the debacle at the banquet and then abandoning Alanna were followed now by seeping, icy cold, and the relentless throbbing in her shoulder and down her arm.

Her prayers merged into the rhythm of the oars. The whispered commands and discussions around her disappeared into the distance, and the cold receded. Even the pain in her shoulder didn't bother her as much.

She closed her eyes and drifted, enjoying the slow warmth spreading over her.

She could finally rest. Finally. She was warm and safe. And so tired. So very tired. Now she would sleep. And forget she'd left Alanna.

The wind rocked her gently, and she remembered an old lullaby her mother sang so many years ago. A song from the earliest days of her people. Remembered it as if she could hear it even now.

Lullaby, close your eyes,
When you sleep, baby,
Dream of me.
Darling child, close your eyes,
We are safe here,
Safe and free.
Lullaby, baby girl—

"No." A rough voice broke into her dream, but she refused to allow it. She kept her eyes closed and chased that feeling, that detached warmth, back down into the darkness.

Someone shook her. "Wake up, Keely."

What? Why? She tried to open her eyes, but that made her shiver, and the shivering jostled the arrow. Bard. She heard a low, pained groan and wondered if someone else was as miserable as she was.

"No more sleeping for you," Tor stated, lifting her into his arms, the chain clanking between her and Nim. Bard, it hurt like a bitch. "It's time to go."

Wait… had they stopped? Were they walking?

The arrow digging into her shoulder roused her, but she kept her eyes closed, wishing she could go back to the safe, warm dream. "Just leave me."

"No." Tor stopped walking. Thank the Bard. But then there was a tug as her chained arm was pulled to the side.

There was a loud clang somewhere nearby, and she flinched. The thick arms under her knees and around her back tightened, holding her more firmly. "I've got you, Keely." Tor's voice was deep and reassuring but threaded through with concern. "One more."

There was another loud clang, too loud to sleep through, and suddenly the tension on her arm relaxed and then they were moving again.

She forced her eyes open to see that Tor was carrying her through a genteel home. Flickering lamp and candlelight gleamed off polished woods and heavy drapes. "Where are we?" Her words came out as an exhausted whisper.

"Reece found us somewhere to stay," Tor replied.

She was too exhausted to ask anything more. Instead, she let her head drop down onto his chest. Let her eyes drift closed.

Tor's voice rumbled in her ear. "Sorry, Keely, I can't let you do that. Stay awake for me."

"I don't want to." Bloody hell. Did her voice sound as miserable and whiny to him as it did to her? She forced herself to keep her eyes open.

Tor chuckled, and the sound reverberated around her. "We need to get the arrow out and help you warm up. Then you can sleep."

When last had anyone held her? So, so long ago. She was the strong one. The capable one. The person everyone could depend on. It was so much easier that way. If she didn't need anyone, they could never leave her all alone.

She should tell him to put her down and walk the rest of the way. But she was too tired, too sore, and too heartbroken over leaving her friend.

"Here we are." Tor pushed open a door with his foot and carried her into a cozy room with a comfortable-looking bed and wide wingback chair, all decorated in rich browns and greens. The room was lit by a lamp and warmed by a small, cheerful fire, and a fresh set of clothes lay waiting at the bottom of the bed. It was almost too perfect to be real.

"Can you stand?" Tor asked.

She wanted to say no, to enjoy being held just for a few more moments, but that wasn't her. She could—would—make herself stand. "Yes."

Tor lowered her gently to the floor in front of the fire, leaving an arm around her, stabilizing her, as she found her feet. "You have to get out of those wet clothes. Jeremiel left a shirt and some clean trousers, but—" He paused as if looking for the right words.

"But the arrow is pinning the jerkin into my shoulder," she finished for him.

Tor grunted. "Yes."

She frowned, looking for a solution, but knowing there wasn't one. She couldn't do it alone. Damn. "I'm going to need some help getting undressed."

Tor dipped his chin. "I'll go get Nim."

"Bard, no." Nim was in no state to come and help her. And the last thing Keely wanted was to pull her away from Val and Tristan, especially after accusing Nim of intentionally abandoning Alanna. That had not been her finest moment.

She swallowed. And then did her best to straighten her spine. "Can't you help me?"

"What about Val?" he asked slowly.

Val? What did Val have to do with anything? Oh…. She let out a small snort. "Val is not my lover."

"But—"

"Val loves Alanna."

Tor gave her a confused look. "He… what?"

Keely tried to smile. "He loves Alanna. They love each other. But she couldn't…. Not with Ballanor as her husband. Val is a friend. I just said that because—" She shrugged. "I thought I was going to die anyway, and it might have helped Alanna. She's suffered enough."

Tor blinked slowly, one hand raising to grip the back of his neck as he watched her silently. The fire hissed and crackled as the moment stretched on, and she realized that he was not going to say anything. Because he was horrified that Val and Alanna loved each other—a Verturian and a Brythorian? Or because….

She sighed. "They did not plan the massacre at Ravenstone."

He narrowed his eyes. "I didn't say they did."

"Yes. Well. I'm sure you were thinking it."

"No, I—" He dropped his hand from his neck and cracked his knuckles instead. "Okay. I blamed them before. Not now."

"Not now?"

He shook his head but didn't say anything more. And it was enough. He had rescued them, after all. And she still needed help.

First, she had to get rid of her breeches so she could sit down without destroying the chair with muddy water. Then they could focus on her jerkin and the arrow.

"I need you to pull my breeches down," she prompted. "I can't do it with one hand. The leather is soaked, and they were already too tight. They're Alanna's."

Tor glanced down at her breeches and then immediately looked away and took a small step back. Damn. He really was honorable. Keely lifted a heavy woolen blanket off the bed and wrapped it over her shoulders to hang down to her knees. She never asked for help. Not unless there was absolutely no other choice, and right now there was no other choice. "I need your help, Tor. I don't ask often, so make the most of it."

"Are you sure I'm the best person?" he asked slowly.

No. She was not at all sure. The last man she'd been even partially naked in front of was Niall. And that was ten years ago. But she was too exhausted and too cold to stay as she was, and her shoulder was on fire, her fingers tingling with waves of burning pins and needles. She couldn't do it alone. "Yes. I'm sure."

He nodded, once, and then knelt in front of her and helped her out of her boots. She balanced herself on his shoulder with her good hand, and he tucked his thumbs into the waistband of her breeches and tugged.

It was hard work, the tight, wet leather clinging to her cold skin, and she had to shimmy her body to help him pull the breeches down. They stuck, and he grunted as he shifted his thumbs and tried again.

Bard. She wasn't at all sleepy now. Even with the relentless ache in her shoulder, she was acutely aware of his big hands, the heat of his fingers where they ran down her legs, how close he was to her body.

The breeches suddenly came away, and she stepped out of them, one foot at a time. He stood and lifted the sodden leather away to dry beside the fire, returning as she sank into the comfortable armchair.

"What about your jerkin?" he asked slowly.

There was only one solution. "Cut it off."

Tor watched her for a moment but then nodded. "Okay." He pulled out a lethal-looking dagger and began slicing through the laces while she held the blanket swathed around her body and over her chest.

It was a strange kind of dance. Trying to hold the blanket out of the way but at the same time cover herself. All while keeping her injured shoulder still. She was deeply, intensely aware of the closeness between them. Of how big he was, and yet how carefully—tenderly almost—he was helping her.

If he hadn't been so close, she might have thought he was unaffected. His face was stoic, completely shuttered, and he hadn't said a word since he'd taken out his knife. But she could see his Adam's apple bobbing as he swallowed. Could feel the way his breath picked up. And she knew that he was as aware of her as she was of him.

Eventually, he was able to pull the pieces of the jerkin away, leaving only a small circle of leather surrounding the shaft of the arrow.

Tor helped her to thread her good arm into the dry cotton of the shirt that had been left for her, working it over the top of the blanket, and cleared his throat. "Will you be alright if I go and get Rafe, our healer?"

Keely leaned her head back against the chair, fighting the urge to say no, she would not be alright if he left. Bard. What was wrong with her? First, she wanted him to hold her. Now she wanted him to stay. This stranger. This *soldier*. She forced herself to reply. "Yes, I'll be fine. Thank you."

"Don't go to sleep."

She chuckled. "I won't."

He narrowed his eyes at her, still not moving for the door, and she let out a huff. So, this was what it was like to be coddled by a burly, frowning mama duck. It was strangely soothing. "I won't go to sleep. I promise I'll wait for the healer."

Tor nodded silently and left.

The room felt so much colder without him in it. So much lonelier. But that was her life. That was what she was used to. A long line of lonely rooms.

For a moment, she let herself imagine what it would be like to have a man like Tor run his fingers down her legs in a different way. To touch her with desire. To look up at her with those dark eyes filled with heat instead of worry. To have someone care for her and protect her.

It was a nice dream. But not for her. She trusted him with her life, but not with her body. And not with her heart. Never again would she risk that kind of devastation.

Tor was back within a couple of minutes, accompanied by a friendly-looking Nephilim with deep purple-blue eyes, wide shoulders, and a leather case in his hands.

Tor gestured the man forward. "This is Rafe. He's the healer."

Keely chuckled. She'd gathered that much already.

Rafe smiled in response. "Tor says you were shot."

"Yeah." She pulled the blanket back so he could see the arrowhead embedded in the front of her shoulder. It had started to bleed again, and her arm ached relentlessly.

"Where's the shaft?" Rafe asked.

"I broke it off."

Both men frowned, but it was Rafe who replied. "That must have hurt."

"Hurt a lot less than having the head constantly pulled

by the shaft."

Rafe nodded slowly. "Been shot before?"

Actually, no. But there'd been plenty of former soldiers in Verturia who had. Soldiers who had fought against men like Tor and Rafe. Maybe even fought against Tor and Rafe themselves.

She wanted to blame them. Bard knew she'd spent long enough hating the Blues under Ballanor. But she'd also watched Val and Alanna together. Seen him sacrifice everything for her again and again. She couldn't blame Val, and she couldn't blame his friends either. No. She blamed the kings who'd sent them there to die.

Damn, she was maudlin.

She shook off the thought and did her best to grin. "Not myself, no. But I know my way around a bow and arrow. Crossbow even better."

Tor narrowed his eyes at her, as if aware that she had forced herself to smile when it was the last thing she felt like doing, but he didn't say anything. Instead, he moved to stand at her side while Rafe opened his case out onto the bed. Inside, she could see bottles and bandages, gleaming knives.

"I'm going to have to cut it out," Rafe said softly. "But I'll do what I can to… encourage it."

"Encourage it?"

Rafe shrugged, and she looked at Tor instead. "It's a Nephilim healer thing. They don't explain."

Rafe poured something into his hands and carefully rubbed it into his skin. A sudden astringent smell made her eyes water as he looked through his case and selected a blade.

Keely looked away. Pain was one thing. Watching it happen was something else entirely. She felt Rafe's hand settle beside the arrow, but instead of the sharp pain she was expecting, her body filled with a slow, spreading warmth. Far more soothing than the darkness she'd drifted into earlier.

She gritted her teeth, waiting for the pain to start, and turned her head toward the window. "Will you open the curtains, Tor?"

"Of course." He pulled the heavy fabric back, letting in the cool air. Bard. She had always loved the open air. It was one of the things she'd missed the most when they left Duneidyn—feeling the wind against her face as it blew down off the mountains. Well, that, and feeling safe.

It was pitch-dark outside the window, and the lamplight shone on the glass, turning it into a hazy mirror. She could see the room, herself, and Rafe working on her arm. But mostly, she could see Tor.

He was everything Niall was not. Tor was big and muscular and gruff where Niall was lean and always smiling. Tor, unlike Niall, was a man of very few words and rigorously contained emotions. His face was hard, but his mouth was full and soft. Bard. She should *not* be looking at his mouth.

Rafe tugged something in her shoulder, and pain crackled down her arm. And then Tor was there, picking up her other hand and holding it in his.

She concentrated on that. On the feeling of his rough hand in hers. On his solid, anchoring presence. On the low rumble of his voice when he spoke to Rafe. He had an amazing voice. So deep and resonant, she could feel it vibrating through her entire body.

She concentrated on the feeling of his hand, on the sound of his voice, and she kept her eyes firmly on the window—watching Tor.

Chapter Three

KEELY STRODE across the clearing and peered down the path. Still empty. Damn it to the Abyss. Should she stand there staring into the quiet woods? Or do another lap of the clearing?

Nim and Tristan were talking quietly on one side of the small glade while Mathos stood on the other, staring up at the passing clouds. Tor sat just behind her. All of them were waiting impatiently for news of Alanna. To find out whether the Hawks' desperate rescue had succeeded.

Keely had left Alanna behind and Ballanor had wasted no time in arranging her friend's execution. Val had taken the other Mabin and flown back to Kaerlud to save her, but the rest of them had to wait.

She bit her lip—a bad habit she had developed after Niall had died. One she had tried to break, but never quite managed—she had needed it, that sting, the bite of pain reminding her she was still alive. It kept her grounded in what *was*, rather than lost in what should have been or might have been.

"Why don't you find something to do?" Tor rumbled from his seat on the log behind her. "It'll help."

She spun around and glared at him—him and that deep voice, richer and smoother than the dark chocolate of the Sasanians. The voice that had anchored her in the icy churn of the heaving ocean and rumbled quietly beside her as Rafe drew out the arrow.

Tor had cared for her in the farmhouse that had been their brief refuge. He'd helped her hide when Grendel had found them, and he'd ridden beside her as they made their harried escape, following Nim as she flew off to find and rescue Tristan with the other Mabin, killing Grendel in the process.

He had stayed with her as they fled north, staying off the roads, keeping to the shadows, looking for somewhere to hide until they could rescue Alanna. Tor had helped her to set up a tent when her exhausted body had rebelled and the agonizing ache in her shoulder threatened to overwhelm her, and distracted her when the constant fear for Alanna made her want to throw her head back and howl.

It was Tor who had woken her from her broken sleep, bringing her to the campfire where Jeremiel was explaining that Alanna was going to be executed that day; that her friend was due to die at noon. Tor who had helped the Hawks plan the mission, sitting beside her, his strength a solid, reassuring wall that she wished she could lean on. And Tor who had looked her in the eye and promised that he trusted the Hawks to get Alanna back. He'd promised her like he believed it. And, Bard help her, she believed *him*.

She couldn't remember anyone spending that much time quietly supporting her in her entire life.

Ordinarily, she wouldn't need it; ordinarily, she wrapped a wall of competence around herself, too high for anyone else to consider breaching. But she hadn't been able to maintain that wall with Tor. He'd helped... and she'd let him.

A riot of emotions seethed through her, one after the other: guilt, shame, sorrow, fear, all woven through with hope. She was responsible for Alanna. And Alanna was going to die if the Hawks didn't reach her in time.

Keely had come to Kaerlud as Alanna's maid because it was the only role that Prince Ballanor would accept—no companions were allowed for the Princess of Verturia, but servants were another matter. Or rather, one servant.

In reality, their mothers were cousins, and they were friends, though Alanna was a little younger and a lot sweeter. Keely felt responsible for her. And she had bloody left her. Oh, she knew all the reasons why it had been the right thing to do, but it didn't help. Not now, standing alone to watch the empty path.

Val had taken Jos and Garet with him when he left to rescue Alanna. Ballanor's new army was decidedly lacking in Mabin soldiers, and the poorly trained new Blues hadn't seemed to be aware that they'd left the skies wide open. That was how they'd get to Alanna. Tor's plan was for Val and the other Mabin to sneak into Kaerlud, flying in via the cemetery, grab Alanna from the main square and then fly her back out.

It was a good plan—the right plan—but only those with wings could go. All Keely could do was wait. She was forced to watch them leave, unable to help, unable to do anything useful at all. And if there was one thing that she really, truly hated, it was waiting for someone to come back. It was even worse than watching them leave in the first place.

The last time she'd sat around waiting... Bard. Even all these years later, the memories were just as clear and poignant as if it had happened only days before. Keeping busy. Watching the road. Helping with the tenants and managing the farm. Feeding the chickens. Alone. Watching the road. Telling herself that Niall was fine. That he would come back. That he had promised her, and he kept his promises. Watching the road.

Waiting and watching the road day after day until the messenger came, carrying Niall's signet ring, dried blood crusted on the emerald.

Bollocks. This was exactly why she didn't think about it. She had pulled herself back together and built herself again, piece by piece. She'd built her life into a new shape. It was a shape that would forever hold the empty space where the man she'd expected to grow old with should have been, but it was a bearable shape, nonetheless. And yet, here she was, watching the road once more.

Tor grunted, and she turned to look at him. What had he wanted? He tilted his head and raised an eyebrow as if expecting an answer... oh yes. Find something to do.... What in the Bard's name was she supposed to do?

She tried to think of an amusingly sarcastic reply but failed. She was too distracted—her thoughts jumping and skittering with as much agitation as a flock of unruly chickens let loose in the yard with a falcon in the sky. Bloody hell, why did she have to think of chickens? She hated chickens.

What was happening at the palace? Had Val and the others reached Kaerlud in time? Was Alanna still alive? What the hell was she going to do if—

Damn. Tor was right; she needed something to take her mind off Alanna and Val and what in the Abyss was going on in Kaerlud. She looked around for something to do but all the squad's possessions were packed, and the horses stood saddled and ready. As soon as the Mabin returned with Alanna, they would be moving out.

But only if they reached Alanna in time. If they could get her free. If they managed to evade the mass of guards arrayed against them. If…if…if…. She swallowed heavily against the ache in her throat and pushed the thoughts away. They would rescue Alanna. And escape. She had to believe it. She couldn't lose another person she cared about.

A woodpecker drummed vigorously somewhere in the woods. The noise thudded in her brain as she paced the small clearing, biting her lip, her eyes returning to the small path that was the only way into and out of their hiding place. Still no one there. As there hadn't been on any of the previous thousand times she'd checked.

"Maybe you could help me with this thread?" Tor tried again. "If you want."

She stepped up to the log he was sitting on. "What are you doing?"

"Mending my shirt."

She glanced at the cotton undershirt he was holding, noticing the neat row of stitches mending the collar and the series of small, ripped holes down the front that Tor hadn't sewn together yet. And was that…? She pointed at the faded brown stains. "What happened there?"

Tor shrugged without answering and then held out a needle and strand of creamy flax thread, both almost lost inside his massive hands. She took them, her fingers brushing against his warm palm, and squinted to thread the needle before passing it back.

Keely sank onto the log beside Tor, ignoring the shiver that small touch wanted to send down her spine, and looked at him more carefully. He was focused on his mending, eyes on the needle as it slipped in and out of the shirt, his stitches surprisingly small and tidy for someone whose fingers swamped the needle so completely.

He clearly didn't plan to say anything, but it was obvious he'd been hurt. "What happened?" she asked again.

He stayed silent for a long moment, but eventually he lifted his eyes and answered, "Gatehouse."

Nim and Tristan looked up from their conversation while Mathos pushed himself off the tree he'd been leaning on, everyone focusing on Tor.

"Gatehouse?" Tristan asked quietly.

Tor shrugged, ignoring them all.

Nim had already told Keely about how Tor had sacrificed himself to save a woman in the food market—yet another of the deeply honorable things he'd done—but in all the stress of the past few days, it seemed no one had thought to ask him if he was hurt. Damn. She hated the idea that he had been wounded, had been suffering, all while taking care of her.

She twisted to look at him more directly. "Lift your shirt."

Tor grunted. "Not wearing one."

She rolled her eyes. "Then take off your jerkin."

The needle paused, hovering over the fabric as his dark eyes focused on her. Bard. He was completely still and utterly silent. But the intensity of that look captured her. A look that dared her to tell him to take off his clothes again.

Bard, she wanted to. She wanted to touch him as much as she wanted him to touch her. She cleared her throat and tried to sound unaffected. "Take off your jerkin, Tor."

Tristan stood with a grunt, breaking the moment. "What didn't you tell us?"

Tor looked away, releasing her from his gaze, and set aside his mending before slowly unbuttoning his jerkin and pulling the sides apart. Damn. She had never imagined he would be hiding such heavy, defined muscles, rippling as he moved, or such horrendous bruising.

Before she'd had time to think about it or stop herself, she reached out and laid her hand onto the mass of purple and green, wishing she could soothe the half-healed cuts and abrasions.

Tor flinched as her cold hand touched his warm skin, and she moved to pull her hand back, but he caught it with one of his own, holding it against his belly as if they were the only two people in the world. Just him and her. Her hand pressed against his skin, feeling the hard ridges of muscles flexing as he shifted.

"I'm sorry." Her words came out as a whisper.

He shook his head. "I'm not."

Bard. She stared at him, completely disoriented. Wanting to push herself closer. Wanting to get away. When last had she felt like this? So flustered—so mesmerized—by a man. She blinked. Not a man. A soldier.

Mathos reached them, and she tugged at her hand, needing distance. Tor released her and turned to his friend just as Nim and Tristan arrived. "It's not a big deal," he said quietly as he picked up his mending.

"Why didn't you tell me? Or Rafe?" Tristan demanded.

"Or me?" Mathos added.

Tor shrugged, still stitching his shirt. "Wasn't all that important. Not with everything else going on."

Tristan frowned. "Make sure you ask Rafe to take a look."

Tor nodded his agreement. Thank the Bard. In the many hours they'd spent together, he had never once mentioned that he'd been hurt. He must have been bleeding and in agony when he hauled her through the icy waters of the moat, yet he hadn't hesitated or complained. The thought of him hurting in silence bothered her. Bothered her in ways she didn't want to think about.

Tor tied off the last stitch and then slipped out of his jerkin to pull the newly mended shirt on before putting his jerkin back over the top and tying the laces. Then he reached into a satchel beside him, picked up a small linen bundle, and passed it to her.

She wrinkled her nose at him. "What's this?"

"Spare shirt."

Mathos chuckled. "Forgive him, Keely. It's his special talent—saying something completely true and yet utterly unhelpful. Sometimes I think he does it on purpose so that he doesn't have to say what he really thinks."

Tor narrowed his eyes at Mathos but softened when he looked back her way. "For your friend. She'll need something to wear when she gets here."

Bard. After days of ignoring his own needs to take care of hers, now he was taking care of Alanna too. She cleared her throat again. "Thank you. That's really…. Thank you."

He didn't reply, simply sat beside her, his leg warm and solid where it pressed against hers as her nerves slowly ratcheted back up and her eyes began to dart toward the path once more.

He was still sitting quietly beside her when Jeremiel jogged into the camp with Reece. "They're coming. Jos flew ahead to warn us, we need to go. Right now."

Keely stood so quickly, she would have stumbled if a heavy hand hadn't reached up to hold her hip and stabilize her. Tor rose slowly beside her, a comforting warmth at her shoulder as she focused on Jeremiel.

"What about Alanna? Did they…?" Keely paused as the words stuck in her throat.

Jeremiel gave her a quick nod. "She's alive but unconscious. Val's carrying her."

Keely wiped a shaky hand down her face, wishing she could collapse back onto the log, just for a moment. But Tristan was already barking orders to move out and she was up on her borrowed horse and cantering down the path before she could fully process that Alanna would be okay.

Within minutes there was a sharp whistle, and they reined the horses in, guiding the big stallions to a safe stop as Val landed heavily on the path ahead of them. Alanna was gripped tightly against his chest, Jos and Garet following close behind.

They were smeared with dust and dirt and blood, their faces drawn, and sweat dripping down their necks, but their eyes were clear and relieved. Jos was even smiling.

Alanna was safe in Val's arms. His grip on her friend never wavered despite the grayish pallor of his face and his painfully stiff movements. Val looked as if he'd spent the day walking through the fires of the Abyss, as if all his wounds had reopened and each step was agony, but he also looked as if his world had righted. As if he could finally breathe.

Val leaned down and pressed a gentle kiss to Alanna's forehead, and it was all Keely could do to keep herself from crumpling into a heap and weeping. She had been so afraid, still was afraid—not for herself, but for Alanna.

Bard. Her friendship with Alanna had snuck in under her defenses, and for the first time in years, she was vulnerable to loss.

She swallowed hard, watching Val as he held Alanna. He settled himself into his saddle then carefully arranged Alanna to keep her comfortable and secure as they escaped, using his wings to balance them both so that he never had to let Alanna go.

Val loved Alanna. It was there in everything he did.

What would it be like to feel that again? To love someone and know they loved her back. To know she could trust them. To see them and see her future.

Keely pulled her cloak tight against the sudden cold and nudged her horse forward, following the Hawks. She had seen too much to think of love in terms of certainty. Loving a person didn't keep them safe. Having your love returned didn't protect you from their loss. She'd learned that the hard way.

Niall had broken her heart on the day he left for war. And then he'd died on the battlefield and shattered her completely. She couldn't risk that kind of destruction. She never wanted to haul the broken mess of her heart and her life back together, one mangled piece at a time, ever again.

Except... except that Val and Alanna were meant to be together. They were meant to take the risk of choosing each other. She knew it with every fiber of her body. Their love was worth it.

Keely closed her eyes for a long moment and accepted the truth. That kind of love was worth the cost.

She was thinking about Alanna and Val, but for some reason, when she opened her eyes, they settled on Tor as he rode through the woods beside her.

Chapter Four

Why was the camp so quiet?

Tor abandoned oiling his sword—the Bar-Ulf sword he had somehow managed to hold on to despite everything that had happened—and looked around the circle of neat tents. Everything was peaceful; they'd been on the road long enough to settle into an easy rhythm even with three new, female, squad members.

Nim and Alanna were peeling carrots and chatting about how much they were looking forward to the famous hot spring baths at Eshcol. The rest of the squad were doing chores. The small tracks leading away from the clearing, overhung with autumn trees bright with reds and golds, were quiet and empty. All was as it should be... but it still wasn't right.

There was noise. Nim and Alanna laughed, Jeremiel and Garet called out as they came back from patrol, Reece grumbled loudly about something, yet again, and horses nickered. But there was no singing.

Keely had a surprisingly low singing voice, full of depth

and emotion. And she sang everything from heartbreaking laments that reminded him of all the grief of the frozen battlefields of the north to ribald tavern ditties that would have been perfectly suited to the Kaerlud docks. She even murmured love songs to whichever horse she was riding that day for the long hours of their relentless march toward Eshcol.

Her songs followed him everywhere. He would look up and see her—her vibrant hair tied back into a fiery braid, her jade-green eyes sparkling as she met his gaze—and it felt as if she was singing directly to him. His days had come to revolve around those moments. Those flashes of brilliance among the gray.

They would reach the temple soon—within the next two days—and the knowledge scratched like a thorn inside a glove. He wanted to reach Eshcol. Something new and primal had been stirring within him and he needed Keely to be safe. Keely and the rest of the Hawks, now including Nim and Alanna. But he didn't want to think about what would happen when the journey ended. Didn't want to imagine what it would be like when she was gone, and his days went back to foggy numbness.

And *that* was the problem with the camp. Keely wasn't singing. In fact, Keely wasn't there at all. Where was she? Why wasn't she sitting with Alanna or chatting to Rafe, helping and offering her usual witty observations?

Frankly, it was some kind of miracle that Nim was still there; by now he would have expected Tristan to have whispered in her ear and for them to be off in the woods together. Those two really needed their own house—somewhere well out of hearing distance—and about a hundred years alone together. Although, given the way they looked at each other, maybe a hundred years wouldn't be enough.

As for Val and Alanna. Gods. Val spent all daylight hours in the air as far away from everyone as possible, while Alanna spent all day checking the skies, and then she spent all night in Val's tent without him realizing. Alanna needed to tell Val how she felt, convince him that what they had meant something, before Val left for good.

Tor wouldn't blame him. Val had been clear that he loved Alanna—how much clearer could you be than sacrificing your entire life? But she'd told him to leave. And if there was one thing Tor was intimately acquainted with, it was exactly what it felt like when the people who were supposed to love you told you to leave.

He pushed the rising swell of confused emotion away. He wasn't going to think about what he'd lost, or what it had felt like to be disowned. If he didn't think about it, he didn't have to experience that blinding misery, could ignore the barbed pain in his heart where he used to have a family. Where he used to have some sense of certainty.

He had been brought up not to show his feelings. Or even acknowledge that he had any. And, for the first time, he understood—ignoring the pain made it all go away.

Which was exactly why Keely was dangerous. She was the flame that should not be touched. She was too bright, too vivid. With every day that passed, every song she sang, every twinkle of her intelligent eyes, every time she went out of her way to help his squad or take care of Alanna, she climbed further under his skin.

Tor looked around the small clearing again. Where the fuck was she?

He stood, stretched out his stiff legs, and slid his sword into its scabbard. The Hawks were trickling in to help make dinner and finish their chores—all except Val, who was probably doing yet another long sweep of the surrounding woods. Everyone who should be in camp was. Which meant she was alone. And it wasn't safe, even for someone as capable as Keely.

Alanna grinned over at him and then gestured behind her with her thumb over her shoulder, pointing toward a lighter stretch of woodland a little way from their camp.

Was he that obvious? He paused, wondering whether to pretend he hadn't been looking for Keely after all, and then decided that was ridiculous. They had spent many hours together. They were friendly. Friends, even. Of course he would wonder where she was. Exactly the same as he wondered where Mathos was. Or Tristan.

Specifically *when* he might have wondered where Mathos or Tristan had gone was irrelevant. He'd definitely done it. At least once.

Anyway, all the Hawks, including Keely, fell under his protection. It was merely his duty to check on where she was. The fact that he spent half his waking hours remembering what her bare skin felt like under his hands was beside the point.

He grumbled under his breath as he shoved his hands in his pockets, but it didn't stop him from following the path Alanna had indicated.

He found Keely in a small glade, the pale afternoon sunlight streaming around her. The ground was littered with fallen leaves, muffling his footsteps, but she still spun to face him before he'd fully entered the glade, lifting a crossbow, and pointing it straight at him.

He stopped instantly. Her grip was firm and confident, and if she released, he'd have a bolt through his heart in an instant.

They stared at each other for a moment, and then she lowered the crossbow, pointing it safely away toward the ground at her side. Her posture was one of strength and experience, even though she still seemed to be protecting her shoulder slightly, and he remembered her mentioning that she had some skill with shooting.

"Archery?" he asked, stepping closer.

She raised one eyebrow. "I wasn't allowed weapons in the palace. I've been feeling out of practice."

Bloody Ballanor. He could only imagine how awful it had been for Keely, a maid, with no status, no power, and not even a weapon to defend herself, in Ballanor's court.

"No wonder you hated it," he admitted quietly.

"Hated what?" she asked in her soft Verturian accent.

"Hated Ballanor. The court. Brythoria." He paused, not wanting to include the guards, although he knew he should. "All of it."

She shrugged again. "At least it's over." She hefted the crossbow in her hand, taking its weight. "And now I've got a weapon."

He grunted. "I see that."

She raised her eyebrows, waiting for him to say more.

"I'm glad," he admitted.

She grinned back at him, pleased with his answer, and he couldn't help adding, "You said that you shoot." Gods. Mathos was right, he did have a habit of stating the obvious. But the obvious always seemed so much safer than saying anything else.

"Yes, I used to. I'd like to start again."

Late afternoon sunshine streaked across the small glade and the trees were filled with the evening calls of birds, and suddenly it didn't seem so quiet anymore.

He stepped closer, wishing he could have put a crossbow

in her hands long before, wishing he could apologize for the time she'd spent in Ballanor's court, but unable to find the right words.

She was so strong. And so beautiful. The golden sunlight caught her hair like a halo, and he ached to run his hand through the silky strands. When he'd pulled her into his arms in the moat, her damp hair had smelled of heather—woody and slightly floral—and he wondered if that soft scent would surround him if he gave in and reached for her.

How many hours had he spent remembering the torture of cutting her jerkin away? Balancing the knife so that it cut smoothly, never jarring her or pressing into her more than he absolutely had to. Utterly, acutely aware of her. Every breath, every movement. The way her elegant hands gripped the blanket, like a woman might grip her sheets as she lost herself in pleasure. If he had leaned forward, just an inch, he would have been able to run his tongue over that perfect skin; pink and flushed from the cold.

"Shall we have a competition, then?" she asked eventually.

Yes, they had to do something. Because otherwise he was going to take another step forward, and another, and then he would be close enough to touch her. He had to remind himself that he had no right to touch her. No right to reach toward her, despite how much he wanted to. How desperately he wanted some of her light to shine on him, to ease the cold he'd wrapped himself in.

He nodded, focusing on her question. "What's the prize?"

She chewed on her lip, considering, drawing his eyes to her soft mouth, those pink lips. What could he do to ensure the prize was a taste of that small smile?

"Whoever loses has to pluck the birds for tonight's meal," she said eventually.

"Okay," he agreed, working to keep his eyes on hers, not drifting down to her mouth.

He was tempted to offer a handicap, something to even out the odds—how could a girl shooting on a Verturian farm ever have the experience of a soldier shooting every day? But he had a very clear idea that Keely would not be impressed by the suggestion that she wasn't good enough, and he kept his thoughts to himself. "What are the rules?"

"We're shooting at crabapples," she said, gesturing to the other end of the glade. She had compensated for the small size of the glade by choosing tiny autumn apples, mottled in yellow-greens and streaky reds. They were balanced on a low tree branch, eight in a row. "Most hits wins."

He nodded toward the loaded crossbow. "You can start."

She grinned, eyes twinkling, turned toward the row of crabapples, and lifted the crossbow to tuck it into her shoulder, widening her stance. She breathed slowly, sighting down the barrel, and then pulled the trigger.

The bolt whistled through the air and smashed through the first crabapple with a spray of juice and apple flesh.

Damn. He'd known she was good by the way she handled the crossbow, but she was way better than he'd expected. He would have to really concentrate if he wanted to win.

She handed him the crossbow with a smile, and he loaded the next bolt, aimed, let out a breath, and fired. The second apple exploded in another syrupy shower. Thank the gods.

She dipped her head. "Not bad. I was thinking of

offering a handicap, but I can see now that would have just been insulting."

He barked out a laugh. She must have suspected that had been what he was thinking. Not anymore, though. "We're pretty evenly matched," he admitted.

She hummed her agreement as she took the crossbow back, touching him briefly over the stock. Her hands were slim with long, elegant fingers, and so very competent.

She lifted the crossbow sighting carefully, breathed out, and fired. But her bolt missed, rattling the apple as it flew past.

"I knew there was a reason I didn't trust crabapples," she said with a huff of laughter.

"You don't trust crabapples?" he asked, amused.

She wrinkled her nose at him. "Of course not. How can you trust a fruit that's so sour on the inside? They pretend to be little apples, but you can't even eat them covered in sugar and pastry."

Tor nodded slowly. He'd never had a view on crabapples before. Mostly, he just wanted her to keep looking at him. To keep speaking to him as if his opinion mattered to her.

She passed the crossbow over, still smiling.

He loaded the bolt, sighted carefully, and fired, splintering through the tiny apple with a shower of juice.

Damn, it felt good. He was tempted to say something about the sweetness of victory making up for the tart crabapples, but he held it in.

"Go on." Her eyes sparkled. "You can gloat."

His lips twitched, and he fought to stop himself from grinning. When last had target practice been this much fun? Honestly, nothing in his life had been as enjoyable as this, for longer than he wanted to remember.

"Remind me what the prize is," she said as she took hold of the crossbow once more.

"Plucking."

She snorted, not at all delicately and Tor froze. He was pretty sure he'd said plucking. He thought back. Yes, he'd said plucking. Not fucking. But now all he could think of was that smooth, bare skin under his hands. Gods.

She loaded the next bolt. "Well, I'd better be sure to win."

She smashed the next one and gave a small bow of victory as she handed over the crossbow.

He raised the weapon, trying desperately to clear his mind of images of Keely, naked, skin flushed as he.... He shook his head. He had to concentrate.

He sighted. Fired. And missed by at least an inch.

She looked at him, chuckling in commiseration. "I warned you about those crabapples."

Keely was the perfect opponent. Challenging, but playful. A good sport when her shot missed, complimentary toward his successes, gracious about her wins. They were tied on two hits each and a small part of him wanted her to win—wanted her to have that moment of joy—but a much bigger part wanted to take the victory. He wanted to show her what he could do, to prove that he was good enough to be there in that clearing, shooting apples with her.

She reached for the crossbow but didn't lift it immediately, simply stood still, carefully considering the last two apples on the branch.

Somehow, he'd moved closer to her during their game, and now she was in touching distance. She was tiny compared to him, her head just a little over his shoulder, lean and lithe, the complete opposite of his heavy bulk. What would it be like to reach out and pull her closer?

Would she come into his arms? Or would she push him away?

She threw him a glance filled with laughter, and then loaded a bolt and lifted the crossbow. She took her time sighting, minutely correcting herself, and then let the bolt fly. Not into the next crabapple in the row, but into a dead branch a few levels higher in the tree.

The bolt struck home, shattering the old branch, which fell in a heavy cascade of dry wood and brown leaves to crash into the last two apples and throw them to the ground.

She looked at him over her shoulder, tilting her head questioningly as she raised one fiery eyebrow, and he couldn't help his surprised laugh.

"Good enough?" she asked cheerfully.

What could he say? The rules had been that the most hits won, and she had, undoubtedly, hit the most. He gave her a small salute, still chuckling. "My lady, you are the winner."

She grinned back and patted his arm. "Don't worry, next time we can compete with weapons you're more comfortable with… needles, perhaps."

Maybe it was because he'd been enjoying himself. Maybe it was the ripe, tart-sweet scent of crabapples in the air or the afternoon sunshine. Or maybe it was entirely her. But something made him step even closer and lower his voice. "Needles, Keely? I assure you, I have a perfectly good sword."

She let out another amused huff, looking up at him with twinkling eyes. "Yes, I'm sure your sword is very… big."

It was the first time he'd seen her completely relaxed, her face lit up with joy and amusement, and he wished he could pull the tie from her braid, run his fingers through her bright hair, tip her head back and taste that smile. Take some of its joy into his own body.

She hoisted the crossbow over her shoulder and went to look for the bolts they'd used, leaving him alone with the aching tightness in his breeches. But even as he watched her stride away, he knew there would be no "swordplay" between them. She was not the kind of woman who messed around for one or two nights. And how could he ask for more when he had nothing to offer her?

His future, his home, his place in the world were all gone. His own family didn't even want him.

Keely made him feel things. Made him want things. She broke through the numbness he had wrapped himself in, and he couldn't bear to even imagine what it would be like if —when—she told him he wasn't enough.

Chapter Five

ONE MORE DAY of traveling and they would be in Eshcol. One more day and then Keely could finally get clean. Finally find some clothes that fitted. Just one more day, and they would be safe and free. And then what?

Keely glanced toward Val's tent and smiled. Her friend finally had the love she deserved.

She didn't know whether to thank Reece or strangle him for the nasty little jibes that had resulted in the epic argument between Val and Alanna. The argument that had cleared the air and revealed the truth. Alanna loved Val and he loved her in return. And now they had disappeared into Val's tent to continue their—ahem—discussion. Perhaps she should strangle Reece *and* thank him.

Keely leaned back on her hands, enjoying the knowledge that Alanna was happy. She was glad for her friend. Alanna deserved every moment of joy she got.

But it also raised the question—what about Keely? What would she do? It was hard to look back over the last decade and realize she had built nothing for herself. She had walked away from her own life and made Alanna her priority, and now Alanna didn't need her anymore.

A year ago, she would have smiled brightly, wished Alanna the best, and moved on. But now the thought made her heart ache. Something about the last weeks had changed her. Maybe it was standing in Ballanor's court, certain she was going to die and wishing she had really lived. Maybe it was watching Val and Alanna struggle and fight their way toward each other, and the love they both deserved. Maybe it was the way she felt when Tristan looked down at Nim with the slightly stunned expression of someone who hadn't ever imagined they could be so lucky.

Whatever it was, it had made her look back at the last ten years of her life and wonder what the hell she was doing. She had put her dreams away when Niall died, and now, for the first time, she was starting to think it might have been a mistake.

Coming with Alanna to Brythoria hadn't been a mistake. Doing everything she could to protect her friend hadn't been a mistake. No, she would never regret being there for Alanna. But assuming it was better to never have anything of her own, deciding—at the ripe old age of nineteen, when Niall died—that she was better without love… *that* had been a mistake.

She had told Alanna to fight for Val, and she had meant it. But what kind of hypocrite did that make her? She'd given up on love long ago.

And while she was being honest with herself, she had to admit the rest. If Alanna and Val's newfound happiness was a challenge to her long-held independence, Tor's presence was cataclysmic.

The more time she spent with him, the more she liked him. She liked his careful words and his deep, reassuring voice. She liked his kindness, his quiet humor, his loyalty, and the strong moral core that drove everything he did.

She also liked his big hands and heavy muscles. The tanned skin on his neck that she had spent far too many hours imagining sinking her teeth into. She wanted him, wanted his body against hers, bringing her to that place where all thoughts and worries were suspended by the fierce pleasure running through her. And she wanted him to hold her afterward. Wanted to curl into his warmth and stay there. But could she take the risk of caring for another soldier? She still didn't have an answer.

She looked around the fire again, watching the Hawks as they chatted and relaxed. All except Reece, who was sitting a little out of the circle, yet another wineskin in his hand and a surly look on his face. He was behaving just like the other soldiers in Kaerlud—like an arrogant, entitled bully.

Reece scowled back. "What are you looking at, queen's maid?" He took another long sip from his wineskin and then gestured to the camp around them, leering toward Val's tent. "Not even the queen's maid anymore, are you? Now you're nothing at all."

Bard, even half-drunk it was as if he'd been reading her mind. Well, Keely had lived among Ballanor's cronies for months and had never given them the satisfaction of seeing how they riled her; she wasn't about to start now. "What's your problem, Corporal, you got sour grapes in there with your never-ending wine?"

Tor and Mathos looked up from their nearby conversation while Jeremiel quietly put his empty plate down. Any one of them would step in; that was the Hawks for you. But she didn't need help; she'd been looking after herself for years.

"At least I own something," Reece replied with a sneer, lifting his wineskin in a mocking salute. He gestured toward her, taking in the too-tight breeches borrowed from Alanna and the too-loose shirt she'd been wearing when they fled the farmhouse. "You don't even have your own clothes, former maid."

Keely raised her eyebrow at Reece. "I wasn't really the queen's maid, you idiot. I was always her friend. My mother is cousin to Queen Moireach."

Reece snorted unkindly. "Sure. And I'm King Reece of the Fish Street Docks, at your service."

Ass. She stood up and faced him squarely. "You know, Reece, we all felt sorry for you with what happened with your girlfriend. But you should realize that this childish tantrum you've been throwing doesn't impress anyone, and it's getting old."

Reece stood up, swaying slightly. "Not my girlfriend anymore, just a fucking liar. Like Alanna. Like you. Gods, I'm so bloody sick of liars."

The rest of the camp went silent. Tristan stood slowly, his scales flickering up his arms in a wave. Damn. Did Reece not understand the danger he was in?

Keely waved the Hawks away. She didn't need their help, and anyway, bullies had to be handled in person. "*You're* the one who's been pretending to be something you're not. You forget, Reece, I lived in the palace for months. I saw your little drama unfold."

"I never lied!" Reece took an unsteady step closer, indigo scales ruffling along his arms as he jabbed his finger at her, the wineskin still gripped in his other hand.

Before she could grab that hand and break the finger pointing in her face, Tor was there. Not between them, not threatening Reece in any way, just standing at her shoulder quietly, watching. Keely turned, ignoring Reece to look at Tor suspiciously. "What are you doing?"

He raised his eyebrows innocently. "Nothing."

She glared back at him. "I don't need any help."

His ridiculously full lips twitched. "I don't doubt it," he agreed gravely. "I've seen you shoot. But when you take him down, which I know you will, I plan to have the best view."

Keely rolled her eyes, trying not to show how much his quiet support meant. He was standing beside her, not taking over, not fighting her battle, but lending his strength should she want it.

Reece looked between her and Tor, his eyes bloodshot in his pale face as he staggered back a step and let out a rough, unamused chuckle. "Gods. I don't know why I bother." He waved his hands between them. "When this ends badly, don't say I didn't warn you." And then he turned and stumbled away into the darkness.

There was a long, weighted silence around the campfire until Keely sighed and shrugged. "That went well."

Everyone chuckled, and she smiled back. This was what it felt like to be part of something. To know that the people around you had your back. She glanced at Tor. This was what it felt like to trust someone.

His face was as stoic as always, but when they sat back down, he sat right next to her. Close enough that his thigh was touching hers. Close enough that she could feel his warmth.

"I'm sorry about Reece, Keely," Tristan said from across the fire. "If you have any problems, any problems at all, just tell me."

She nodded. "Thank you."

Tor was silent, but he shifted even closer. Her eyes dropped down to his arms, to where the red-and-black tattoos rippled over the bunching muscles. He had stood beside her so many times. Would he ever take that next step and wrap those heavy arms around her? Could this be the future she hadn't known to look for?

The squad had planned for Alanna and the Hawks to spend a couple of days in the Temple of the Nephilim at Eshcol and then head west, toward the rough, sparsely populated mountains of Tegeingl. Take themselves as far away as they could get from the reach of the new king and the devastation of the war in the north... and Keely had a place with them, if she chose. Or she could leave Alanna and the Hawks and make her way back to Verturia.

This was the moment that she had been coming to since she had stood in Ballanor's great hall wishing to live. She had to make a choice based on what she wanted for her life. And, Bard help her, she was starting to want Tor to be part of that life.

Another bloody soldier. And not only that—Nim had told her all about what his family had done. He was a soldier who had worked his entire life for his parents' approval... and then they'd disowned him.

But even knowing there were wounds in his past, even though his life was dangerous, she was starting to think he might be the man she could lower her defenses for. And she wanted to know if he could lower his in return.

She turned to watch him in the firelight. "I'm thinking about what to do after Eshcol," she admitted.

He watched her carefully, entirely focused on her words.

"I'm considering whether to turn west with the Hawks, toward Tegeingl, or carry on north, back to Verturia. It's been a long time since I've been home," Keely said softly.

"I've heard rumors that things are getting worse in the

north," Tor admitted. "And if Ballanor restarts the war, it will get even more dangerous."

"Are you saying that I shouldn't go north? Or that I should try to get there as quickly as possible?"

"What do you want to do?" he asked quietly, his face serious but not giving her any clues as to what he was thinking.

She bit her lip, trying to decide how much to reveal, how vulnerable she was prepared to be. Why was it so much easier to risk her life than to risk her heart?

"I haven't seen my mama for a long time," she hedged. "My da died years ago, and she's been living in the castle at Duneidyn. It might be nice to see her. Maybe spend some time in the mountains. I do miss the mountains."

"There are mountains in Tegeingl," he observed.

"Yes. There are." She huffed out an amused snort. Just as Mathos predicted, a completely accurate statement that didn't help her at all. "The Hawks will be there, and Alanna too, of course," she added.

He nodded slowly. "The Hawks would love for you to stay with them."

Was he saying that he would love for her to stay with them? It sounded like it. Especially after mentioning that there would be mountains in Tegeingl.

"What do you think I should do?" she asked, just loud enough for only Tor to hear.

He looked at her for a long moment, his dark eyes filled with some complicated emotion she couldn't read. "I think you should do what makes you happy," he said at last. He lifted his hand, almost to her face, as if he was going to brush his fingers down her cheek, but then he dropped it and glanced away.

Do what made her happy. Was that his way of saying she should go with them when they turned west?

What made her happy? She hadn't been happy, not truly happy, for a long time. No, that wasn't true. She had been happy spending time with Tor.

It was time to start living again. To let herself take risks. It was time to open her heart and choose. And she chose to stay with Tor.

Chapter Six

TOR WATCHED Keely as she rolled her eyes and laughed at something Mathos said. Gods. He cracked his knuckles, one after the other, and forced down the urge to wring his friend's bloody neck. All of his friends. Starting with Mathos and moving swiftly on to Reece.

Every day he spent with Keely, he wanted to be with her more. But he would never ask for it. Not now. Not with her going back to Verturia and leaving him behind. She had turned those clear, jade-green eyes on him and asked what he thought, and he hadn't had a clue what to say. Fucking words.

Should he ask her to stay with him, when she had as good as told him that she wanted to go home? Should he tell her that his entire existence felt gray, and the only ray of light that broke through the haze was her? That his life was now defined by his duty to the squad—the Hawks were all he had left—and if Tristan said they would be retreating to live on the moon tomorrow, he would simply tighten his saddlebags and follow.

He could still hear their words. *Our son, Tor, son of Pellin, son of Bar-Ulf, died this day.* He wasn't dead, of course not, but something inside him *had* died. Some understanding of the world and his place in it.

He was a disowned former guard with nothing to his name and no future to speak of. The Hawks were heading west into the wild mountains, far from the homes they'd known. How could he ask her to be part of that? And if they ever, by some miracle, made it back to the palace, what then? What future was there for her—a Verturian in a Brythorian court? A court run by people like his parents. People who would never accept her, let alone appreciate her.

No. He couldn't ask her to stay. Even though it would break something in him for her to go. She would be much better off going back to her own home as she planned. She would start a new life—singing as she worked, rolling her eyes, hunting with that lethal crossbow, and laughing at her own jokes while she cared for all the people around her. She would be far away from him, but she would have a good life. He wanted her to have that.

He had told her to do whatever made her happy, knowing it would send her away. And now he had to sit and watch her laugh and joke with the rest of the squad while the evening somehow turned into an impromptu celebration around him.

Alanna and Val had finally… whatever it was they'd done. There had been shouting, then there had been murmuring, then Val had lifted Alanna into his arms and marched through the camp to deposit her in his tent, fastening the flap behind him.

Which of course led Tor to immediately picture what Keely would look like in *his* tent. That red-gold hair spread out over her creamy skin. Following the scattering of freckles down her chest. His hands would engulf her pert breasts. Gods. He would—

"What do you think, Tor?"

He blinked, trying to clear his head, and looked at Mathos. "About what?"

Mathos chuckled, as if he could guess the direction of Tor's thoughts before he interrupted. "I was just telling Keely that although the angel Muriel gifted the Apollyon with all those muscles, in the end, we should feel sorry for you, living without drake-given wings like the Mabin or the Tarasque's inner beast to keep you company."

Tor grunted. It was exactly the kind of stupid argument Mathos liked to start, and Tor had years of practice at ignoring him.

"I don't know," Keely disagreed, grinning. "I think there's something to be said for a man who doesn't flap about the place."

Mathos gave her a smug look until she continued. "Or sparkle in the sunshine like one of the palace jewels."

Mathos grumbled, and everyone laughed as Tristan passed around a full wineskin. Probably one of Reece's. Damn, he'd wanted to take his friend's head right off his shoulders. But Keely was just fine standing up for herself— exactly as he'd known she would be.

Gods, he liked her strength. The way she stood her ground. And under all that bravado, he liked her generosity. Her easy good humor. Her loyalty to her friend.

Tor took his swallow and passed the wine on. Maybe it was better if he didn't spend his time thinking about Keely. Especially as she'd be leaving after Eshcol… and they would reach Eshcol in the morning.

Mathos heard his grumbling curse and raised an

amused eyebrow. And Tor knew that within seconds he would be the punchline of a joke he didn't want to hear. He stood and said goodnight instead. Made his way into his small tent, and then lay for hours in his bedroll, not sleeping. He stared at the canvas roof of his tent and wondered what would happen when they reached the temple.

Would Keely go north to find her happiness without him as he expected? Or would she change her mind and head west with the squad? What was she doing? Was she already in her tent? Getting ready to go to sleep? That loose shirt of hers drove him insane. Just a small tug and it would be off her shoulder. He could run his knife through that thin cotton far more easily than the heavy leather of her jerkin, strip it all away, and finally see her.

What would she look like with her hair unbound? He would thread his fingers through it, spreading it over her shoulders as she dropped to her knees and opened his breeches. She would look up at him, those big green eyes sparkling as she ever so slowly took him into her mouth and—

Gods.

He kicked off the blankets and spent a long moment considering taking his aching cock into his own hand. But then he reminded himself that he wasn't supposed to be thinking about Keely, and especially not Keely naked, and cracked his knuckles in frustration instead, before shoving his hands behind his head and keeping them there.

The night was long and exhausting, filled with half-formed fantasies and seductive dreams that he pushed away again and again. It was a relief when Mathos called him to take the early patrol and he could finally throw off his constricting blankets and escape the confines of his tent to breathe the fresh, earthy air. Even the softly falling rain was better than being trapped alone with his thoughts. Reece had done him a favor when he asked him to take his patrol.

Tor followed the narrow woodland paths, listening to the birds call and the wind rustle softly through the trees as the rain grew heavier until it fell in steady sheets over the woods.

By the time he returned to the camp, the squad were standing in their oilskins, huddled against the trees, eating a rough breakfast, and trying to stay out of the rain. Everyone except Reece. Bloody Reece. He'd asked Tor to do his patrol for him and now he hadn't bothered to come back from wherever he'd disappeared to.

Keely passed him a bread roll stuffed with bacon, which he took gratefully as the squad bantered light-heartedly, ignoring the cold and wet—it certainly wasn't the first time they'd marched in the rain—until Tristan dusted off his hands and called them all to attention so he could outline their plans.

Garet and Jos had already flown over the first part of their route west, but the rain was ruining visibility, and it was impossible to see far enough to judge the safety of the road. They would stick to forest paths as they pushed forward for the last few miles until they reached the protection of the Nephilim. Keely would be riding with him. One last, torturous chance to have her near. To put his hands on her and dream of what might have been.

They took turns, sometimes riding, sometimes walking, but as the mud grew thicker and the path more treacherous, they decided to let Perseus carry them both for a while.

Gods. He hadn't held Keely in his arms since the night they'd escaped from the palace. He'd been attracted to her then; now, he couldn't think of anything else. Her muscular body settled against his with torturous pressure, made infinitely more overwhelming by her gentle movements as she rose and fell with Perseus's ground-eating trot.

She sang as they rode, just loud enough for him to hear, and the low melody raised the hairs on the back of his neck as he lost himself in the feel of her. The rhythmic rise and fall of her voice, the surge of Perseus beneath them, the slide of her body against his. She surrounded him like a dream. The kind of dream he never wanted to wake up from.

The rain fell steadily while the low clouds and swathes of heavy mist turned the forest into a ghost world of grays and reaching branches. Icy drops ran down his face and under the collar of his oilskin, even inside his sleeves.

In front of him, Keely's hair darkened to a deep, burnished copper, and her pale skin flushed from the stinging rain and cold wind. She must have been freezing, and she still favored her left arm, but she never complained. In fact, she hadn't complained once. Not about her wound. Not about living in a tent. Not about hunting for their dinner with the other archers. No, she was a warrior all the way through.

She would be fine wherever she went after Eshcol. And yet… he didn't want to let her go. He wanted her to stay where he could stand beside her and protect her. He wanted to know she was safe.

Tor snorted to himself. That wasn't entirely honest. Yes, he wanted to know she was safe. But he also wanted the right to slip his hands under her cloak and run them up her sides. Wanted to pull her closer until she knew exactly what she was doing to him. He wanted her to be *his*.

Keely swiped a lock of wet hair out of her face and turned to look at him with twinkling eyes, distracting him from his increasingly uncomfortable saddle. "What are you snorting at?"

How could he possibly answer that? He shrugged instead, and she rolled her eyes in response before looking away again, sliding across his lap yet again.

"How's your arm?" he asked, trying to distract them both.

"Fine." She rotated her shoulder as if to prove it had healed, but he saw the tiny flinch she tried to cover.

"Mm-hmm. I'll ask Rafe to have a look."

"I told you that it's fine," she retorted firmly, but she looked over her shoulder as she said it and he saw the flicker of warmth in her eyes, the surprise that someone cared enough to want to help.

She spent so much time looking after Alanna, and now the Hawks. Who looked after Keely? "When we stop—"

He swallowed the rest of his sentence as Jos crashed onto the path in front of Mathos in a flurry of splashing mud and rain, and the line of Hawks skidded to a shocked halt. "They're here, Captain, fuck!"

Gods. It couldn't be. They were so close to Eshcol—to freedom. His arms tightened around Keely reflexively. He couldn't let her get hurt. Wouldn't.

The line crushed in as they all surrounded Jos, his face stark and haggard under his rain-slicked hair.

"Report!" Tristan demanded from the front of the line.

Jos spread his legs, clasped his hands behind his back, and quickly explained. "Visibility is almost nothing, but I thought I'd do an extra mile or two to check our access into the temple. And I saw... fuck... he's here. Ballanor."

"How many?" Val asked, wrapping his wing over Alanna and pressing a rough kiss to her shoulder.

Gods, Tor wished he could do the same with Keely.

Jos grimaced. "At least three companies of mounted palace guards. Blacks and Blues. Coming fast. Every few minutes, a quad of guards peels off into the woods to track from behind. There's no way back."

Garet landed heavily beside them as Jos finished, wings trembling as he panted out, "Right behind us."

Mathos was almost entirely covered in shimmering burgundy scales as his beast responded to the threat. "Can we outrun them? Make it to the temple?"

Garet shrugged. "Maybe."

Tor threw a glance at Keely. At her grim face and clenched fists. He couldn't bear for her to be captured. Thank the gods there was still a chance they could reach the temple.

Tristan raised his voice, his face harsh and set. "Mabin in the air. Dead run. MOVE OUT!"

They were moving even before Tristan had finished the command. Mathos led the way, Tristan and Nim behind him, Val and Alanna immediately behind them, and then him and Keely riding together.

The path branched, and Alanna swerved left, splitting the group, and Tor followed her. Far better to separate and give the horses space to run. But they were still too close, the path they'd chosen too narrow, too slick with mud and dangerous with roots and branches, for all of them. The horses were frightening each other, vying for space, and they could so easily lose their footing and then all of them would be lost.

Keely saw the danger at the same time as he did. Seconds later, she flung her arm out, pointing to an overgrown animal track branching away from the path they were on, and he pulled hard on the reins, forcing Perseus to turn a sharp left.

Low branches, brambles, and twining vines riddled the cramped path. The woods pressed in so close that Perseus had to force himself through the tiny gap, his mad gallop soon slowing to barely more than a trot as he fought the mud and the forest.

Tor gripped the reins, his concentration split between Keely bent low over Perseus in front of him and the rest of the squad somewhere behind.

Hoofbeats thudded away from them as whistles cut the air, horses neighed and men shouted. There was an exultant howl far to the right, and he had to grit his teeth, forcing himself to hold their course. Someone had been captured, but it wouldn't do them any good to turn back. Whoever was caught needed them to stay free, to get away. And to live to come back and rescue them.

The path ahead curved further west, away from the temple, and they followed it down a rocky embankment into deeper thickets. He pushed Perseus onward as the ancient trees grew even closer, blocking the light, and the noise of their hunters faded away behind them.

Slowly the rain eased and birds began to sing, calling to each other through the dense foliage as they fled onward.

An hour passed, maybe more, before Tor allowed himself to believe that they were safe. He hadn't heard anything other than birdsong and the thud of Perseus's hooves for long enough to feel certain that no one had followed them onto the almost invisible path. And by now the heavy rain would have helped to wash away their tracks.

Keely had been bent over Perseus during their initial flight, but now he realized she wasn't even watching where they were going. Her head was bowed, lost in the swathes of her oilskin, and she was utterly quiet.

Keely, who had a comment about everything, whose wry

observations about the people and places around her regularly had the Hawks chuckling, who sang to herself constantly… was silent.

"Whoa." He pulled at Perseus's bridle and brought him to a stop.

If anything, the movement made her hunch even deeper into her cloak. Gods. Had he missed another arrow? Or perhaps she'd opened her wound? Fuck. He should have been paying more attention.

"Keely? Are you hurt?" he asked softly.

She flinched, but she didn't turn.

"Keely, look at me. What's wrong?"

"Nothing." It was a whisper, almost too low to hear, but full of agony.

"Keely, if you don't look at me right now, I swear to the gods, I will lift you off Perseus and check you for myself."

She turned her head away, muttering, "Fuck you, Tor."

That was it. The adrenaline-fueled flight through the woods, his fierce need to protect her, the horrifying idea that she was wounded, all combined into one driving necessity.

He slid down and flung Perseus's reins over a nearby branch, then he flicked Keely's foot out of the stirrup, grabbing hold of her thigh with his other hand in case she decided to kick, and pulled.

She slid sharply to the side with a muffled screech of rage, but he was already lifting her. He swung her around into his arms, gripping her tightly with one arm around her back and the other under her knees, holding her against his chest, and strode up the narrow path.

She writhed and twisted, trying to break free, spitting some of the worst curses he'd ever heard. She was a strong, lithe woman used to hard work and exercise, but he was heavily muscled, even by Apollyon standards. He was much stronger than her, his arms easily the size of her thighs. He could have stood there all day without breaking a sweat while she flung herself at him.

Finally, she quietened and looked at him. Gods. It was far worse than he had imagined. The misery in her eyes nearly achieved what all her twisting had not—he nearly dropped her.

He had never once seen her cry, not even when they pulled the arrow from her shoulder, and she still held on to her tears even now. But her face was twisted into a mask of grief, her eyes suspiciously wet as she fought to hold in her emotion.

"Keely, gods, please tell me what's going on."

"Alanna." The word was so quiet that if he hadn't been holding her against his chest, he wouldn't have heard it. "She finally had her dream. She had Val. Did you see her this morning? She was so excited."

"Keely…." Fuck. He didn't know what to say.

"And I left her. Again."

He stepped them sideways until he could gently lower her into the fork of a huge spreading beech tree, freeing his hands to cup her cheeks and tilt her face up toward his. "No, Keely, we didn't leave her. We stayed safe so that we can get back to rescue them. It was the right decision. You know it, and I know it."

She swiped at her eyes with the back of her hand. "I do know. Of course I know. But… I left her before, and she nearly died. I'm supposed to protect her. I feel… I can't. Bard." She lowered her voice to a rough whisper. "I couldn't bear it if she died. Not now. Not when she's so close to having everything she ever wanted."

"Gods." He let out a rough breath. "I'm sorry, Keely. It

must be awful, worrying about your friend, especially after everything you've both been through."

She looked up at him, her eyes glistening as she bit her lip, torturing it with her teeth. "Aren't you worried?"

Yes, he was. But he controlled his emotions—he always had. He kept his feelings locked down, and his mouth closed, it was how he'd survived year after year on the northern battlefields. What he couldn't protect himself from was how soft and sad Keely was. How lost she was without her usual fiery confidence.

He wanted to reassure her. He wanted to tell her that everything would be okay. But he couldn't lie. Couldn't find it in himself to tell her that everything would work out. Not this time.

He wanted to tell Keely he wouldn't leave her. That he would find a way to keep her safe. And that he would do everything he could to help her in whatever way she needed. But he couldn't find the right words. And he didn't know if it was what she wanted to hear.

Instead, he dragged his thumb down her bottom lip—it was slightly bigger than her top lip, just enough to give it a tiny pout—tugging gently until she released it. And then he lowered his mouth and kissed it better.

He had been too frightened for her, too affected by her grief. He wanted to touch her and reassure himself that she was safe. And he wanted to take away her pain, even if it was only the pain in that tender lip.

She gasped, and he froze, holding himself still, waiting for her to push him away. Expecting it; knowing that she was a dream he could never really have. Knowing that he should never have allowed himself even that small taste.

Instead, she smoothed her small hands up his chest and

around his neck—and pulled him closer. Gods. He stepped into the V of her legs and they wrapped around him, her mouth opening under his. Their tongues slid against each other slowly, tasting, sipping, as their bodies leaned even closer together.

He could feel her muscles moving in her back, her arms tight around his neck, her strong legs holding him tightly against her. She was everything he had imagined, and so much more.

He pulled the tie out of her braid and wove his hands through her hair, angling her head as he slanted his mouth over hers, falling into a slowly rising tide of heat.

His cock pulsed heavily against the leather of his breeches, nestled hard against her core, and he rolled his hips as he lowered his mouth to suck on her neck. She tasted just as sweet as he knew she would.

She arched against him, head tilted to the side, giving him access to that throbbing pulse, and scratched her nails over his neck. The sharp sting brought him back. Just enough. He dropped a tender kiss on her reddened skin and stood, still holding her hair gripped in his fist, to rest his forehead on hers. "Gods, Keely."

Her clear, jade-green eyes looked into his, pupils blown wide. "Don't you want this?"

"I do. Fuck. You must know how much I do." He wanted it—this thrilling, exhilarating, terrifying feeling of being alive that was almost overwhelming in its intensity.

He had spent so long keeping all his emotions tightly locked down that now even pleasure was daunting. And Keely, with her brilliant, burning fire, could blow him apart completely. But he still wanted it.

"Then don't stop," she whispered.

His breath shuddered out as he tried to keep a grip on himself. On her. He lowered one hand to her hip, his fingers pressing into her skin. He needed control. Without it, it would be too much.

"Please." Her accent softened her husky words. "All this time, you've given me what I needed. We've become something, haven't we? I want to forget, for a moment. I need this…. Please."

She needed him. Needed *him*. And if she needed him, then maybe she would stay. He pressed himself even deeper into her body and closed his mouth over hers once more.

Chapter Seven

KEELY WRAPPED her legs around Tor and pulled him closer. He was so big against her, his heavy muscles rippling as he held her pinned against the tree. His skin was hot and firm, his lips moving over hers in confident sweeps.

It had been so many years, so many cold, lonely years, since anyone had touched her.

She wanted to forget, that was true. But mostly she wanted Tor. She wanted to feel his powerful body against hers. Wanted him to be hers.

She had wasted so much time. Bard. Alanna only got one night with Val. One night. If Keely only had one night left, she wanted it to be with Tor.

Tor was worth it. Yes, he was a soldier, but he was so much more than that—he was a warrior, with a warrior's ability to survive. He had fought his way to the very top of the Brythorian guards, and he was still fighting now, after everything. And through all those battles, he had never lost sight of his honor.

She ran her fingers up into his cropped hair and tilted

her head back, exposing her neck, allowing him to press hot, open-mouthed kisses along her collarbone, scraping his teeth gently down the tendons of her neck, nipping and sucking.

His fist still gripped her hair as he pressed her back into the tree, his teeth on her neck an exquisite needle of pain that flooded her belly with heat and held her whole being captivated by the intoxicating sensations he was rousing.

Bard. This was so much more intense, more potent, than anything she had ever experienced before. All that strength, that well of formidable control, focused entirely on her.

She couldn't think. Couldn't worry about the future or regret the past. All she could do was feel. And it was exactly what she wanted.

He leaned back, pinning her on the branch with his hips as he pulled open her oiled cloak and untucked her loose cotton shirt. He flicked his finger through the laces and shoved the cotton roughly to the sides. Her breasts were small enough that she didn't bother to bind them, and her nipples pebbled as the cold air whispered over her skin.

Tor let out a long groan of appreciation before lowering his head to take one puckered nipple into his mouth, his free hand reaching up to massage her other breast.

She arched back, gripping his head, holding him against her, and he rewarded her by giving her nipple a sharp tweak between his thumb and forefinger. He tugged with his teeth on the other side at the same time, twin shafts of delicious fire.

She whimpered and pushed her hips forward, feeling each pinch of his fingers, each swirl of his tongue as molten lava snaked down into her core.

Tor ran his mouth back up and onto hers, and they

groaned together. Keely lowered her hands to fumble with his jerkin, still lost in the heat of his mouth, finally managing to pull it open and slip her hands under his shirt against his bunching muscles. She stroked over his velvet skin, sliding her fingers through the rough hair spread over his broad chest, over the hard points of his nipples, and shivered. Cold air and hot flesh combined with fear and grief, hunger and connection in a swirling maelstrom of feeling and freedom.

She ran her hands lower to pop open the buttons of his breeches and slide her hand inside. Bard, he was huge. As thick and heavy as the rest of him. She had a moment's doubt, but she was pulsing with need, her body a fiery mass of desperation, and she let the thought go. She licked her lips and wrapped her hand around his shaft.

His hips shuddered, and he breathed hard as he lowered his forehead to hers. "Are you sure, Keely?"

"Yes."

He watched her closely. "Keely. I want...." He swallowed. "I like to be in control. Is that—?"

She looked into his potent gaze, those dark, serious eyes, and nodded. That was exactly what she wanted. "Yes. All of it."

He stepped back, gently placing her on her feet, then quickly stripped off his jerkin and shirt, then laid his jerkin out over the fork in the tree branches.

He helped her wiggle out of her boots and breeches and then lifted her back onto the smooth leather, still warm from his body. Damn. He was still protecting her.

He stepped back into the V of her legs and lowered his mouth to hers for another scorching kiss, his hands stroking gently up and down her sides, raising goose bumps in flurries where his calluses teased at her skin.

"Touch me." His voice was a heated murmur against her ear.

She wrapped her fingers around him, so thick and hot, and he immediately wrapped his own, much larger hand over hers, holding her firmly. Holding her still.

His tongue swept through her mouth, again and again, her nipples dragging through the rough hair on his chest as she squirmed. Then he nudged forward, still gripping her hand over his cock, until he was rubbing against her clit.

His heavy cock pulsed in her hand, but she was helpless to move with his fist over hers; all she could do was feel as he stroked her, hot flesh against hot flesh in a constant barrage of sensation. All while his mouth owned hers.

His free hand rose to cup the back of her head, his fingers tangling in her hair, angling her mouth into his as he took his time; long, slow sweeps of his tongue on hers, as if he was tasting her. Luxuriating in her. While his cock rubbed aching circles around her clit.

There were too many sensations. The long pulls of his mouth. Her pulsing clit. Her chest rising and falling in rough pants. The tingle of her scalp from his tight grip on her hair. Her slowly rising desperation for him to be inside her. "Tor. Please."

"Not yet."

Keely's hips moved forward helplessly, searching for more as her kiss grew sloppy. She ran her free hand up his arm, reveling in the flex of muscles as he tortured her again and again, and she gripped his arm, trying to pull him closer.

He growled and held firm, still circling, nudging, almost where she wanted him, but not quite.

He ran his mouth down her neck to bite her shoulder, and she shuddered helplessly. And then he took her nipple between his teeth and sucked as he finally pushed his cock into her entrance.

She gasped in a shaky breath. He was huge, and it had been a very long time. But he stopped there, holding his hips still as his hand in her hair pulled her to arch back and his tongue flicked out to taste the underside of her breasts. Bard. She'd never known how sensitive she was.

He let go of her hand, leaving her to grip his cock, and swirled his thumb around her clit as he pushed the rest of the way into her with a long, achingly slow thrust.

His tongue still played along her breasts, his thumb still rubbed those maddening circles, but otherwise, he didn't move. Her walls fluttered around him, trying to suck him deeper, and she tipped her hips, desperate to relieve the building pressure.

She needed…. Bard. She needed him to *move*. Her body shuddered as a slow, devastating ache traveled up her spine and her core clenched. She was so full. Thrillingly, gloriously full. But she needed more.

He lifted his head and took her lips in a rough kiss, his thumb on her clit driving her insane with the same relentless, steady circles. She gasped and pulled back until her mouth was just touching his, their tongues flicking against each other as they shared air, and she tightened her legs, nudging him forward with her heels.

He growled, deep in his throat. "This is mine."

Bard. That voice. That intensity. She whimpered. "Please. Please, Tor."

His voice, impossibly, deepened. "Be still."

She forced herself to hold still, breathing his air, nipples so hard they hurt, her core fluttering around him as his thumb never faltered. She had never been so desperate.

He chuckled against her mouth, and then he started to

move. A long, slow glide away, and then another deep thrust back into her. Slow and smooth at first, but then faster, thrusting in heavy drives that left her panting hard.

He pumped into her in a driving rhythm that rocked her body. She was already so close, so desperate. She just needed one more…. His teeth found her nipple and tugged, and everything came together in one blinding, staggering climax. She threw her head back, moaning helplessly as her entire body spasmed around his.

He stayed with her, fingers wrapped in her hair, thumb pressing hard against that throbbing bundle of nerves, never faltering as she rode out her orgasm to the very end. And then, in a smooth glide, he grunted and pulled out, painting her belly with streams of come almost in the same movement.

He pulled her close, their flushed skin locked together as she trembled. They were sweating and sticky and glorious. She wrapped her arms around his back, tucking her head under his chin to listen to the heavy thudding of his heart as it gradually returned to its usual slow rhythm.

He dropped a soft kiss on the top of her head, and she laughed. Sated, and safe, and surrounded by Tor.

Bard. She hadn't imagined anything could be like that.

He spun her out of the tree and into his arms, knocked his jerkin to the ground and then, still holding her, sank down onto the leather. He leaned his back against the ancient beech with her sitting across his lap, bare legs hanging down over the side of his thigh.

They sat like that, holding each other in the quiet woods, and, despite everything, she felt safe and cared for. Hopeful, even.

Tor dropped another soft kiss onto the top of her head,

his arm tight around her shoulders. "Are you warm enough?"

"Yes, thanks. You?"

He chuckled against her hair. "Perfect. Just... perfect."

She tilted her head back and looked at him. "Why do you sound surprised?"

He huffed out a breath, his eyes dark in the dim light of the wooded hollow. "I didn't think there was a chance for this."

Honestly, she hadn't known if there would be. And she owed him that honesty. "These weeks together—you and me—I wanted... this. But I've learned to be careful. Especially of men in uniforms."

He ran his thumb slowly over her bottom lip. "I wish you'd never been hurt."

Bard. It was almost too much, his kindness, after the mind-shattering intensity of what they'd shared.

"I'm not... I guess you noticed that wasn't my first time."

He grunted, shrugging. "He was a soldier?" he guessed.

"Yes." She spoke softly. Bard. *Was.* How could that one word hold such a world of hurt?

"And he left you?"

"In a way. He chose to join the army." She let out a long, slow breath. She was still overwhelmed and strangely vulnerable, and it was a struggle to keep her voice even. "He died on the border during the war with Brythoria."

His head fell back against the rough wood behind him. "Gods. I'm sorry."

Shit. She hadn't intended for him to feel responsible. Geraint had started the war that sent him there, and good men had died on both sides. "Not your fault," she murmured gently.

"Maybe not, but I'm still—"

"Don't be sorry," she interrupted. "I guess I just never thought I'd find myself with another soldier." She smiled, trying to lighten the mood. "I've avoided all soldiers very successfully until now."

He chuckled, his arms warm and heavy around her, the sound of his breathing in her ear. Soon they would have to get up. Start making a plan to find Alanna, help the Hawks. But she wanted just one more minute of peace first. One more minute with Tor.

"What do you think it will be like in Tegeingl?" she asked, trying to convince herself that they would easily find the others. That they could free them, if necessary, and then head west like they'd planned. "You promised mountains, but I don't really know what else to expect."

"Tegeingl?" he grunted, looking confused.

"Yes." She huffed out an amused breath. "You know. The place we were aiming for?"

He looked down at her, a deep line creasing his forehead. "You're coming west?"

What?

"Yes, of course," she replied slowly. "We'll be together. Obviously, we need to rescue Alanna and the others first. But you said I should do what made me happy, and I realized that I wanted to take a chance, I wanted for us to maybe try…." She let her words trail away as the reality of his reaction slowly sank in. The reality of what it meant that he was so surprised. "You didn't think I should come with you?" she asked, hating the uncertainty in her voice.

"That's not it at all." He watched her carefully, eyes even darker than before. "I wanted you to come with us. I wanted…. I mean, this was… incredible."

She pulled her shirt closed, a chill chasing across her

skin as she prompted, "Incredible? As in impossible to believe?"

He grunted, the silence extending around them uncomfortably.

She stood up and pulled on her breeches and boots, needing to get dressed. Needing the protection of her clothes while she tried to understand why the man who had been so intently focused on her five minutes before now looked as if he would rather be anywhere else in the world.

Tor watched her quietly from his place on the ground, the warmth between them evaporating into the cold, dark woods.

She looked down at him, unable to let it go, her voice rising in annoyance even as she tried to keep calm and understand. "Please explain this to me."

He shook his head slightly. "This was perfect. *You* are perfect. But you're going to leave, aren't you? You're going back to Verturia. You told me you wanted to go north."

"No." She shoved her hands into her pockets. "I asked if you thought I should go north. I wanted to stay." She swallowed, forced herself to say the words. "I had decided to stay with the Hawks. With you."

Tor nodded slowly as if he didn't quite believe her. "But you just said that you don't want to be with a soldier. And I —I don't know anything except being a soldier."

She blinked, trying to understand. Had she said she didn't want to be with a soldier, or just that she was surprised? What did he really mean? Did he *want* her to go north?

Her heart thudded heavily in her ears as she tried to process this sudden change. She wanted to start again, to have dreams and hopes again, wanted to make a new life, one with companionship and pleasure. Maybe more one day.

Had her realization that she wanted more in her life led her to read too much into what was happening between them?

She had thought he wanted her in the same way she wanted him. Not as a random fuck, but as someone who meant something to her. But maybe that wasn't what he had been looking for at all?

"What do you want, Tor? What are *your* plans?" she asked carefully.

Tor chuckled, but the sound was entirely without humor. "Gods, Keely, a plan is one of the many things I don't have. I used to be the man everyone came to for strategy, but now... now I struggle to see past tomorrow. I don't have a plan. Not for... anything."

She rubbed her lips, still feeling the rawness from his kisses, the burn of his stubble on her throat. "What exactly didn't you plan, Tor?"

His voice lowered, coming out rough and miserable. "I didn't plan to be a mercenary or disowned or a fugitive from the king. I certainly haven't got any plans to leave the Hawks, and, although I spent a lot of time imagining it, I didn't plan—" He glanced up at the tree behind him, his words trailing off into silence.

She stiffened as the air punched out of her. How could he include what had happened between them in his list of losses?

She folded her arms over the aching tension in her chest. "You didn't plan to fuck the queen's maid up against a tree."

His eyes shot to hers. "Yes. No. I mean... I hoped—"

She stared down at him, speaking slowly as she forced

her voice not to shake. "Just so that we're completely clear…
you wanted to fuck me, but you expected me to leave the
next day. You didn't expect any kind of future with me?"

His eyes were wide, fists clenched tightly as he slowly
pushed himself to standing. His breeches were still
unbuttoned, his chest bare, his face tightened into a deep
scowl as he wrapped a big hand around the back of his
neck. His face was bleak and grim. But he didn't say
anything.

Keely dropped her head, her shoulders slumped, her
voice a rough murmur. "I thought you wanted… I thought
we…." She shook her head sharply, not finishing her
sentence.

How could she have been so wrong? Misread the
situation so cataclysmically?

She waited. Wishing—hoping—that he would tell her
she was wrong. That he did want her for more than one
unexpected afternoon.

But he didn't. He just stared at her with those dark eyes.

She had thought they were building something together.
She didn't know what exactly, but something. Something
promising. But all he'd wanted was a quick screw with
someone he thought was leaving.

Bard. This was exactly the problem with needing
someone. With starting to think you could rely on them.
When you discovered the truth—that you were on your own
—the pain was devastating.

She turned away from him, not prepared to stand there
in the silence as he stared at her for even one more second,
and started walking back down the path toward the Temple
at Eshcol. Leaving him behind.

She didn't know what she would find. Whether the
king's soldiers still roamed the woods or perhaps the famous

Nephilim Clibanarii warriors. And she didn't care. Alanna needed her, and she couldn't bear to stay with Tor.

Keely scrubbed her hands across her burning eyes and forced her chin up. Whatever happened, she wouldn't cry. She. Would. Not. Cry.

She kept the tears in all the way through the dark, cold woods until they were found in the early hours before dawn by a group of kindly Nephilim soldiers who brought them back to the temple.

She kept the tears in during Val's battle with Ballanor and the king's death. Even when Val fell to his knees in front of Alanna and asked her to marry him, Keely held on to the joy she felt for her friend, clung to the proof that there was right in the world, that there was love, even if it wasn't for her.

Keely did her best to carry on as usual. To ignore the way Tor now skirted around her and never spoke to her. To pretend she couldn't see the grief in his face when he looked at her. The dark rings under his eyes that suggested he was sleeping as little as she was. The way he continued to care for her. Apple pies that suddenly appeared on the menu. Ramiel arriving to offer the use of their shooting range if she wanted to borrow a crossbow. A new shirt and breeches that the Nephilim acolyte swore had been requested for her specifically. And she still didn't cry.

On the day Tor and Mathos rode away to look for Princess Lucilla, she waited for him all day. Waited for him to come to her and say something. Anything. She waited for him right up until Haniel told her that Tor and Mathos had taken their leave after lunch and were already miles away.

That was the first day she cried. Helpless, aching sobs that burned her throat and rattled through her chest until her face was swollen and her nose red and raw. That was the first day she chose to skip the meal she didn't really want anyway and stay in her room alone.

Nim came to see her, telling her more about how badly Tor's family had hurt him. Alanna dragged her outside, promising to help her hide the body when she finally decided to kill him. But she didn't want to kill him. It had been abundantly clear he was suffering as much as she was.

She spent the long weeks alone. As much as she loved Alanna and was coming to care for Nim, two happy couples were more than she could bear.

And she didn't feel like herself. That first catastrophic flood of tears had opened the gates, and now she wanted to cry all the time. Worry for Tor left her feeling constantly unsettled. Her lack of appetite and the lonely meals she snatched by herself meant she was increasingly queasy, and the sleepless nights were leaving her more and more exhausted.

Then Tor came back. He and Mathos had found Lucilla but they'd been ambushed by Dornar.

He was exhausted, hungry, and dirty from his flight across the kingdom, but alive at least. Within hours of his return, they were leaving for Glevum where they would meet the *Star of the Sea* and sail down the River Habren to look for Mathos and the new queen.

Within seconds of stepping onto the gleaming, orderly deck, she knew that the past weeks hadn't even begun to scratch the surface of suffering.

The ship rolled and heaved, assaulting her with motion, with the flickering of sunlight on the water, the pungent aroma of soldiers and weapons, salted meat, and freshly caught fish. Her simmering nausea churned up in an uncontrollable, acidic wave, and she only just made it to the rail before she vomited up everything she'd eaten that day.

And then she kept vomiting until there was nothing left but bile.

She wiped her mouth with the back of her hand, dropped her forehead to the rail, and let the bitter, lonely tears flow down her cheeks, dripping onto the polished wood and into the dark waters below.

Chapter Eight

TOR TOOK A STEP BACK, and another, not sure where he could stand that would allow him to avoid the celebration happening in Queen Lucilla's reception room without being rude.

A mere three weeks had passed since the *Star* had sailed down the Habren River and rescued Mathos and Lucilla, and now the queen was safely on the throne—crowned the day before in a glittering ceremony—with Mathos beside her.

Almost the first thing Lucilla had done on taking back her palace was to reinstate the Hawks and give them all promotions. The entire Royal Council, Tor's parents included, had been disbanded and sent away, and Lucilla was creating a new council to govern the kingdom. Mathos was a baron—a fucking baron—and consort to the queen, while Alanna and Val were married and about to travel north to finally ratify the treaty that would end the war.

The palace itself felt different, this room especially. The dark paintings and heavy drapes were gone, replaced with cream and cobalt-blue in a room designed to be comforting and warm. It was bright, even, despite the rain lashing at the windows, the wind rattling across the walls, and the darkness of encroaching winter.

But that warm comfort didn't reach Tor. He would have been more comfortable outside, where the cold and dark were the perfect accompaniment to the black frost that gripped his soul. The frost that surrounded everything he did, infected everything he said, and showed no sign of thawing. His duty to the Hawks was the only thing keeping him moving, but he couldn't bring himself to laugh or smile. Not even for them.

A massive fire gave off a gentle golden light, and the myriad of lamps and candles flickered warmly on the Hawks as they bantered with each other, drinking red wine from silver goblets and helping themselves to food from the huge trays left for them on the polished central table. Meat pies, rich with spice and buttery pastry. A whole salmon roasted in honey. Autumn berries drenched in cream. Gods. It was almost impossible to believe.

A few short weeks ago, they'd been mercenaries, living in exile, with no homes, no future, and very little hope. And now, here they were. Back in Kaerlud. In the palace with the new queen.

It was like a dream. Surreal and strange and hard to get a grip on. Or it would have been if it weren't for Keely. Keely, who would soon be traveling north with Val and Alanna. Keely, who haunted him like a living, breathing nightmare entirely of his own making.

They hadn't had a single real conversation since the disaster in the woods. She was icily polite, but nothing more. And he couldn't blame her. Honestly, he hadn't given her the chance to say anything more. Not since she'd turned around and walked away from him, facing the dark woods and Ballanor's soldiers rather than spend one more moment with him.

She had been so warm and soft and perfect in his arms as he sank against the tree. His breeches still unbuttoned, her shirt open, her bare legs resting on his. All he'd wanted was to hold her on his lap. To feel her breathing. See her pulse fluttering in her neck.

She had tucked herself against him, her head under his chin, and for one exquisite moment, everything in the world had been right. And then he'd opened his fucking mouth.

He could have apologized for what he'd said, but, day after day, he didn't. How could he, when he still didn't have a future he could offer her? When he might open his mouth and say something even more hideous. *You didn't plan to fuck the queen's maid up against a tree.* Gods.

Instead, he had wrapped himself in numbness and silence. He avoided her. Didn't speak to her. Didn't sit with her. He had kept away from her in the Temple of the Nephilim after they returned from the woods to find their friends already there. Avoided her during Val and Alanna's wedding. Timed his visits to Reece, recovering in the infirmary after the horrendous beating he'd received, to ensure he was alone. And then ridden away with Mathos to look for Lucilla without even saying goodbye.

His time with Keely was precious to him, and he couldn't bear to hear the final words that would end it forever. If he never gave her the chance, then she couldn't say them. If he stayed away, he couldn't say the wrong thing, and she couldn't say goodbye.

And yet, it was also relentless, abject torture. The time they'd been apart had done nothing to reduce how much he wanted to be with her. If anything, the torment of not being able to touch her had made him even more aware of everything she did.

He couldn't stop himself from looking for her, from checking she was safe. And he couldn't shake his profound gratitude that Alanna, Val, and Keely would all be coming back after the treaty was signed. It was the only thing that gave him any relief. She had decided to stay with the Hawks —she had said so.

Alanna and Val had been clear that they would come back in the spring. And Keely would follow her friend. She wouldn't leave her. The knowledge settled something in him. Keely would come back, and maybe they could try again.

Keely was wrong about what she'd said that day. He did want to be with her. Did want to hold her and touch her and talk to her. Every single day. He didn't want one meaningless fuck and to part ways. Not at all. But instead of telling her that, he'd let his fears for the future, his belief that she would never truly want him back, speak for him.

He'd failed her. And the truth was, as much as he wanted to give her whatever she needed, he was still failing her. She'd become increasingly withdrawn. Her creamy skin was now permanently wan, with dark smudges under her eyes in her too-thin face. She wasn't eating enough—he'd just seen her turn away yet another offer of food and drink. She had turned away the pastry. Gods, Keely loved pastry. And she never smiled. But the worst of it all was that she had stopped singing. The silence pressed down on him, shredding what was left of his heart.

That glowing spark of fire and defiance that had made her so vibrant was gone. And he had no idea how to get it back. He wanted what they'd had before. When she had teased him, liked him… trusted him. But he couldn't see how that was possible. And he couldn't bring himself to wish their time in the woods away.

If her silent misery wasn't bad enough, the thought that he was responsible for her suffering—that his words, his actions, had somehow taken something from her—made it infinitely worse. And day by day, he hated himself a little more.

Soon she would be heading north, away from him. Away from the scant protection he could offer, his feeble attempts to make her life more comfortable, for long weeks, months even, before they returned. Who would care for her? Who would check her shoulder, or ensure she was eating? Who else would worry that she never sang?

Gods. Had his silence been an even bigger mistake than his words? The thought settled on him slowly, sinking shamefully into his heart and lodging there.

He looked at her, sitting across the room, looking so pale and quiet, and accepted the truth. Avoiding her had been a mistake. He should have done something—anything—to make things right between them.

Suddenly he was desperate to speak to her. To spend time with her before she left. To apologize and make her see that she meant so much more to him than she thought. But he had no idea where to start.

Tor cracked his knuckles, taking out his frustration on his hands until Mathos glared at him from across the room and he wrapped his hand around the back of his neck instead.

He glanced at the clock on the mantelpiece, wondering whether he could sneak out without being noticed. He didn't want to lurk at the back of the room, watching Keely and feeling like an asshole. He would rather sit alone in his quarters, drinking cheap wine and feeling like an asshole. He needed to figure out what the hell he should say to her. How he could break this terrible silence between them.

"I saw that." Mathos grinned as he walked over and offered Tor a heaped plate. "You can't leave yet. I believe the excitement is about to start."

"Fuck off, Mathos," he replied tiredly, taking the plate and then putting it down on a nearby table.

"No." Mathos stood beside him, leaning his shoulder against the wall as if he owned the place. In a way, he probably did. "It's too much now, Tor. I've been watching you two staring at each other when you think the other won't notice for weeks. You, constantly trying to check on her without her noticing. Keely, spending longer and longer alone in her room. She hardly lasted more than an hour after Lucilla's coronation before she disappeared off by herself, probably to walk along the battlements again."

Tor dropped his head, kneading the tight muscles in his neck with his fingers. None of this was news. "What do you want from me, Mathos?"

"I want you to tell me what happened."

He closed his eyes for a moment. "Nothing happened."

Nothing except Keely wrapping her legs around him and pulling him closer, her mouth hot and demanding. Nothing except the feel of her soft skin, so smooth and warm under his palms. Her body pressed against his, enveloping him. Her sweet pleas almost shattering his control. Feeling as if he had seen the gods, there in that dark hollow. And then realizing that he was mortal after all, and utterly fallible.

He shook his head and repeated. "Nothing."

Mathos frowned. "It's not 'nothing.' Not for either of you. And speaking as the man who nearly fucked up his entire life by walking away from Lucilla, I think you're making a mistake."

Tor stared at his friend for a moment before admitting quietly, "I already made it."

"Then fix it."

"It's not that easy, I—" The room around them fell silent, except for the crackle of the fire, and he stopped speaking to see what was happening.

Gods. Tristan was on one knee in the middle of the room, looking up at Nim. Tristan's face was rough, harsh even, his entire body scaled in glittering emerald and pewter.

"Nim," Tristan's voice rasped. He swallowed audibly and then continued, "I love you, Nim. I... I mean we, my beast and I...." He paused to swallow again. "Fuck it."

Tor had never seen his stern friend look so unnerved. Angry, lethal, brutal, even devastated—yes. But unnerved, no.

Nim stepped closer, her body pressed against Tristan's as she cupped her hand on his cheek. Her wings flared out behind her, the firelight gleaming against the silvery leather. "Yes."

Tristan grunted. "I haven't asked you yet."

"Yes," Nim said, voice soft but clear in the quiet room. "To anything you ask."

Tristan turned his head into Nim's palm and closed his eyes, his scales flickering as they flattened. His eyes opened, and he took her free hand in his. "Will you marry me?"

"Yes." Nim's voice was firm, committed, and ringing with her deep joy, and Tor had to blink against the heated prickle in his own eyes.

Fuck it all.

Tristan slipped a ring onto her hand and then surged up

to wrap Nim in his arms as she giggled and not very subtly wiped her eyes on his shirt. Around them, their friends called out their congratulations, laughing and wrapping them in hugs and sharing their joy.

Val dragged Nim out of Tristan's arms to whirl her in a circle while she shrieked, and then dropped her back in Tristan's arms and clapped him on the back.

The room was overflowing with compliments and excitement, and Tor knew he should step forward and add his own. Knew that they deserved every moment of happiness they had together. Nim and Tristan were perfect for each other. They had fought to be together.

But even so, their happiness stupidly, awfully, stabbed him right in the heart. Right in the tender place where he still dreamed of Keely. He paused, breathing down the shaft of jealousy that he knew was totally unacceptable. Unkind and unworthy of him, and unworthy of Tristan and Nim.

But mostly, he paused because of Keely. When Tristan lifted Nim, Keely had stepped back, her face drawn and her eyes gleaming suspiciously. The woman who never cried had subtly wiped her eyes with the back of her hand.

When everyone else had rushed forward, Keely had walked away, across the room. When Val spun Nim, Keely reached for the door. And when everyone else was focused on Nim and Tristan, she slipped through and disappeared.

The door closing behind Keely broke him from his daze, and he started to move. It was too much. He couldn't bear that she felt she had to leave her friends. She was a fighter. A warrior. He had to remind her.

He had stayed away, but it had been wrong. Maybe his words would make things worse, but he had to try. He had to say something. Had to tell her how much she meant to

everyone—to him—and how cold the world was without
her fire.

Crossing the room took forever. Alanna and Lucilla were
both determined to bring him into their celebration. He
congratulated Nim and Tristan, shook Val's hand, and did
his best to share in their excitement. And by the time he was
finally out the door, the corridor was empty.

Tor strode through the palace, nodding distractedly at
the new guards, hardly noticing the banners and flags still
flying since the queen's coronation. He saluted the Blue at
the entrance to the queen's private wing, where Keely had
also been given rooms, and leaped up the stairs two at a
time before marching down the long corridor to her room
and banging on the door.

His fist thudded against the wood but there was no
answer, no noise from inside at all. Was she even there? He
banged again, listening to the hollow echo.

Where could she have gone? She loved to walk the
battlements, but would she have gone there in the dark? In
the rain? Maybe. He could start there. He was turning to go
when the door opened behind him.

He spun slowly, not knowing what to expect. But
whatever he'd expected, it wasn't this. Not this tired-looking
woman, with her drawn face and suspicious wetness in her
eyes, an array of packed trunks and satchels littering the
floor behind her.

As he watched, she straightened her spine and rolled
back her shoulders. "What do you want?"

"I want to know what just happened."

She lifted her chin. "Nothing happened."

Gods. Nothing. Like the nothing he'd given Mathos.
Like the nothing he'd given her, day after day.

He gripped the edges of the doorframe, feeling the

wood creak beneath his weight. "I know that something is wrong. And I feel... responsible. Won't you... gods. Please, Keely, let me help."

She bit her lower lip. The movement so small and yet so evocative; it wrapped a fist around his heart and squeezed.

She wiped her hands down her face, releasing her lip, and sighed. "Why?"

He leaned forward, forcing himself to keep hold of the frame, forcing himself not to take her into his arms, knowing that wasn't what she wanted. "Why what?"

"Why do you want to help after all this time of pretending that I don't exist?"

"I didn't...I...." He took a breath. He had been avoiding her, they both knew it. "*You* are the one who walked away from me. You hiked through the forest in the middle of the night toward who knew what kind of danger to get away from me."

Her eyes narrowed. "And why was that, Tor? Do you remember?"

He closed his eyes and let his head drop, arms still outstretched like a supplicant. Did he remember? He didn't think he would ever forget. The scene played in his mind in a constant loop of regret and shame.

"Do you remember what you said, Tor?" Keely asked again.

Gods. He had let her think all he wanted was a quick fuck up against a tree when he should have just told her the truth: that he hadn't dared to dream that she would want to be with him, but he would hold her tight for as long as she would allow. That he wanted a future with her, he just hadn't imagined it. He should have admitted that he had nothing to offer her. And then he should have asked for her to stay with him—even if just for a little while—anyway.

He opened his eyes, his hands still gripping the door frame like a lifeline. "I remember."

"And now? Do your plans include me now?" she asked quietly, watching him carefully.

Gods. Everything had changed since that afternoon. Everything. He was back in the palace, surrounded by the Hawks, with all his old status and privileges, more even. And yet he still couldn't find it in him to plan the future. When he tried to imagine it, it faded into nothing. Or overwhelmed him with duties and obligations.

All except her. The time he'd spent with her was the only thing that made sense. He wanted his plans to include her, whatever they might be.

It didn't change that somewhere in her heart she had considered leaving. That she hadn't wanted to be with a soldier. That he was unworthy of her. But still, he could do what he should have done that day and tell her how important she was to him.

His voice was low enough to be a growl as he replied. "That time, with you, it meant a lot to me. I want us to be together, for however long that might be."

She frowned. "Why should I believe you, Tor, when you've done everything possible to show me that the last thing you want is to be with me?"

"Gods. I know. I just... didn't want to make it worse. And then so much happened so quickly... I was caught up in it all, and time passed, and every day that went by it got worse. And I didn't know how to fix it."

Her eyebrows raised. "And now you do?"

The wooden frame creaked under the strain of his grip. He didn't know how to fix it. But avoiding his feelings, avoiding her, wasn't working either. "No. I don't know anything. I only know that I can't live like this. I can't bear watching you from across the room when all I want to do is touch you. I want us to try again… to be together. Friends, if that's all you need. To be anything you want, for however long you'll have me."

He looked her in the eye and tried to show her how sincere he was. "Please."

For the first time her expression softened, and she took a small step forward.

"And then what?" she asked in a low voice.

He forced his fingers to loosen. "What do you mean?"

"What do you imagine for us? Can you even see a future where we're together?"

He let go of the doorframe to grip the back of his neck. He had nothing to give her except honesty. "I don't know what having a future even means."

"Why not?" she asked, a hint of her old fire creeping back into her voice. "Tell me exactly what I'm incapable of giving you so that I can understand."

He flinched. "There's nothing you're incapable of— gods, Keely, I've never doubted that you can do anything you want. That's not it. It's my whole life that feels out of control."

He tightened his fingers on the muscles at the back of his neck, holding on. How could he explain when it didn't even make sense to him?

"Why now, Tor?" Keely asked quietly. "Why are you saying all this to me now?"

"Because I can't stand for you to go back to Verturia with Val and Alanna without speaking to you. Because I spend all day thinking about you and I need you to know that I want to be with you." His voice dropped to a whisper. "I miss you."

She swallowed. "I miss you too. But Tor, these weeks—"

She shook her head slowly. "My life is more complicated now. Before, I wanted to know that I meant something to you. I wanted to feel that there was a chance for us. But now… now I need to know that you can truly see some kind of future together."

Fuck. The hurt gleaming in her eyes nearly broke him. And he understood. So much had changed so quickly, it was no wonder she wanted to be more settled—especially after the months she'd spent living in fear under Ballanor's rule. She had talked about wanting a home, and he wanted to give her one. But he wasn't sure that what he had was enough. He had no name to offer. He had a room in the barracks, the uniform he wore, and his grandfather's sword, but nothing else in the world. And Keely wanted—she deserved—more than just another soldier.

She lifted her hand as if to reach out toward him, but then dropped it back at her side, and he felt the loss of that almost-touch in his soul. Long seconds passed as she watched him, and he watched her. She was looking for something, or deciding something, but he didn't know what.

Eventually, her spine straightened, and she lifted her chin, shoulders squared as if she was facing a battle rather than talking to him from the warm safety of her room. "Come with me, Tor. We can travel north together and figure things out between us. I would like to… to try again."

Gods, he wished he could go north with her and leave everything else behind. Wished it with every cell in his body.

But wouldn't that make everything worse, knowing he had failed in his duties yet again and abandoned his new queen without enough protection? Geraint had died under his care; how could he leave Lucilla while she was vulnerable? How could he leave the Hawks—the men who had stood by him after Ravenstone—when they needed him?

He shook his head, fighting off the almost overwhelming temptation to leave it all behind and follow Keely. "I have responsibilities here. Commitments. I wish that I could leave them behind and be with you, I really do."

The softness in her eyes faded. "You wish you could… but you won't? You won't even ask if you can be assigned to Alanna's guards so that you can perform your duties with me? So that we could spend this time together?"

Gods. That wasn't what he was saying. He was needed at the palace. They were massively under-resourced; Tristan and Jeremiel had interviewed all the Blues and been forced to remove vast swathes of Ballanor's appointments, and the Hawks were now trying to replace them without compromising on Lucilla's security. Who would he be if he failed them now?

In truth, he also needed the time to find himself again and make a life worthy of Keely. He needed to prove that he was good enough for her. She had walked away from him once already, and he couldn't bear to go through that again. It would be better for her to go north, then, when she came back, everything would be different. "I have to stay here because this is where I'm needed, but when you get back, we can talk. Really talk. I'd like to—"

She lifted her head and looked him in the eye, a weary resignation settling over her face, and he swallowed the rest of his words. She didn't seem to have heard anything past his refusal to leave Kaerlud anyway.

"Bard." She spoke softly, almost to herself. "This is where you're needed. Here. Not where I…." Her sentence faded into nothing.

Gods. This was going as badly as he had feared. "Keely, please. Give me some time to figure everything out."

Her eyebrows drew together. "All these weeks weren't enough?"

Damn. How had he left her alone for so long? What had happened to all that time? What the fuck was wrong with him?

He was sure he hadn't asked the question out loud, but she answered him anyway. "Shall I tell you what I think, Tor?"

He dipped his chin slowly, and she continued. "I think that what your parents did to you was despicable. I can't even imagine what kind of a person would treat their child like that."

His parents? What the hell did they have to do with anything?

Her voice wobbled, but she didn't stop. "I think they wounded you in ways that you haven't admitted, even to yourself. You've never allowed yourself to grieve. And until you do—until you let yourself truly feel the depth of what they did—you'll never accept what's happened, and you'll never be able to move forward. When you numb yourself, when everything is one big fog, it's easy for the days to pass in a blur. I know because I've done it myself."

He fought the urge to crack his knuckles and kept his focus trained on Keely as she continued, "I think that you'll never trust me to care for you, to accept you as you are, because *they* didn't. And that's why you can't see a future for us."

She sighed. "But Tor, I need that from you. I need you to want a future with me. I'm not expecting you to commit your whole life, or even your whole heart, but just… that you'll try."

Keely clasped her hands in front of her belly, twisting her fingers together in a way that told him far more than her firm voice and clear eyes. "And here's something more for you to think about," she continued. "Even if your parents came back to the palace tomorrow. Even if they suddenly realized how cruel they were and fell to their knees apologizing for what they've done... they still wouldn't approve of me."

Keely held his gaze. "You have to make a choice. Hold on to what's left of the past, of the dreams you used to have, or create new ones. And I get it, Tor. I do. I know what it is to be so lost, so deeply hurt, that it's almost inconceivable to even imagine a future again."

She looked impossibly tired and vulnerable, standing in the doorway to her room. But her shoulders were back, her chin lifted, and she didn't falter. She was still the woman he'd first seen hurling her defiance at Ballanor.

"Who are *you*, Tor? Who do you want to be now that you're standing on your own feet without them? Don't make the mistake that I did and wait ten years before you answer that question."

She wiped her hands down the outside of her legs as if her palms were damp. "I'd thought that maybe, one day, I would stand beside you—that we could stand together—but now.... Bard. The truth is that you don't want me enough to risk it. What you feel for me is not enough to pull you out of that fog. And a vague promise that you've missed me is not enough for me. Not anymore."

He shoved his hands into his pockets, hunching his shoulders helplessly. He didn't want that to be true. It couldn't be true. He *did* want her enough to take the risk. He was trying to do the right thing for them both. Wasn't he?

But she wasn't done.

She looked at him, her jade-green eyes seeing all the way through him. "Once upon a time, I fell in love with a boy. It was a springtime love, of youth and stolen kisses, but it was still love. His family wanted him to fight in the border wars, but he didn't want to go—he was a musician and a farmer, not a soldier—and he was in love with a girl who wanted him to stay. But he left, like they asked him to, like they expected him to. In the end, their approval was more important to him than anything else. And he died there, Tor. Your family took their approval away from you, and it's killing you too."

He stared at her silently, trying to find some kind of response, but failing. He needed to speak. Knew he had to open his mouth and say something. His silence had cost him all this time with her already. But he couldn't process the feelings churning inside him. Couldn't deal with his confusion, the multitude of swirling thoughts. He couldn't find the words he needed.

Long moments passed until she sighed, a long, sad release of breath. "Can you think about it, at least? There's more… more to discuss." Keely swallowed. "Will you come and see me before we leave? Please?"

He dipped his chin in slow agreement, not quite able to say the words. She waited, the silence growing heavy around them, but he couldn't make himself respond.

"Okay," she whispered eventually, stepping back. "Goodnight, Tor." And then she closed the door in his face. And bolted it.

Chapter Nine

KEELY LEANED AGAINST THE DOOR, biting her lip, and staying silent as the oak creaked with Tor's weight.

She could imagine him—palms pressed against the wood, those sinuous black-and-red tattoos highlighting the bulky muscles on his forearms, eyes the color of midnight focused intently on the closed door.

Oh, he could take the door off the hinges if he wanted to, but he never would. Her body and her space were completely safe with him. But not her heart—the very part of her she'd sworn not to risk again. And look at her now.

The door creaked again as his weight lifted, and then his heavy footsteps thudded on the soft carpeting. He was leaving. It was what she wanted. Wasn't it?

She counted to twenty-five before finally allowing herself to step softly across to her bed, avoiding the filled trunks and satchels lying in orderly piles, to crawl onto the neatly made covers and lie, face down, steeped in her misery.

Bard. She had been so proud of her strength. Of

keeping her eyes dry, and her heart safely guarded for so many years. And Tor had ripped that all away.

She should have known better. Should have known to keep him at a good safe distance, known not to start dreaming again. And yet... she had still hoped. And every time she thought she might finally be getting over him, he did something to remind her why she had liked him so much in the first place.

He missed her. He spent all day thinking about her. He wanted to be with her. And damn it all, she wanted it too. But he'd hurt her. And he still couldn't see a real future for them. And now... well, now the future was all she could see.

A gentle knock sounded at the door; nothing like Tor's demanding thumps, but she really didn't want to see anyone. She kept quiet, hoping they would give up and go away.

"It's me and Lucilla," Alanna called softly from the corridor. "Please can we come in?"

Keely pressed the heels of her palms into her stinging eyes and cleared her throat. "I'm... um...." Bloody hell. Why couldn't she think of a good lie?

"We'll help with... whatever it is," Lucilla added.

"Or we can wait," Alanna agreed firmly. "Take as long as you need."

Keely sighed. There were two of them, they weren't going to go away, and she didn't have it in her to argue. She got up, grumbling to herself as she stepped over boxes and slid back the bolt to open the door.

The two women walked in quickly, as if they were worried she might close the door again. Thankfully, they kept any comments about her red eyes and chewed lip to themselves. And, even better, they hadn't taken it on themselves to bring her any food.

It had been bad enough sitting in the queen's reception room with the pungent aromas of cooked meat and spice, salmon, and fresh crab pastries. Fish. Bard, she couldn't even think of it without wanting to heave.

Alanna sat in the cozy armchair under the window, while Lucilla sat on the side of the bed, both wearing loose woolen dresses and boots and wrapped in blankets. Neither of them looked even vaguely royal. They glanced meaningfully at each other and then at the array of packed boxes covering the floor.

Keely sighed again and walked to stand beside the window. She turned to face into the room and perched on the sill, trying to smile. Damn. When did it get so difficult to smile? Her face felt weirdly contorted as her cheeks pulled into a grimace.

Alanna gave her a long, careful look, and Keely swallowed against the ache in her throat.

"You can say it. Whatever it is," Keely said quietly. Did her words sound as dejected to her friends as they did to her?

Alanna rose from her seat to wrap her arms tightly around Keely's shoulders, pulling her into a hug. Bard, she needed a hug so badly. And now she was going to cry.

"Keely, my friend, we want to help," Alanna said quietly as she pulled away to sit back in the armchair. Giving her the space she needed to hold herself together. "Tell us what you need."

What did she need? So many things. But nothing that Alanna or Lucilla or anyone else could help with. This was something she had to deal with on her own.

"We saw Tor follow you," Alanna admitted quietly into the silence.

Keely swallowed against the lump in her throat as she forced her voice not to wobble. "We spoke."

"I take it that didn't go well?" Lucilla said gently.

She shrugged. This time she didn't even try to smile.

Lucilla shook her head. "Gods. Was it that bad?"

Keely snorted sadly reminding herself that Alanna and Lucilla had come because they wanted to help. They were her friends. For so many years, she had cared for other people, without sharing her own fears and losses. But now she didn't want to hold it all in anymore.

She scrubbed her hand tiredly down her face. "I thought a lot about what you said, you know, when Mathos was being an ass. About fighting for him, about how you knew you'd done everything you could."

"And did you decide to fight for Tor?" Alanna asked as Lucilla dipped her chin in understanding.

Keely bit her lip. "I… yes. I asked him to come north with us to Verturia. To give us a chance to figure out what we were to each other."

"And he said…?" Alanna prompted.

"He said that he missed me, that he wanted to be with me, and he wanted to come, but that he had responsibilities here. That he needed more time to figure everything out."

Lucilla choked. "More time? More than he's already had?"

Yes. That was what she needed to hear. Someone to tell her she wasn't being unreasonable. That she wasn't making a terrible mistake. Keely shrugged again, but this time her shoulders felt a little looser.

"Gods." Lucilla folded her arms, face twisted into a dark glare. "I think I should dismiss him from the palace guards, that will give him time to think—"

"No. Please, Lucilla, that would just make it worse. He's

genuinely struggling—you should have seen him, he looked so lost. He's miserable too." Keely spoke slowly, sorting through her thoughts. "I suspect that, deep inside him, he still wants to get back to the time when the world made sense. And I understand that; I really do."

She glanced at Alanna, knowing her friend would remember. "I stayed on the farm for nearly a year thinking that there might have been some kind of mistake and Niall would be coming back. That he would look for me there. It took my father's death and Mama moving to Duneidyn before I could accept that he was gone."

Alanna frowned. "But this is different. Tor's parents looked him right in the face and disowned him."

Keely shook her head. Grief was never logical.

"But what about when the—" Lucilla started, only to swallow her words as Alanna cleared her throat loudly, cutting her off midsentence.

Keely turned to look at her best friend; at her wide eyes and determined glare. And then she turned back to Lucilla, noting the deep red flush climbing up her throat. Lucilla gave Alanna a sheepish look before quickly looking away. Damn.

"You know!" Keely whispered raggedly.

Her heartbeat thrummed in her ears as her palms grew clammy. Her stomach heaved, and she fought it down. Fought back the rising bile and the aching spasm in her throat. That awful nausea that had become her constant companion. They knew. When she hardly even knew it herself.

Did everyone know? Did Tor know? No. He couldn't. He would have said something.

In seconds, Alanna was out of her chair and wiping Keely's hair back from her eyes, using her sleeve to dab at the drops of perspiration on Keely's forehead, her other hand settling in a reassuring weight on her shoulder. "Do you need a pot?"

Keely shook her head helplessly as Alanna wrapped her arms around her once more, holding her tightly. "Oh, Keely, my friend. We're here for you. Whatever you need. You know that, don't you?"

And then the tears came. The tears she had held back all through her conversation with Tor—even when he'd left and she was truly alone—burning her eyes and her throat as she sobbed. She rested her head on Alanna's shoulder and wept.

She let herself go completely, let herself fill with grief and loss and fear and the still-churning nausea. For the first time in years, she let her friend comfort her. Let herself lean on someone else.

Eventually, her sobs quietened and Alanna led her to the bed and settled her, propped up on pillows against the headboard, a soft woolen blanket over her knees like a child. Lucilla passed her a cup of water, and she took a small sip as the need to be sick faded. She wasn't going to hurl, thank the Bard. But she still had tears leaking down the sides of her face.

"I keep crying," Keely admitted, swiping at her face with her palms. "It's bloody annoying."

Alanna chuckled and took her hand gently as she settled onto the bed beside her. "That's normal, I think."

"Nim's going to put a basket together for you," Lucilla said from the bottom of the bed. "She's putting ginger root in it for tea, and ginger cookies for snacks, for you to take with you when you head north. She said it might help with the nausea."

Keely blinked. "How long have you known?"

"Only the last few days," Alanna admitted. "We thought you were still struggling with seasickness and whatever happened between you and Tor. But then you left dinner early one day, and Nim realized it was when they served the herring in—" Alanna noticed Keely's heavy swallow and stopped speaking.

"We wanted to give you a chance to tell us," Lucilla admitted quietly, "but we started to wonder if you would. Mostly we just want to help."

Keely's eyes burned. They wanted to help, but she didn't quite know how to take it.

"What did Tor say about the baby?" Alanna asked softly. "When you spoke to him earlier."

Her throat ached as she replied. "I didn't tell him…. I was going to, but then he started talking about how he was needed here, not with me, and I…." She took a trembling breath. All she'd been able to think about was how she was begging another man to choose her—and failing.

Bard. She couldn't think like that. She had more important worries than her pride.

"Are you going to tell him?" Alanna asked eventually.

"Yes. Of course." She straightened her shoulders and tried to fill her voice with confidence she didn't feel. "He needs to know. And… the, uh… the—"

She swallowed and tried again. "The baby must have the chance to know its da." Bard. It was the first time she'd said the word out loud.

Baby.

It was strangely terrifying, as if she'd made it real by saying it. But, at the same time, she felt lighter. A massive weight had lifted, at least a little. She'd said the word she'd been avoiding as if it was a curse. She'd said it, and the world hadn't ended. The fire still crackled in the hearth, her trunks were still packed, Alanna and Lucilla hadn't run from the room. She could say it. Baby.

"I asked Tor to think about everything and come to see me before we leave. I'll tell him about the baby then. And I'll ask again if he would like to come with us."

Alanna and Lucilla nodded slowly, but there was more she still had to say. One more thing to admit. "If he doesn't want to—if Tor chooses to stay here—I've decided to go home."

Alanna stilled while Lucilla frowned. "Home to Verturia?"

"Yes. I haven't been back to the farm in years, but… it's time. I want to see my mama, to walk along the walls at Duneidyn, and then… then I'll go back to the farm where I grew up."

Alanna watched her carefully. "And what will you do on the farm?"

"I don't know. Oversee the crops. Raise some chickens, maybe." She had a bit of money saved. She was going to do this, and she was going to be fine. They were both going to be fine.

Alanna snorted softly, shaking her head.

"What's wrong with chickens?"

"You hate chickens."

Keely shrugged. "That's just because they're bloody stupid." There were other reasons. More complicated reasons, but she didn't need to explain those. She gave Alanna an apologetic smile. "I need to make a home."

"I guess I always thought you'd be coming back with us," Alanna replied gently.

She wiped her eyes and tried to lighten her voice. "You're busy with Val now, and I had been thinking of going back to visit anyway. I'd already been thinking that I really should start making a life for myself, not just follow you around."

Alanna's hand tightened on hers, squeezing her fingers. Keely half expected Alanna to argue, but all she did was hold her hand, silently giving her support. Bard. It was enough to start the tears again.

"You can make a home here," Lucilla argued for both of them. "You already know that I'd love for you to join the council. You're honest, intelligent, and thoughtful, you're great at seeing the broader picture, and you have an excellent sense for when people are talking bullshit. I told you all of this when I invited you the first time."

Keely shook her head. "I would have been honored to be on your council, Lucilla. But it's too hard. I don't want to spend every day here watching Tor while he pretends not to be watching me."

Tor made her vulnerable. He made her imagine what it would be like to have things that he wasn't ready to give her. And that *hurt*. No. He hadn't asked for any of this, and she wasn't going to manipulate or pressure him into it.

Lucilla snorted sadly. "I genuinely think he cares for you."

Keely pulled her blanket up higher wrapping it over her shoulders. Caring for someone wasn't enough. If there was anyone in the world who understood that, it was her. "So do I. But he has to figure out what he wants."

She leaned over and picked up a sealed letter from her bedside table, spinning it over as she handed it to Lucilla so that they could all read Tor's name clearly written in black ink across the front. "If anything goes wrong, if I don't get to tell him, for whatever reason, will you give this to Tor for me, please? Maybe, just, give him a couple of days after we go to find his feet."

Lucilla took the letter. "But you'll be in Verturia—"

"If he wants to come and see us, he can. And if he's too busy or he'd rather stay here, that's his choice too."

She would be away from him, away from the weakness she felt around him. Away from his deep voice telling her he missed her… but not enough. Away from the tiny, fragile hope that had begun to grow in her heart, and then been shattered.

Lucilla nodded slowly. "Of course. I'll keep it safe and give it to Tor for you."

"Thanks." Keely let her shoulders slump, suddenly exhausted and desperate to slide down properly in her bed and sleep. Sleep and forget everything. Bard. She couldn't remember ever being so tired before in her life.

She had done everything she could. She had asked Tor to go with her. She had arranged to speak with him. She was leaving a letter in case anything went wrong. "You're right, you know," she said softly to Lucilla. "This is better. I fought for him. Whatever he decides, I'll know that I tried."

The only thing she wasn't prepared to do was stay in Kaerlud. Waiting and wishing, constantly looking out for a man to come back to her—only to get her heart broken—wasn't for her. She couldn't do it again.

Within the next few days, he would know everything. And if he didn't want to join them in Verturia, she would start again. She would find herself again. She would be the strong mother that the tiny spark of life growing in her belly deserved.

Chapter Ten

TOR SWUNG HIS GREATSWORD TWO-HANDED, starting low and sweeping up in a wide circle over his shoulder and back down. Then he switched to the other side in another huge arc. And switched again.

His arms burned and sweat ran down his face despite the icy wind curling through the empty early-morning parade ground, but he kept swinging.

It was the Bar-Ulf sword—passed down to him when he left to join the military—a sword that represented centuries of family history. And yet, despite all the wealth and power his grandfather had accumulated, here he was, exercising alone on the parade ground. He'd been disowned, Keely was gone, and the Hawks were hardly speaking to him. What would his grandfather think? Probably exactly what his parents had thought. That they were better off without him.

He swung the heavy sword again. And again. Wide, muscle-tormenting, back-breaking arcs. Normally it was a meditation for him, a time, each day, to push his body and calm his mind. But not today. Not on any of the days since his final conversation with Keely.

They wounded you…. You have to make a choice…. You don't want me enough….

He swung harder, hefting the heavy steel up and over, around and down, and then again on the other side. Relishing the pain. *You'll never be able to move forward.* Gods.

He swung his sword until he could smell his own sour sweat, until his arms were shaking with exhaustion. And then he swung it again.

Your family took their approval away from you, and it's killing you.

You don't want me enough.

The words boiled through his brain, and he couldn't make them stop. No matter how many hours he spent swinging the heavy sword, drilling the new guards, drinking alone in his room, he couldn't forget.

Three nights since she'd said goodnight and closed the door in his face. Two days. And one dawn. The longest, most torturous hours of his life.

Because she was right. He had wanted the safety of the days before his life went to shit. He'd wanted his certainty back, wanted to feel as confident of his life as he had before Ravenstone. And maybe he had even held a tiny, conflicted hope that his family would take him back.

But she was wrong that he didn't want her enough.

He had fucked up because saying the right thing was so bloody difficult. And he'd really fucked up by leaving her alone for so long. The long weeks away from her had made her doubt the truth of how much he wanted to be with her. And who could blame her?

She didn't trust that he wanted her. And he couldn't make himself believe that she would stay with a man like him. Discussing it again, repeating the same words again, wouldn't have helped.

Which was why he hadn't gone to see her before she left.

He still couldn't leave his responsibilities. The look on her face when she'd asked him to travel to Verturia and he'd said no had nearly broken him. He couldn't go through that twice. And, if he was being honest, he couldn't bear to say goodbye.

He had watched from the battlements as they prepared to leave. Keely, Alanna, and Val leading the way. Jos and Rafe just behind them. A squad of hand-picked guards forming up at the rear. They were newly recruited cavalry soldiers, all vetted by Jeremiel and Tristan, all proud to be wearing their brand-new Blues. But *he* didn't know them.

He had forced himself not to charge down the stairs and insist that they take more soldiers. Even better, take more of the Hawks, men they knew they could trust on the long road north.

But Tristan was needed in the palace, Mathos would never leave Lucilla, and Garet and Jeremiel were working with the new Blues. Recruiting, training, overseeing—while Jeremiel took the role of senior truth seeker, responsible for determining exactly how the soldiers and staff had behaved under Ballanor.

Which left Tor. He could have asked to travel with the squad to Verturia. Maybe he should have? Keely had asked him to go… and she'd been hurt that he had stayed behind. She'd tried to hide it behind her stiff shoulders and her firm gaze, but he knew her well enough to know the truth. He knew how good she was at masking her pain and pretending she wasn't bleeding.

It was another reason why he hadn't gone to see her. He was already halfway convinced that he should go north with her. If she asked again, he probably would have abandoned his commitments to be with her.

He had made himself watch, looking down at her while she stood beside her horse long after everyone else was in their saddles. Almost as if she was waiting. Maybe even waiting for him. She'd looked up, once, and he'd almost imagined that she'd seen him, but then she'd turned away again.

He'd had to remind himself that time apart would help. That he could use it to get himself together, to mold himself back into someone worthy. That he was protecting them both. He'd leaned against the stone, using it like an anchor, and forced himself to watch her ride away.

But, in the time since she had left, he'd slowly realized that he'd been wrong. The time apart was not helping. He was not getting himself together. Instead, he felt as if he had taken his sword to his chest, carved his heart out, and sent it with her.

Their party would be traveling slowly to account for the wagons and the carriage that would be accompanying them. They'd been traveling for two days so far, so that gave another four or five before they crossed through the pass into Verturia. Then another day to the capital at least.

Unless there was snow. Or heavy rain. Or problems on the road. Or reivers… bands of roaming outlaws looking for easy riches. How tempting would the obviously wealthy travelers be to men and women starving since the war? Or… fuck. He couldn't let himself think about it or he would go insane.

Alanna, Val and Keely would stay in Verturia for midwinter, waiting for the spring thaws to open the passes before returning. They were going to be the worst damn months of Tor's life. But when Keely got back, he was going to tell her how much he needed her. That he *did* choose her. That he wanted her, not just enough, but far more than enough. Her laugh. Her fire. Her strength. Her friendship and her trust. Her body against his.

He would tell her that he finally understood—it didn't matter what the future looked like, so long as they faced it together. But, damn, it was going to be a long, dark winter first.

He let his swings falter and then stop, dropped his sword to the earth, and let his head hang, his gaze fixed on the steel digging into the frozen mud as the sweat cooled on his back. And finally accepted the truth: he should have gone with her.

"No answers there, mate," Mathos drawled from behind him.

It was the first time any of the Hawks had spoken to him outside of completing their duties since the night he'd followed Keely from the queen's rooms. Their silence had hurt. They were his only family now, and they were treating him like a stranger. But, in a way, he welcomed it; it was exactly what he deserved after the pain he'd caused Keely.

He turned to face his friend, lifting the heavy sword to wipe it clean on his breeches and slide it into its scabbard. "Where do you suggest I look then?"

Mathos shook his head, frowning, as if Tor should already know the answer. "Lucilla wants to see you. She's in the council room."

Tor looked down at himself, at his muddy, sweaty leathers, his skin stinking of last night's cheap wine and the morning's brutal workout. "I'll be there in ten minutes."

"Fine. Don't be late." Mathos spun around and walked back to the palace, not even bothering to make a joke or snide comment as Tor followed him in.

Tor had been closer to Mathos than anyone else on the squad, but now his friend seemed to want as much distance between them as possible. The rest of the squad were clearly annoyed, but not like Mathos and Tristan—Val too, before he left. Gods, they were furious with him. He couldn't blame them; Lucilla, Nim, and Alanna were friends with Keely. But he had never felt so alone, or so unsure of himself. Honestly, he would have preferred it if the squad took their anger out on him with their fists.

It took slightly longer than ten minutes, but by the time he strode past the pair of guards at the door and into the council room, at least he'd changed into a clean tunic and washed away the worst of the stink.

He paused, taking in the massive table covered in papers and plans. There was a plate balanced on one side holding a half-eaten breakfast roll. Queen Lucilla, wearing her chosen uniform of breeches, boots, and embroidered tunic, was leaning over a plan of the palace beside Tristan.

By the sound of it, they were working on a series of changes Tristan had recommended for the Blues. The Clibanarii barracks at the Temple of the Nephilim had inspired him to change the way the palace guards lived and trained, and he was busy explaining the work he was hoping to start in the spring.

Tristan finished his sentence, and they both lifted their heads to look at Tor where he stood in the doorway. Tristan with his usual scowl, immaculate in his new uniform, the queen with a somber, assessing expression.

He gave a polite bow. "Your Majesty. Supreme Commander Tristan."

"Tor. Thank you for coming." Lucilla turned to Tristan. "These look good, thank you. Please tell Mathos the work is approved and that he should get the steward and the Master of the Treasury to sit down and start working on finances."

Tristan grunted, his lips twitching up. "Mathos will be so pleased."

Lucilla grinned back as Tristan gathered up his papers and gave a short bow before excusing himself without even glancing at Tor. But then her smile faded.

Tor kept his hands clasped behind his back, legs apart, slightly braced, and waited. Lucilla muttered something under her breath, but it didn't seem like she was talking to him, so he stayed quiet. Eventually, she lifted an envelope from a pile on the table and held it out to him. "Keely asked me to give you this."

He took it slowly. The thick paper was folded and sealed with dark wax, his name boldly scribed in black ink in Keely's handwriting.

"What is this?" he asked carefully, feeling the overworked muscles in his shoulders bunching as he fought the urge to wrap a hand around the back of his neck.

Lucilla ignored his question. "Why didn't you talk to her before she left?" she asked.

"I…." Gods. Because it was too hard. Because he couldn't have her, not until he could offer her what she needed. Because he might have fallen to the ground and begged her to take him with her.

He couldn't find the words to explain any of that, but he owed his queen the truth. "Because I didn't want to say goodbye," he admitted.

Lucilla hesitated for a moment, her dark eyes searching his. She walked slowly across the room and settled her hand on his arm. It was the first kind gesture from anyone since Keely had left.

"Do you realize that she's not coming back?" Lucilla asked softly.

He shook his head. Not coming back? No. That was a mistake. He cleared his throat and forced his voice to work. "I beg your pardon?"

"Keely's gone. She's not coming back with Alanna and Val when they return in the spring."

He shook his head again, trying to clear it as much as to deny Lucilla's words. Keely *was* coming back. She had to come back. Gods.

Alanna was her best friend, and Alanna had promised to come back and support Lucilla as she learned how to rule the kingdom. Yes, Keely had been thinking about going to Verturia—that's what had started this whole mess—but she'd chosen to stay with the Hawks. She'd told him.

She was coming back, and he was going to tell her how he felt. They were going to talk and…. Gods.

"She *is* coming back. After midwinter. I can't… I mean —" His words faded away in confusion.

Lucilla's expression softened. "She said something about a farm with chickens."

Tor blinked. "She hates chickens."

It didn't make any sense. Why wouldn't she come back? He was going to explain. To ask for another chance. She knew that… didn't she? But… he hadn't gone to her. Gods. Did she think he'd already made his choice, and that he hadn't chosen her?

Lucilla shrugged sadly. "Go and look at her room."

He shoved the letter into his tunic and bowed, unable to think of anything to say, before spinning around and marching up to the queen's wing.

Keely's door was open. Maids were inside laying sheets over the furniture, and they'd opened the window to let in the cold morning air. The room was bleak and freezing. And everything Keely owned was gone.

She had brought her life with her when she came down to Brythoria with Alanna, expecting to stay forever. And then she'd lived in the palace for nearly a year after Alanna married Ballanor. But every single thing she'd owned and used in all that time was gone.

He put a hand onto the wall and leaned heavily on it. How could she be gone? How could she leave and not say anything?

Will you come and see me before we leave? Please?

Fuck.

Her letter burned against his chest. It would be her goodbye. Her final words to him. And he didn't want to read it. She would have tried to do the right thing. She would have told him she was leaving, forgiven him, and wished him well. That was Keely's way—always looking after everyone except herself. And he couldn't bear it.

He didn't need to read her final goodbye to know that Lucilla was right, Keely wasn't coming back. There would be no reunion. No chance to explain or beg for another chance.

He pushed off the wall and walked away as a deluge of guilt and grief threatened to overwhelm him. Keely was gone. The one bright spark in his life—the only person who made him feel any joy—was gone.

It was all he could do to push down the storm of seething emotions and hold himself together. But he did it.

Had he walked these same corridors when his parents threw him out? He couldn't quite recall. Gods.

Somehow, he made it down the stairs, past the guards, and back into the administrative corridors where the stewards, chaplains, and marshals did their work. Without even really thinking about it, he found himself outside the door to Tristan's new office.

He knocked twice and opened the door when Tristan grunted.

The new Supreme Commander looked up from his desk, eyes narrowed. "First Lieutenant Tor."

Tor didn't wait to be asked, he simply stepped forward and sank into the hard, wooden chair opposite Tristan. If he didn't sit down, he was going to fall. What had he done?

He wrapped his hands around the back of his neck and forced himself to breathe. To push his shocked misery far down where he could only feel a small part of it. To take back control of his churning emotions. "Did you know? That Keely wasn't coming back."

Tristan leaned back, scowling darkly, but slowly, as his eyes traveled over Tor hunched in the chair opposite him, his face softened. "I knew."

"Gods, Tristan. Why didn't you say anything?"

A wave of emerald green and pewter scales flickered up Tristan's arms. "It wasn't my place."

Tor let out a harsh snort. They had known. Known she was leaving. Forever. Known that he had fucked up completely by not going with her. And not one of them had said anything.

"I thought you were my friend." The admission scraped out of him. This was his squad, the only people in the world he thought he could trust. The only family he had left.

Tristan leaned forward, his scales gleaming all the way up his neck. "I'm more than your friend, Tor. I'm your brother. And so are all the Hawks. Which is why we've given you the space you seemed to want. You should be grateful that we've left you alone instead of ripping you apart for hurting Keely. You know the code."

Sister to one was sister to all. Gods. And Keely was as good as Alanna's sister. His breath ached in his too-tight lungs. "Maybe you should have," he admitted softly.

Tristan grunted. "Honestly, we probably would have, but Keely asked us to let you be."

Tor let his head drop between his elbows, his black-and-red tattoos blurring into fiery brands over his folded arms. Keely was still protecting him, despite everything.

Tristan picked up his pen and tapped it on the desk, the noise jarring in the quiet room. "Did you know that your father had written to me?"

"What?" He lifted his head to stare at Tristan, bewildered by the sudden change in topic.

"Your father," Tristan repeated. "He would like positions for your two younger brothers in the Blues. He feels that the family should be considered given its—" Tristan looked out the window as if recalling the exact words. "—long and exalted history. He wants a meeting."

"What?" That didn't make any sense at all. Tor was in the Blues. Did they think Tristan hadn't noticed? Were they planning to work side by side with him and still pretend he didn't exist?

"They're hoping to come back to court," Tristan continued. "They've petitioned for a place for all four of them, with their two sons in the palace guard."

"Their two sons," Tor repeated helplessly.

"Fuck." Tristan wiped his hand down his face. "Sorry. You know what I mean." He looked warily across at Tor. "I take it that you didn't know?"

"No... I...." He took a breath. Let it out again. "No."

Gods. How did they do this to him? Make him feel so small and worthless when all he'd done his entire life was work himself to death trying to be good enough. Trying to make them proud. Scrabbling for….

Gods. For their approval. Just like Keely had said.

Tristan dipped his chin, his scales smoothing into skin. "I'll write back and say no."

Tor let his hands drop to the table, allowing Tristan's words to settle. He could ask Tristan to let them come and then use the opportunity to try and build something with them once again. Could make it known that they were only there because of him. Take the chance to recreate himself as the son of Pellin, son of Bar-Ulf. Pieces falling into place, one after the other.

Or he could let it all go, everything he'd once thought he was, and do the only thing that made any sense to him.

He imagined Keely, standing in her shift and defying the king. She would have fought for what she thought was right.

Gods. She *had* fought. She had fought for him. She had told him what she wanted in the woods, looked him in the eye and told him she would stay with the Hawks if he wanted her to, if he could see some future for them. And she had asked him to go north with her to Verturia. And he had let her go. Both. Fucking. Times.

But now the fog was clearing. "They can come if they like. I'm not going to be here."

Tristan raised an eyebrow. "You're not?"

"I need to take time off. Urgently…. Please."

Tristan snorted, but his eyes were understanding. "Actually, the queen has already approved a leave of absence for you. She's even provided you with a letter, under her seal, commanding all outposts between here and Verturia to provide you with anything you need. You can travel fast, changing horses, maybe catch them before the border."

Tor stood, surprised and grateful and desperate to get on the road. "Thank you. And please give my thanks to the queen."

Tristan put his hand out to shake. "You're still our brother, Tor. Be careful up there—the reports I'm getting aren't good. When Geraint ended the war, he stripped back the barracks to skeleton staff only, calling most of the senior officials back to Kaerlud. When they left, they took their protection and their money away with them. The reivers are worse than they've ever been, and one man alone on the road will be an attractive target."

Bloody hell. That was what Keely was riding toward. He had to get to her.

But Tristan wasn't finished. "And Tor, be careful with Keely."

"Yes," he answered immediately. "I will." It was more than an answer to Tristan, it was a vow.

He had to find her and convince her that he was worth forgiving. It would be bloody difficult after everything that had happened between them, but she was worth the risk. And, if nothing else, he would be with her, watching her back as she traveled through those beautiful, bleak, dangerous moors and into the mountains of her homeland.

He stood and brought his fist to his heart—the Apollyon way of recognizing Tristan as family—and then turned to go. Keely's letter crackled against his chest as he jogged out the study and down to the barracks to pack.

Chapter Eleven

KEELY LAY in the dark listening to the ancient wood of the abandoned farmhouse creaking in the wind. The whole structure shuddered and moaned, reminding her of the hideous days she'd spent retching on the *Star of the Sea*. Who knew someone could throw up so many times and still function?

At one point the Nephilim captain had offered her a rope so that she could tie herself to the rail while she vomited over the side as the ship heaved and rolled beneath her. She'd lashed herself to the rail and leaned over, staring at the churning gray water, wishing that Tor would hold her hand again. But he never had.

Keely sat up in the pile of blankets and wrapped her arms around her legs. Thank the Bard that the hideous nausea had finally eased. Getting off the ship had made a world of difference. And Nim's basket of ginger cookies and insistence on regular snacks and rests had helped too. For the first time in weeks, she had a little more energy. A little more interest in the world.

If only she could get a grip on the ridiculous tears that seemed to leak out of her eyes at every opportunity. Nim had told her it was entirely normal, and that she had once treated a woman in her village who was pregnant in spring and couldn't stop crying because of baby animals. Baby bloody animals. Somehow that was meant to reassure her. Instead, it had made her think of baby animals and her eyes had welled up. Damn it.

Keely sniffed and wiped her eyes with the back of her hands. She was strong. She had been strong her entire life, and now she had a tiny person who needed her strength even more. She straightened, lifting her chin. She would be whatever the pea needed.

Yes, she'd started calling it the pea. Which wasn't the best name in the world. But still. What else was she going to call it? Torlett? Dun-Tor? She snorted. And then her eyes leaked a little more.

How could she possibly still be missing him so much? Everything in her wanted to turn around and go back. To stand in front of him and force him to see that they had a chance to build something rare. Something precious.

But didn't you walk away first? a quiet little internal voice prodded. *Aren't you walking—running—away now?* She truly hated that voice.

Had she run away? Maybe. But wasn't it sensible? Wasn't it better to give him the space he so clearly wanted? And, most importantly, wasn't it better for the pea? The child would be better off with a stable home and a parent who was dedicated to her. That had to be her priority.

Or was it really that she'd made herself so vulnerable to Tor that now she needed as much distance from him as humanly possible so she could repair her broken walls?

Did he even realize how vulnerable she'd felt? Would it

have made any difference to tell him that she was afraid? That even contemplating being with someone was an enormous step for her. That asking him to come with her had taken her so far past her usual boundaries that she might as well have been on the moon. For him, it had been no big deal. But for her... it had been everything.

Keely closed her eyes for a moment. Damn. Of course it would have made a difference. Tor always listened, and thought, carefully. He would have tried to understand. Maybe he would have done things differently.

He hadn't come to see her. But hadn't a part of her suspected that he wouldn't? Wasn't that why she had written the letter—because she knew he would hate to say goodbye.

She'd waited and waited. And then, somehow, she'd known. She'd looked up and seen him on the battlements. He had watched her, unable to truly stay away. He wanted her, but he was afraid... and if there was anyone who could understand that fear, it was her.

Maybe she should have stormed up those stairs and forced him to listen. Told him the truth, all of it. Opened her heart and let go of her pride.

But she hadn't.

She'd been a coward where Tor was concerned. For the first time in a decade, she had wanted to be with someone, had allowed herself to imagine a life with them. Had begun to build tiny dreams of the future. And then, when he hadn't immediately leaped to making promises, she'd folded and run.

Keely sighed. She should have stayed, that night in the woods. Given him a chance. She knew he struggled to express emotions. And she also knew how wounded he'd been by what happened after Ravenstone. And yet her own vulnerabilities, her own terror of losing someone she cared for, had overridden everything. Including her good sense and any courage she might have had.

And now she'd left again. Damn.

"You are stronger than this." She whispered the words into the darkness, and then, slowly, wrapped her hands over her flat belly. "*We* are stronger than this."

She rubbed her eyes, grabbed her satchel off the floor, and pulled out one of the ginger cookies that Nim had given her. Nim must have spoken to Alanna about taking their trip slowly because they seemed to take an inordinate number of breaks and rests. And Alanna's attentive kindness, even Val's gruff concern, had given her some comfort.

Yes, she was going to have a baby. And yes, Tor had chosen to let her go. The thought of doing it all on her own was daunting. But she had been on her own all this time. She could do this.

Somewhere outside, a rooster crowed in the darkness. And then another joined in. Bloody chickens. Anyone who thought roosters only woke up at dawn had never kept the stupid fowl.

These birds must have been left behind by the farm owners when they abandoned their home—too close to the fighting and the growing numbers of reivers roaming through the war-struck north—and they had made themselves a home in the decaying rafters of the outbuildings. Now they were celebrating whatever had taken their fancy while the rest of the world tried to sleep.

Well, Alanna and Val were trying to sleep, anyway. Given the noises she'd heard through the thin walls, it wasn't that surprising that they were both still passed out. Finally, her best friend had the love she deserved; that she had denied herself for so long.

Keely looked down at her belly. "We deserve it too, little

pea," she murmured. "But don't worry, your old mama is going to give you so much love. So, so much love. Whatever happens, we'll have each other."

Damn. Now she'd made herself cry again. She'd cried more since falling pregnant than in all the years before. Even when Niall died, she had kept her tears to herself.

She wiped her eyes with the sleeve of the shirt she'd worn to sleep in. It was one of Tor's—the shirt Alanna had borrowed when she was first rescued—Alanna had given it to Keely instead of giving it back to Tor, and now Keely slept in it every night.

"Look at this, little pea," she murmured toward her belly. "See the ridiculous things your mama has started to do."

She wiped her face and looked longingly at the blankets. It would have been nice to get some more rest, but she knew she'd never get back to sleep.

She lit the small lantern she'd left on the floor beside her bedroll and then pulled Tor's shirt over her head and tucked it safely back into her satchel before dressing in a dark green blouse, topped by a jerkin, with her leathers. She tied her hair back in a tight braid, and then pulled on her boots, gloves, and a heavy woolen cloak.

Creeping softly so that she didn't wake Alanna and Val, she let herself out of the farmhouse, holding her small lantern up to light the way.

Two guards immediately spun to watch her, and she gave them a polite nod as they slowly relaxed.

Winter dawn would be late, and getting later as they traveled further north, but there was a lightness in the sky, a subtle glow along the far horizon, that suggested the sun would rise soon. A milky sweep of stars gleamed across the sky, and she tilted her head back, enjoying the fresh bite to the wind and the quiet of the early morning.

She picked her way past the glowing embers of the fire and waved at Rafe, who was sitting on a log, warming himself. He lifted the mug he'd been cradling in a salute, and she smiled back.

She should tell Rafe about the baby. He would be kind; she knew he would. He wouldn't tell anyone. Although at this point, probably everyone knew. Val, Tristan, and Mathos, certainly… and Tor.

What had he thought when he read her letter? Was he relieved that she had gone? Had he read it with that stern look she knew so well and then carefully folded it and packed it away to return to the responsibilities he already had? The other commitments he'd made, and the life he was trying to rebuild.

Or had he growled and marched away, angry that she'd left? Those big arms flexing under all that red-and-black ink as he gripped the back of his neck like he always did when he was overwhelmed by too much emotion? Had he been disappointed in her cowardly way of telling him that he was going to be a father? Did he wish, now, that he had joined her on the road?

Who knew?

Either way, she should tell Rafe. He would know if there was anything she needed to do. Anything she should prepare. Babies were not her specialty, but she could learn. She *would* learn.

A quad of their guards walked down the road, just returning from a sweep of the perimeter, and nodded politely as she lifted her lantern higher and made her way down the rutted track to the dilapidated barn. The chickens had woken her, and now she was going to face them.

Keely walked into the barn, wrinkling her nose against the smell. Possibly it had been a cow byre at some point, but now it consisted mostly of rotten old boards, stinking of chicken shit, with just enough remaining beams that the flock could roost safely away from foxes.

The birds fluttered along the beams, eyeing her warily from their perches, lifting their wings and clucking nervously. They weren't at all sure about her, and, Bard knew, chickens were insane at the best of times. A couple of roosters, excited about the lantern light, crowed loudly.

Keely leaned against the door, letting them get used to her as she watched them. It had been her job as a child to collect the eggs. The kind of early morning—*get out of bed right now, Keely!*—job that a teenage girl could really resent on a winters' day.

There had been servants that could have done it. Her mother was a cousin to the queen, however distant, while her father was a very wealthy landowner in his own right, but her father had the idea that everyone should have a job to do, and the chickens were hers. Even when she was old enough to have real responsibilities, the chickens had stayed under her care.

Niall had helped. He would stride over the grassy fields between their farms and vault over the low fence to help her with the chickens. Well, mostly he made her significantly slower, but she wouldn't have traded that time for anything.

He was nothing like Tor. Long, lean muscles, golden blond hair, and a sharp wit. Everything was amusing to him. And Bard, he'd made her laugh. She'd laughed until her sides ached and her face grew stiff from smiling. And then he would kiss her. There in that warm, quiet barn, all surrounded by chickens.

When he died, that joy had died with him. All that

warmth had gone, and she had been sure she would never get it back. Never wanted to get it back, if losing it hurt so much.

Bard. How was it possible to love someone and hate them so much, all at the same time?

Ten years had passed since she had begged him to stay. She had wept and argued and pleaded. Begged him, as his betrothed, as the woman who would always love him. Asked him to change his mind and choose her.

But he had left anyway, and six months later they had brought his signet ring back to give to her, his body buried somewhere on the other side of the mountains.

She had been so angry with him. And so guilty that she was angry, when he was dead. She had walked around, numb and broken for months. And then her papa had died —another blow to her already damaged heart—and her mama had decided to go back to Duneidyn and asked her to follow.

She had packed up and left the farm, hoping to never see another chicken in her entire life. Or another beautiful, life-changing, heart-stealing boy. Especially not a soldier.

She had stayed away from men and the hurt that came from caring for them. Right up until Tor. Dark to Niall's golden light. Serious and stoic to Niall's easy good humor. But just as devastating.

Keely sighed. And now she was thinking about farming chickens. Why? Because it was the only thing she could think of. Because she wanted to go back to that time when she had felt warm and safe and invincible. Like she could do anything and be anything. Before life had taught her that it didn't work out that way—that every day was going to be a fight—and the only thing she could count on was her own damn self.

Bard. She stalked out of the shed and slammed the rickety door. This little trip into her memories was supposed to be cathartic. Not make her feel worse. She looked around, wanting space and air, and distance from her thoughts.

The sun had climbed over the top of the horizon, and she could make out a narrow path winding up behind the outbuildings. It led up a low hill, the first of many, rising ever more steeply away, up to the huge, towering mountains of the north.

Her feet found the path, and Keely followed it almost without thinking. She liked to be high above the world. She had spent hours on the tallest battlements, first in Duneidyn and later in Kaerlud, leaning into the wind, surrounded by open space, as she let the cold air blow away her worries.

She followed the path up, her eyes on the blue-purple mountains in the distance. The steep mountainous ridges that had protected Verturia from invaders—including neighboring Brythoria—for so many years.

And now they would be the border between her and Tor. Tomorrow, they would cross into her homeland, and she would have truly left him.

She turned and gave Rafe and the soldiers milling around the fire a quick wave, pointing toward the hill, miming that she was going for a walk. They waved back in acknowledgment, and she turned to pick her way up the rocky path as the roosters complained behind her.

It was hard walking, the hill steeper than it had looked, and the path was rutted and littered with rocks and stones.

Halfway up, she turned and looked back to see Jos flying a wide sweeping loop over the farmhouse and down to the thick line of trees that flanked the long driveway back to the road, checking for danger. It was beautiful to watch, the powerful flight of a strong Mabin, as the sun climbed higher, picking him out in golden light.

She was panting by the time she reached the top of the first hillock, but it was worth it. The world spread out, a sea of sprawling heather rippling in the early morning light, the low dells and hollows wreathed in heavy mist as the nearby hills rolled upward into mountains in the distance.

This was the feeling that she missed. The feeling that the world was in front of her, ready to be taken. For so long, she had lived without a future. Was she going to give up now, when she had finally glimpsed what she wanted?

She closed her eyes and let herself imagine Tor holding a baby. Those big arms, covered in ink, cradling their child. She could work on the council like Lucilla had suggested. Finally do something real to end the misery of the war that had taken Niall's life. And maybe, one day, the friendship and attraction between her and Tor could become something else. Something more.

She sank down onto a low mound of rocks, breathing in the cold air and watching her exhaled breath puff into clouds of vapor, and accepted what she had to do—she couldn't stay in Verturia. She was going to have to go back after this trip and speak to Tor properly.

She let herself settle into the stillness of the morning. Cold stone at her back, fresh air on her face, and the slow spread of relief at having made the decision. She snuggled more deeply into her cloak and lifted her eyes to watch a pair of peregrine falcons climbing higher and higher until they were tiny dots almost too far away to see.

Jos paused in the air over the road for a long moment and then dipped down out of sight on the other side of the farmhouse. It was cold, and she'd have to go down soon. And she was starting to feel the first stirrings of hunger, which she now knew better than to ignore. But not quite yet. She could take two more minutes of peace.

A sudden commotion at the farmhouse snagged her attention. Guards were calling out to each other, their words whipped away by the wind.

From her perch, she could see the back of the house and the tumbledown rear of the shed, as well as the pair of guards who were settled on the far side of the outbuildings, patrolling inside the thick gorse hedge that protected the farm. But not what was happening out the front.

Jos still hadn't reappeared, and she started to worry. Had there been bad news? It was early, but if a messenger had left the barracks at Staith before dawn and ridden hard, they might just be arriving now.

Was everything okay at the palace? Lucilla and Nim were there with the other Hawks. And Tor.

Keely stood, shaking out her limbs and rubbing her gloved hands together, watching the farmhouse. And then she saw him. Emerging from between the buildings, wearing heavy leather armor covered in a thick gray cloak, and starting to climb up the path toward her.

He looked up, saw her, and paused. He was too far away for her to see his eyes, to make out his expression, but she knew he was looking right at her.

Bard. Tor had followed her after all.

Chapter Twelve

TOR FOLDED his bedroll and tied it to the back of his current horse with swift, efficient movements, despite his staggering exhaustion.

Brutal hours in the saddle, day after day, snatching a few hours of sleep—in unfamiliar barracks when he could, beneath a hedgerow when there was no other option—had taken its toll. But dawn was close, and it was time to get back onto the road.

The last four days were a blur of galloping horses—changed at every barracks along the bleak Great North Road—freezing mud, rain that poured in cold rivers down his face and under his oilskin, hasty meals of dried meat, and broken sleep.

But he knew he was close. He would catch up today, he was sure of it, and something relentless inside him drove him on. He had to see her before she crossed over into Verturia.

The mountains growing hour by hour in the distance

felt like the point of no return. As if she would disappear entirely if she crossed over without him.

He pulled his thick woolen cloak tighter, covering his knives but leaving easy access to the greatsword at his hip, slung his crossbow over his shoulder, and then launched himself into his saddle.

The stallion, whose name was lost in the fog of swift changes, whickered and huffed as he nudged him into a steady trot, slowly warming them both after the cold nighttime hours. Leaving behind the grim poverty of Staith.

He had to move fast enough to catch them. He'd fucked up so many times, but not this time. There was only one thing in his life that made any sense. Only one thing that he wanted—Keely—and he wasn't going to be too late.

The sun crept higher, bringing the hills around him into focus, the mountains behind them growing clearer. He bent low and focused on the road as he pushed the unfamiliar horse into a ground-eating canter.

He was just starting to think it might be time to slow to a trot and allow the stallion to rest when he saw the glint of sunlight on a Mabin in flight over a copse of trees up ahead. Jos, by the look of him. He raised a hand in greeting and was relieved to see his gesture returned, then pushed on, swiftly covering the last mile.

He reached a turnoff to a rutted drive that curled away, perhaps to a farmhouse judging by the moss-covered roof peeking out above the trees, as Jos landed lightly beside two Tarasque guards standing sentinel over the drive.

His stallion blew hard, flanks quivering as they slowed to a walk, and he looked up to greet the three men. "Morning."

Jos grinned. "I wondered how long it would take you."

Tor shrugged. What was he supposed to say?

"Do you want to see Keely first or go and say hello to Alanna and Val?"

"Keely."

Jos dipped his chin. "Good." He swept his hand back, gesturing up the drive. "Come on then."

Tor slid from his horse, and they walked together up the rough drive.

"You didn't push on to the border," Tor noted. Staith wasn't that far behind them. In fact, he'd expected them to be quite a bit further up the road already.

It was Jos's turn to shrug. "We've been taking the whole trip pretty easy. Alanna's orders. She wanted everyone to get a good rest before the last push up to the passes."

They reached a series of tumbledown outbuildings, ripe with the stink of chickens and noisy with their clucking, leading up to a house that was far more ramshackle than he'd expected. The front wall was caved in at one side, and the roof sagging heavily. But it was no doubt significantly dryer and more comfortable than the spiky hawthorn hedges he'd been sleeping under.

Jos pointed out a narrow path that wound between the buildings, then up toward the hills behind them. "She went for a walk. You'll find her up there."

Tor frowned at his friend. Didn't he know about the danger? "You let her walk alone?"

Jos huffed out an exasperated breath as he tilted his head toward the far side of the farmhouse. "Two guards had their eyes on her the whole time, plus I was in the air." He paused for a moment and then grinned. "And I'm not sure I'd use the word 'let' around Keely."

"Hmmm." Maybe. She loved walking up in those high places, but now he was here she'd have better security to do it.

He stood, looking at the path. She was only a few minutes away. After so much desperate effort to reach her, it suddenly seemed impossible to take that last step.

Jos gave him an understanding look. "Pass me the reins and go and see her—she'll want to see you, I promise." And then he snorted. "Just, maybe, take a weapon."

Definitely not; a weapon would only give her ideas. Thicker armor, maybe?

Tor clapped Jos on the shoulder in thanks and then handed him the horse's reins. He made his way past the chicken shed and then onto a narrow, rocky path that led steeply up the first of a series of hills leading to the mountains. He stepped over a particularly rutted channel, and then looked up.

She was standing further along the path toward the top of the first hill, close enough that she would hear him if he shouted, but too far away for him to read the look on her face. She had seen him, was looking right at him, but he couldn't bring himself to call out.

He'd spent long hours in the saddle planning all the things he would say to her, but now he couldn't remember any of them.

He wanted to run to her, grab her, hold her against him. But he didn't want to frighten her away. Didn't know how she felt about seeing him again after he'd refused to travel with her. After she'd decided to stay in Verturia.

She had asked him to come with her. That must mean something. Surely? Or had their time apart reminded her that she didn't want to be with a soldier? Had she realized how little he could offer her? He was about to find out.

Small stones clattered away behind him down the steep path as he strode up the hill toward her.

Gods, she was stunning. Her red-gold hair was fiery in

the early morning sunshine and her back was straight, chin up, shoulders squared. She looked ready for battle—or flight. He had no idea which. He only knew that nothing could stop him from going to her.

And then she started to walk. Toward him. Not away, thank the gods. She slid on the rough stones, speeding up and he broke into a rough jog, taking the last few yards even faster.

He opened his arms, and she ran into them. Gods. He was holding her, wrapped up against him, in a way he'd thought he'd lost forever. She was warm, and alive, and embracing him so tightly he could feel her entire body pressed against his. Her arms around his waist, her head tucked under his chin, the soft scent of heather surrounding them.

"You came." Her voice was rough and strained against his chest. And then she shuddered, drew in a shaking breath, and shuddered again. And he realized she was crying. His warrior was weeping helplessly in his arms.

All the feelings he'd been pushing away so successfully threatened to overwhelm him. His guilt and fear, the hope that had kept him going hour after hour.

He fought for control as he swung her up, cradling her in his arms, and strode up the rest of the path before lowering himself to the ground, holding her safely in his lap while he leaned against a large rock.

So much like he'd held her that day. And yet so different.

He pulled his gloves off, needing to touch her, and stroked her hair while her muffled sobs slowly subsided. Eventually, she leaned back, her face puffy and red, her eyes bloodshot, nose swollen. She was utterly beautiful.

"You were right," he admitted softly. "I was trying to find myself again. So much of what I'd believed turned out to be a lie. But, Keely, I do know that I want to be with you. I do choose you."

She wiped her eyes with the backs of her hands, her voice still rough with tears. "I choose you too."

"Even though I'm a soldier, Keely?"

Keely bit her lip, but she didn't look away. "Yes."

Gods. He wanted to believe that he was enough. Wanted it to be true so badly.

He ran his thumb slowly over her reddened bottom lip, wishing she had never been hurt by him or anyone else. Then he threaded his fingers through her hair and cradled the back of her head as he looked into her beautiful jade eyes. "The last weeks have been terrible. I should never have let you go without begging you to stay. Not outside Eshcol, not for all those weeks, and definitely not from Kaerlud. Will you give me another chance?"

"Yes." She didn't hesitate. "That's all I want."

There was more to say. Much more. He needed to ask what she wanted. Whether she still planned to live in Verturia. And how that might work given his commitments to the Blues.

Deeper, so far down that he was hardly even aware of it, he wanted to ask her why she wanted him. To ask for some reassurance that he was enough. But he was drowning in feelings he had no idea how to deal with. What they had was fragile, and he didn't want to say the wrong thing. Again.

Instead, he tightened his arms around her, grateful beyond words that she was giving him another chance.

Chapter Thirteen

KEELY HELD TOR, reveling in the scent of him, strong and male, as well as the pinpricks of teasing pain along her scalp from his fingers sifting through her hair. The deep rumble of his voice as he murmured her name and the gentle scrape of his beard. It was the first time she'd ever seen him unshaved.

He had come for her. He had come for *them*.

He had looked so impossibly serious as he'd jogged up toward her. Dark rings under his eyes, mud splattered over his breeches. He'd ridden long and hard to get to her. And he had made the choice to do it.

He was wrapped around her, his hand in her hair and his lips pressed against the top of her head. And she couldn't help thinking about the last time he'd had his fingers on her scalp… the last time they had been so close.

The warmth between them grew, his heart rate picking up under her ear, and she lifted her face to press a kiss onto his throat, and then ran her lips up, along his jaw, and finally onto those full, firm lips.

Tor groaned. His mouth opened under hers, and he kissed her back, running his tongue along hers in a long, leisurely taste.

For the first time in long weeks, she felt like herself. But perhaps a new version of herself. Somehow lighter, more vulnerable but also more alive.

Tor deepened their kiss, and she twisted, feeling his length pressing into her thigh, warmth rising through her belly. Yes. This was what she wanted. To touch him and feel his skin. To reassure herself that this was real.

She whimpered, pushing herself closer, and suddenly found herself pulled back, gripped in his big hands, while they both panted.

"Not here." He tilted his head to the side of the farmhouse, and she remembered the two guards who had watched her climb the hill.

"My room?" she asked quietly.

"Gods, yes."

She scrambled off his lap and gave him a moment to adjust his breeches before leading him down the slope. As soon as the path widened, he came up beside her, matching his pace to hers. His dark eyes crinkled at the sides as he threw her a small smile, and she couldn't help smiling back as they hurried down to the old farmhouse.

They emerged into the front courtyard to see that several of the guards were milling around while Alanna and Val conferred quietly with Rafe and Jos.

Damn. She hadn't expected a committee.

Tor settled back into a more stoic, shuttered expression, his shoulders slightly hunched, the warmth that had been growing between them now cooling under the watchful looks of the Hawks as they joined their friends.

"Tor." Val nodded, but he didn't smile.

Rafe, however, was more welcoming, clapping him on the back. "It's good to see you." He grinned at Keely. "I think we're all very pleased you're here."

Val grunted and opened his mouth to say something, but Alanna nudged him with her elbow and spoke first. "We *are* all pleased to have you here."

"Took long enough," Val muttered just loud enough for everyone to hear, and Alanna winced.

Keely could feel the tension thrumming through Tor and she turned and gave Val her strongest smile. "He came, Val. Be glad for us."

Val crossed his arms over his chest, wings drawn back, and scowled down at her. "Keely, when I married Alanna, you became my sister. So, I'm going to do what any big brother would do and ask you, are you completely sure you want this? You know that we'll support you. That you're our family now. I don't think the last few weeks—"

"Yes." She cut him off. "I'm sure."

She was sure. This was all she'd wanted. For them to try. To give it a chance and see where this connection between them might go. And for the pea to know its da.

Val glared at Tor behind her, and for a long moment, no one said anything. Slowly Val's grim face relaxed, and he reached out to clap Tor on the shoulder. "Alright then. Welcome to the family."

Behind her, she felt Tor's muscles go rigid. He was exhausted, and now Val had, unwittingly, reminded him of what he'd lost. Bard. She was finally starting to truly understand him. To understand that Val's casual statement meant something far more serious to Tor. Tor, who never showed his emotions. Who always needed his control.

But she could help. She could get him somewhere to rest

and take a few moments. "Can we get some hot water? Tor's been on the road for days."

Alanna requested for the nearest guards to fill a basin in Keely's room and then, after a glance at Keely, declared that she wanted to stay at the farmhouse and continue their journey the next day.

Alanna didn't even pretend it was for any other reason than to give them time together, but when she pulled Val and the others away to plan a hunt for their dinner and then ordered everyone out of the camp, Keely couldn't feel anything except thankful.

Within minutes the others were gone, and they could let themselves into the farmhouse alone. She led him to her small room. Pale winter sunlight filtered in through a high window, turning the dust in the air into glowing, dancing specks. A basin had been filled and placed on a rickety old table, and the steam from the water curled and billowed.

Tor pushed the door closed behind him and then shrugged out of his cloak and hung it on the hook on the back of the door.

For a moment, Keely felt strangely uncertain. It was so much easier to get swept away in the moment, to allow passion and desire to drive her. But this was something else —this was a decision that they were both making.

Tor pulled the ties from his vambraces and dropped the heavy leather to the floor with a groan of relief. His jerkin followed, and then his cotton shirt, until he was standing in front of her, naked from the waist up, his wide shoulders rippling with heavy muscle. His strong pecs were dusted with wiry black curls, the twining tattoos up his arms seeming almost alive in the soft light. And all her worries faded.

He pulled off his boots and socks, then loosened the top button of his leather breeches and padded over to the water.

He lifted the small washcloth, dipped it in the water, and then used it to scrub his face. A drop of water ran down the side of his throat, following the tendons to his clavicle and her eyes followed its progress before dropping down further.

Her mouth went completely dry, but the rest of her was melting.

Keely forced herself to look away and slide out of her cloak. Hang it beside his. Pull her boots off one at a time. She slid her jerkin off and dropped it beside her satchel. All while her entire body tingled with awareness.

She took a step closer to him, and he turned, his short hair sticking up in damp spikes, his face scrubbed clean, dark chest hair trailing down to the open top of his breeches. And she forgot how to breathe.

"Do you want this, Keely?" he asked softly. "You're sure?"

She nodded. "Absolutely." She didn't just want it. She needed it. Needed this to be a clear choice. Not a moment of lust driven by fear and grief.

"Then come here." His voice wrapped around her, heavy and demanding, and she stepped slowly forward.

His dark eyes fixed on her green blouse. "Take it off." She blinked, but her fingers reached for the ties.

He watched her silently, his eyes hotter than the darkness at the center of a flame.

She slipped out of her shirt and threw it to the side, then wriggled down out of her leather breeches, and then stood, waiting.

She didn't know what she was waiting for. Or how she knew it was what he wanted. But he was watching her with such open appreciation, that she stood still and let him look.

His heavy-lidded eyes traveled slowly over her, pausing on her swollen breasts, down her belly, and then to the triangle of red-blond hair at the apex of her legs.

His wicked lips pulled up and he stepped forward to wrap his big fingers around her chin and tilt her head up, his eyes locked on hers. And then, so slowly that she could feel the heated air rippling between them, he lowered his mouth over hers.

She sagged into him as his strong arms came around her, pulling her into him and holding her up as his mouth dominated hers.

He let out another long, harsh groan, and she realized that this was what he needed. What they both needed. He wanted to stay in control. And for once in her life, she wanted to be able to let go.

She had only slept with Niall a handful of times. Frantic, giggling couplings, under clothes, behind the shed, in the meadow. Both young and inexperienced, learning their way together.

Tor was nothing like that. He was dark and potent, as if all the emotions he never admitted, maybe even to himself, were boiling beneath his surface, powering his fierce intensity.

He lowered her gently into the pile of blankets on the floor, and she lay there, watching him as he stripped off his breeches and then kneeled.

He sat back on his haunches, looking at her. Not touching her but, instead, devouring her with his eyes as the furnace between them ratcheted higher. Goose bumps broke out over her arms as her nipples tightened into hard buds.

He settled his big hands on her thighs, his eyes on hers. "Open."

Bard.

She let her legs fall open. Felt his approval resonating through her body. And then he leaned down and licked her. A long, slow drag of his hot, wet tongue, all the way past her entrance, through her folds, to press heavily on her clit.

She whimpered, and he lifted his head to frown at her. "No noise. Or the guards outside will hear."

She knew from Eshcol that until he had control, he wouldn't move. And she needed him to move. She shoved her fist into her mouth, and he grunted in approval. And then lowered his head and licked her again.

And again.

Scorching glides through her swollen folds. Parting her. Teasing at her entrance and then away again as her thighs trembled.

He sucked her clit between his lips, a long, devastating pull. She squirmed, desperate to get closer, needing something to fill the growing ache inside her. But he dropped a heavy hand onto her hip and held her still.

He lifted his head and licked his lips. "Show me your breasts. I want to see them. Last time—"

Last time, they'd still had their clothes half on. Last time, her breasts had been a small handful.

She took the heavy mounds in her hands, lifting them as he groaned. She pinched her nipples, rolling them between her thumb and fingers, tugging and scratching along the sides of her breasts as he watched, licking his lips.

Then he used his fingers to spread her open and dropped his head to slowly spear her with his tongue.

Her back arched off the floor, her hips lifted up into his mouth as he used his thumbs to stroke her, still pushing into her with his tongue.

Her hands faltered, leaving her breasts to grip the blankets in tight bunches. Searching for something to hold on to. Bard. She was so close. Her gasping pants shuddered in her ears as he wound her tighter and tighter.

He chuckled in appreciation, his breath hot against her. "Gods. I can't tell you how long I've wanted you exactly like this." And then he licked her again, his mouth and fingers working together to drive her higher and higher as she trembled beneath him.

Lights flickered at the corners of her vision as he pushed two thick fingers inside her, sucking her clit hard at the same time, and a potent wave of ecstasy rushed up through her as she gasped out her climax.

Tor crawled over her, and she lifted her legs to wrap around his hips, groaning under her breath as he slid deep inside her. He lowered his mouth to hers, tasting of musk, of her, surrounding her with his strong, masculine scent.

He slid his hand along her arm, found her hand, and laced his fingers through hers, and then he started to thrust. Slowly at first, long, smooth glides, going deeper and deeper. Then speeding up until her hips were lifting to meet his in a pounding, relentless rhythm. He stroked into her with all the power of his heavy muscles, setting a punishing, consuming pace that drove the air from her body and all thoughts from her mind. He was in her, part of her, the very air she was breathing.

She lifted her free hand up and groped for the wall. Found it and used it to stabilize herself. To hold herself steady under the force of his thrusts.

He reached under her and bunched the blankets so they lifted her hips, angling her so that he ground down on her clit with every heavy stroke, and that sparkling, devastating fire started to build once more.

Then he lowered his mouth to her neck and sucked, growling deep in his throat as he pulled her skin into his mouth, and that low, possessive rumble flung her over the edge once more.

She spasmed around him, whimpering and shuddering, and then, feeling him start to pull out, she tightened her legs. "Stay. Please."

He let out a low moan, his body rigid over hers. "Keely?"

"Stay."

"Gods." He surged forward, pumping into her with short, rapid thrusts until his cock seemed to grow even thicker within her clenching inner muscles. He stiffened, his body trembling as he released into her, flooding her until his seed ran down the inside of her legs. And then he finally collapsed on top of her, his fingers still laced with hers.

He lay like that just for a few seconds, his body pinning hers, before he rolled them to the side, pulling her with him. Holding her in a hot, sweaty tangle.

They caught their breath, coming slowly back down, and he slipped out of her. She tucked her head under his chin, listening to the thudding beat of his heart as it slowly calmed.

He reached over her to grab a blanket and used the corner to help her clean herself, then pulled the other side to cover them both.

"Thank you," he murmured into her hair.

"Thank you too."

"No, I mean, thank you for letting me…. I've never come inside anyone before."

He shifted slightly under her ear, and she knew he was wondering, so she whispered the truth. "It was a first for me too."

He chuckled, a low, pleased sound. Somehow possessive

without being smug. The most carefree and happy she had ever heard him.

For the first time in years, something settled inside her. She was in the right place. Exactly where she wanted to be.

And, for the first time, she was starting to believe he wanted to be there too.

Chapter Fourteen

TOR COULD SMELL Keely's hair and warm skin, the scent of sex heavy in the room. She sighed gently, her body soft and trusting in his arms. Gods, he'd come inside her. He should have been terrified, but instead, it felt perfect. He had chosen her, and she had chosen him back.

He had never known a woman like her. Riding day and night to get to her was the first thing he'd done right in months. Yes, her very existence threatened his control in every way. But she was worth it.

She tilted her head up to look at him, and he smiled back at her. And then felt his smile falter—her eyes were clear, but fine worry lines had settled on her brow. And when she nibbled on her lip, he knew that there was more she needed to say.

All he wanted was to hold her, lying quietly together. After all the weeks of uncertainty and loneliness, he wanted to take a moment to enjoy being with her. But Keely had something on her mind, and if he'd learned anything, it was that ignoring it would not make it better.

He cleared his throat. "You can tell me. Or ask me. Whatever it is, I won't ever lie to you."

She nodded slowly, her eyes traveling over his face, searching. "What did you think of my letter?" she asked eventually.

How the hell was he going to answer that? "I don't really—"

"I mean," she interrupted. "Were you pleased with it?"

He frowned. "No."

She flinched, her eyes going wide as she stiffened. "You're not pleased. But you still came all this way, you still —" She sat up, taking the blanket with her as she shook her head. "I don't understand you. Not at all."

She might not understand him. But he *really* didn't understand her, or anything about what the fuck was happening. "Why should I be pleased with a letter that tells me goodbye?"

"What?" She blinked, and then scraped at her eyes with the back of her hand, but she didn't try to pull away. If anything, she softened slightly.

"Tell me why I should be pleased that you were leaving."

Her eyebrows pulled closer together as she turned her face toward him. "But that's not what my letter said… well, not everything."

It was his turn to blink. "Wasn't it?"

"Didn't you read it?"

"No. I left within minutes of getting it. I've been on the road every second of the day since then."

He wanted to stop there, but he'd only just promised never to lie. "And, honestly, I didn't want to read it. I didn't want to know that you were gone forever. It's still in my pocket."

"Oh, Bard." She started to laugh, a wild, hysterical, slightly watery laugh. The laugh of a person standing on top of a mountain and wondering if they might accidentally jump.

She looked at him and then away as her laugh trailed off, but she didn't say anything. There was something more. Something in her letter. Something that she was now afraid to reveal. Gods. "Keely, you're worrying me."

She bent her knees, wrapping her arms around them, watching him uneasily. "You came for me. Bard. You came to find me, and that means everything. But Tor, there's something you need to know."

The silence extended around them, filled with only the soft sigh of the wind around the rough farmhouse.

"Keely?" he prompted.

"Okay." She nodded to herself. "I can do this." She let out a wobbly breath, cleared her throat, and then spoke quietly. "I'm pregnant."

Gods. Gods. He didn't.... Had he even heard her properly? "You're what?"

"Pregnant. We... ah.... That day—" One of her hands dropped to her belly and cradled it protectively.

"I didn't." He shook his head. "I mean...."

How could he explain? He'd thought he'd protected her. He certainly hadn't intended.... Gods.

She understood immediately and shook her head gently. "You didn't do anything wrong, Tor. I know you tried. Nim said that it doesn't always work."

He sat up beside her, twisting so he could look at her properly. "You're sure?"

And yet, even as he asked it, he knew the truth. It all made sense. Her sickness, her insistence that he think about their future, leaving him a letter, the depth of Tristan's anger. Mathos refusing to speak to him. Val's little "welcome to the family" speech. Because of course Tristan would know. Val, and Mathos. Lucilla too. Gods. They all knew.

Most importantly, he knew deep in his soul that Keely would never, ever lie about something like this.

They were having a baby.

Their baby.

His baby.

And then the truth hit him like an avalanche of ice pouring down his naked skin. They all knew, except him. And they had all known she was leaving anyway. He had come so very close to losing her. To losing them both. "You were going to leave and take my baby away?"

She frowned, biting her lip. "No. It wasn't like that. You had already left to search for Lucilla when I realized. And when you came back, you refused to even look at me. Literally, the last thing you said to me was that you couldn't see a future for us. But I still asked you to come with us to Verturia. I told you we had more to discuss. I tried, Tor." She tilted her head to the side. "I left the letter for you. I wanted you to know. I wanted you to come and find us, but I didn't want to force you to make a decision that you were uncomfortable with."

He leaned back against the wall behind him and tried to think. What she was saying sounded sensible, but it was so hard to get past the fact that she had left and taken his baby with her.

She had said she didn't want a soldier, that she wanted to leave, and she'd acted on it.

He had known it was too good to be true. Known she couldn't possibly want him. Not forever. He had chosen her, but she had always intended to leave him behind and make her way to Verturia.

She'd wanted to be away from him so badly that she was prepared to travel while she was pregnant and live alone with a baby. If she had made it over the border, would he have ever found her again? Would he have ever found his child again? The fear of losing them both rushed over him, fogging his brain.

He wrapped his hands around the back of his neck and squeezed.

Even knowing that she carried his child, she'd still decided to go. Yet another family that didn't want him. How could he ever trust her to stay?

"What?" Her voice shook as she flung herself out of the blankets and stood. "How dare you say that you can't trust me."

Fuck. Had he said it aloud? All of it or only part of it? He was so utterly exhausted, so full of emotion roiling through him. Joy and fear and an unreasonable, unreasoning rage at her for making him so vulnerable.

"Yes, you bloody did say it aloud," she spat as she pulled her clothes on with sharp tugs that would have looked furious if he hadn't been able to see how badly her hands were shaking.

She tried to yank her boots on. Fumbled, and then tried again, eventually succeeding, and then flung her cloak on.

Her lip was so badly chewed it had started to bleed, and the sight made him want to howl.

He had hurt her. Again. But he couldn't seem to make himself stop. All he wanted was a family. *This* family. The one he had chosen for himself. And for a brief shining moment, he'd had it. With the woman he needed and wanted beyond all reason. And she had almost taken his chance away.

It pulled at something dark and twisted inside him. The

knot that had never unraveled. And it brought back all the fear and grief and impotent rage of standing in his parents' reception room as his father called for the guards.

Another person who should have loved him, sending him away. Leaving him alone. Didn't she realize how much power she had over him?

The words fell out of him before he could hold them back. "How could you do this to me?"

"How could *I* do this to *you*?" she repeated with stunned incredulity.

He gripped the back of his neck, trying to find some kind of calm. Enough that he could have a reasonable conversation with her. He knew he wasn't explaining himself. That he was making this worse. But he didn't know how to fix it.

Keely wiped her hand down her face. "I can't believe I trusted you again. I let you into my body. Again. Why does any kind of intimacy turn you into… this?" She waved her hand in his direction.

He stared up at her. Gods. He shook his head. It wasn't intimacy; certainly, that had never been a problem before. It was the power of the feelings she created in him—the uncertainty and need, the very depth and breadth of what she did to him—that's what made him crazy.

He was the calm member of the squad, the considered strategist. Except when it came to Keely. "It's you," he muttered, knowing even as he said the words that they sounded utterly wrong.

She flinched, and there was a momentary breathless pause as his words echoed through the room.

And then she took a step back. "You know what, Tor, fuck you. I did the best I could for *my* baby. You want to hate me for leaving? Well, how about you spend a moment considering that you never, not even once, asked me to stay."

She tilted her chin up, shoulders squared, once more the woman from the king's banquet. All rage and strength.

Fighting for someone else, yet again, no matter how much pain it caused her. Fighting for their child. Gods, she would be an amazing mother.

Before he could finish the thought, she whirled around and strode from the room, slamming the door behind her.

Tor sat frozen. Alone in her room. Surrounded by her scent, by her things, by the coldness of her last words to him.

He rose slowly, feeling as if he'd aged a thousand years in the last few minutes, and washed his face in the lukewarm water, hardly noticing the rough cotton of the towel as he mindlessly patted himself dry. Gods.

No wonder she'd been so obsessed with the future. With him making a real, tangible commitment. She'd asked him, and he'd refused. And she was right. Again. It had never occurred to him to ask her to stay.

And now... now he'd accused her of lying to him. And then stealing his child. Fuck.

Fuck.

There was no way Keely would accept that—from anyone—and nor should she.

He stumbled across to his cloak and felt in the deep pocket sewn into the inner lining to find the letter she'd left him. Such a small thing. Folded parchment, sealed. His name a heavy black scrawl across the front.

He broke the seal and leaned against the wall to read.

Tor,

I'm not at all certain how to start this letter.

It seems, somehow, to be both immeasurably easier to write to you, sitting here in my room alone, rather than facing you in person. And significantly more difficult, here by myself, reminded of exactly how alone I am.

I would have liked to have told you. But, if you're reading this, I've failed to do so. Maybe I could have tried harder. Maybe I'm a coward, after all. I've thought it more than once over the last few days, and I expect I'll think it more in the days to come.

He closed his eyes and dropped his head back heavily against the wall. Gods. She had been alone, and afraid, thinking of herself as a coward. Keely, the bravest person he knew. The woman who had defied a king, knowing she would die, had been afraid to speak to him, the father of her child. She must have been terrified to realize that she was pregnant and all alone. And she *had* tried.

A hot, twisting shame settled across his chest like heated wire, burning and constricting, as he forced himself to continue.

Anyway, I'll get to the point—I'm pregnant. I hope it's abundantly clear that you're the father. There's no one else and hasn't been for many years.

You already know I'm going north with Alanna. I intend to stay there, to make a home in Verturia. I don't know why. Perhaps because it's the only home I've had that was really mine, and now I find I need one. Perhaps because I was safe there once.

I need to know that my child—our child—will be safe too.

I know that you want to stay in Kaerlud. I understand that you have a life you want to rebuild. A life that doesn't include me and a child. And I know that this was never your intention. It was a mistake. I'm giving you this chance to continue your life exactly as you'd planned. I have no desire to live my life as a regret, and most especially not your regret.

Maybe one day, when things are more settled for you, you would

*like to come and visit. My mother will be in the Castle at Duneidyn;
she will know where we are. Ask for Nessia.*

> ~~*I wish that*~~
> *Farewell,*
> *Keely*

Somehow the fact that she had started to express a wish
and then crossed it out hurt more than the rest of the letter
combined.

He hunched his shoulders against the agony of his own
rising self-hatred. Gods. He had broken the fledgling trust
just beginning to grow between them once more. She had
tried to do the right thing by him, and for their child. She
had forgiven him, welcomed him, given him a family. And
he'd thrown it all in her face.

He had to find a way to make this right. Apologize and
beg for forgiveness. Immediately. Unequivocally. Waiting
would be a disaster.

He had to explain that what he'd meant was that she
was everything to him. That he was overjoyed by the idea of
having a family together, and that it was terror of losing her
that had made him react so badly. It was his fear speaking,
not her, nor anything she'd done.

He had to fix this before it got any worse. And then he
had to beg her to give him another chance. Gods. Another
chance he did not deserve.

He dressed quickly, listening for Keely. Had she gone
outside? The house was quiet and still.

Some soldier's sense nudged him. It was too quiet.
Something didn't feel right. Where was Keely?

A shiver of foreboding teased up his spine, and he
quickly strapped on his weapons. Knives. Sword. Crossbow.

Would Keely need a weapon? He rifled briefly through her

open satchel. There were no weapons. But he did find his old, mended shirt. He lifted it, surprised to find it carefully packed in her things, and realized it smelled of sweet heather. Of her.

Gods. She'd been wearing it.

Panicky fear trembled up his spine. She had never given up on him. Not until now. Now there would be no more chances.

He made his way through the empty house and out to the fireside to find Jos and the other guards arriving back from their hunt with a small roe deer, congratulating themselves on their success.

Rafe sat nearby sorting through a basket of wild herbs while Alanna and Val made their way up the drive, back from their walk. But he didn't see Keely.

"Where's Keely?" he asked.

No one answered immediately, although the general hubbub faded.

His muscles pulled up tight along his shoulders as he fought to keep his voice calm. "Where. Is. Keely?"

Rafe stood. "I saw her about ten minutes ago, going around to the back, toward the outhouse. I assumed she'd finished and gone inside to you."

"No. She… left." Gods. Where the hell could she be?

Alanna gave him a worried look. "I'll check."

Within a minute, Alanna was back accompanied by two grim-faced guards. "The guards stationed at the back of the house moved away to give her some privacy. That was when the hunters got back, and they spent a minute talking with the men. After that, they went back to their posts, but never saw Keely again, so they assumed she'd finished up while they were admiring the deer."

Fuck.

This couldn't be happening. Tendrils of fear spread through him. Where the hell was she?

"I'll look." Jos leaped into the air, winding above them in an expanding spiral, searching.

Tor couldn't wait. He had to do something. Anything. He strode around to the outhouse and banged on the rickety door before pushing it open. It was empty. Just like he'd known it would be.

He stepped back out into the watery sunlight and forced himself to breathe. Forced himself to stand, eyes closed, for a moment, calming his thoughts. Making himself concentrate.

And then he opened them again and considered the outhouse. It was hidden at the back of the farm, close to the outer ring of gorse—planted by some long-gone farmer hoping that the thick thorns would form a natural fence to protect the homestead. Behind the gorse was a rocky slope dotted with more gorse, sprinkled with the last of the year's bright yellow flowers, and small stunted trees.

Tor strode up to the hedge. Only when he was standing almost on top of it did he see a narrow path zigzagging through the thorny bushes, perhaps made by the native wild goats searching for a gorse dinner. Gods. The dusty soil on the hillside beyond the hedge had been disturbed.

The hillside was bare for a few dozen feet and then covered in stunted trees and low bushes. It would have been easy to hide. Easy to watch. And terrifyingly easy to grab one small woman and carry her away.

Fuck.

How long had they been gone? How long had they had her? How many of them? Reivers usually formed small groups of three or four, but sometimes as many as ten.

Some of them were criminals fleeing their crimes, some

were farmers who gave up on working the land hoping for an easy profit from theft and extortion, others were soldiers who had fled battle or been set punishment they couldn't bear. All of them were cruel and savage.

Gods. Reivers would—

No. He wasn't going to think of that. Not now, not ever. He was not going to imagine his Keely in their hands. He would get her back. Someone took her up that hill, but he would bring her back down.

"I'll come with you," Rafe said firmly from behind him, and Tor spun to see Val and Alanna too.

"So will I," Val added.

Gods. These men were his true brothers. Standing with him the second he needed them. And they had supported Keely all this time. Would have supported her with the baby —that was what Val had been promising earlier. That was what Tristan had meant when he reminded Tor that they were a family.

He would fix this. He would make it right and give Keely whatever she wanted, even if what she wanted was to be left alone. But first, he had to get her back.

He nodded his thanks to Rafe with a curt dip of his chin, but then he focused on Val. "You can't come. You have to stay with your wife."

Val's frown deepened. "I can help."

Tor wrapped a hand around his neck, squeezing the aching muscles, holding it like an anchor as he fought to finish this conversation while every cell in his body needed to be moving. "Thank you. Genuinely. But Rafe, Jos, and I have scouted together many times. And frankly, you don't have enough guards to split them. You need to take Alanna to the barracks at Staith and then come back with more men."

Alanna wrapped her arms around her belly, holding herself, and Val immediately pulled her closer. Her eyes were soft with distress. "I'm not leaving here until we know."

Tor shook his head trying to keep his last tiny hold on his rapidly fraying temper. "I'm sorry, but you would be a distraction. You're using resources we need."

Alanna drew herself up as if to argue, but he kept speaking, low and resolute. "She would want you safe. She would never forgive herself if something happened to you because you were here. And frankly, we need the men who can't be spared from your protection."

Alanna shook her head, her lower lip trembling, but Jos landed beside them before she could argue further. "The ground's disturbed past those bushes. There's a path that leads further into the hills, toward the mountains."

It was all he could do not to take his friend by his shoulders and shake him. "Did you see her?"

Jos folded his wings behind him, battle-ready, as he replied, "I couldn't get too close without being seen. But yes, I think so."

"What do you mean, you think so?"

Jos's eyes flicked to Rafe and Val and then back to his. "I saw two men on horses, traveling fast. A third, smaller, person was holding on behind one of them, covered in a gray cloak. It could have been her."

Gods. Fuck. She was wearing a gray cloak.

Tor forced himself to think. "Okay. That's good. She's alive and... she's alive." That was the most important thing. They must have been moving since they grabbed her. All he had to do was catch them.

Catch them. Kill them. Get Keely back and then go down on his knees and make her understand that he hadn't meant any of the things he'd said. Not in the way that he'd said them.

He needed to explain that she made him feel things that overpowered him with their intensity. That he had been terrified—and had no idea of how to handle that feeling.

Not because she wasn't enough, but because she was magnificent. Because she was everything.

And the archangels help the men who took her, because their time was almost over.

Chapter Fifteen

KEELY CAME BACK to consciousness with a surge of acidic nausea and a vicious, stabbing pain in the back of her head. She was crumpled in a heap, her face pressed down into the cold ground and she could hear the men who'd taken her. Bard. Just when she'd thought she'd finally reached rock bottom.

"Fuck. Andred is not gonna like this. Not at all," said a whiny, nasal voice.

"Not our fault though, was it?" said a deeper, coarser voice.

Stones clattered heavily as if they were being thrown or kicked. She kept her eyes closed and her body still, trying to ignore the clamminess of her palms and the churning in her belly; the need to scream out her fear and pain. She couldn't afford any kind of weakness in front of these men.

"How could we know there'd be a guard with the princess all the time. Blues in the skies, soldiers all over the place."

"Exactly. And now we gotta move before that Mabin

comes back." Apparently, deep voice was making the decisions. "Andred can decide what to do with her. He wanted to know whether the rumor was true about Alanna coming north. Now we know. And this one can tell him more."

A boot scuffed along the ground, and more stones clattered, followed by a rough, put-upon sigh.

"Fucking Andred. I don't even know why we follow—"

"Yeah. You do. We made our choice."

There was an angry grunt of annoyed agreement. And then a boot nudged roughly into her leg. "Wake up."

Keely groaned, curling herself into a ball around her belly. No point in pretending to be unconscious if it was going to get her hurt.

A rough hand wound itself into her hair and yanked her upright, forcing her head up as she scrabbled to her feet, her head pounding. She wiped her mouth on her sleeve, swallowing hard against the bile in her mouth.

The two men watched her with equal expressions of annoyance. Eventually, the shorter of the two folded his arms over his chest and jerked his head toward the taller, thinner man. "You're riding with him."

"Come on, Garn," whined the tall man. "She looks like she's about to hurl. Can't she walk?"

Garn turned his head slowly, a ruffle of olive-colored scales flickering above his collar, not saying a word.

"Fine. Fuck. Fine." The thin man looked at Keely with hatred. "You're behind me."

No. Definitely not. Getting on that horse was a terrible idea. Going anywhere with these two men was insane, and Andred sounded even worse.

She had promised the pea. She had promised herself.

And Tor—what would he think? That she'd run away with his child? Again. Of course he would.

"No—" She stepped back but caught her foot on a low pile of rocks and almost fell. She wheeled around, trying to regain her feet, and by the time she had righted herself, Garn was standing so close he was almost touching her, his nose wrinkled and eyes narrowed.

"The only reason you're still alive is because Andred might have a use for you," he said quietly, tipping his head toward the ugly crossbow carried by his companion. "Get on the horse or we'll shoot you now."

She ran her eyes desperately over the narrow gully they'd pulled her into. Gray hills rose away from them, strewn with rocks and tufts of winter heather, too steep and exposed to offer any escape. The path itself was rough with stones and sand, hard enough to walk on, unstable and dangerous to run on, and also totally exposed.

There was no escape. Not yet, anyway. She had to stay alive, protect the pea, and then look for a way out.

She made her way to the horse he'd gestured toward and waited. The thin man mounted, still grumbling in a low, curse-filled monologue, and then waited impatiently while Keely hauled herself up behind him.

She had no option but to sit behind his saddle and cling to his dirty shirt for stability, while her stomach lurched and her head pounded brutally. They rode up the narrow trail with Garn riding hard behind them, the two men kicking the horses into a quick trot, moving as fast as possible along the treacherous path.

Within minutes, they reached a fork and immediately branched off away from the farmhouse, always sticking close to the rising hills and rocky outcrops around them.

Keely swallowed, taking slow breaths through her mouth and trying to ignore the stench of stale sweat and dirt. The brutal pain at the back of her head settled into a slightly more bearable ache, and she focused on the path, memorizing the route they were taking and looking for any chance of escape. But nothing could take away the misery pounding through her. It was finally over. That tiny flicker of hope that had stayed with her—against all odds—for so long, had died. She was alone.

No. Not alone. She was carrying a precious life inside her. The pea needed her to be strong. Especially now.

They'd been riding for about ten minutes when Garn suddenly called out and they moved quickly into the shadow of the rocks and rising hills as the two men stared back at the sky. In the distance, Keely could see the distinctive shape of a Mabin in flight. He stayed too far away to be sure, but it looked like Jos.

The Mabin paused in the air, turned toward them, and then flew rapidly back down toward the farmhouse.

Someone had noticed she was missing and looked for her. And now they knew where she was. All she had to do was find a way to get free, and the Hawks would help—Alanna would make sure of it. Val too. They were her friends.

For the first time, it occurred to her that she wasn't actually alone. She had genuine, kind friends who cared for her. People who would look for her and help her. Alanna and Val would come for her.

She wasn't going to think about Tor. That was done.

Soon they were far from the original path, surrounded by tumbled gray rocks and rising mountains. Far from the farmhouse and anyone who might be able to see them, even from the air, unless they were directly overhead.

They sped up, the horses clattering through the narrow

gully, kicking up pebbles that ricocheted back off the high stone walls as they galloped.

What was Tor doing? Was he still sitting in her room, with his back to the wall, dark eyes filled with….

No. She was not thinking about that.

The path rose to the top of the hill they'd been climbing, and they emerged onto a bleak ridge. Mountains rose up ahead of them, much closer now, while down to their right a steep tree-covered slope fell away toward a distant lake.

The lake was huge and dark, nestling between the hills, its far shores hidden in swathes of mist and low clouds. And on the near side, about a mile along the shore, up against a wall of sheer cliffs, was a huge encampment—enough tents for two hundred men, maybe more. It was unlike anything she had ever imagined from a group of reivers. Who the hell were these people?

Her captors pushed their horses into a gallop as Keely clung on, desperate not to fall on that desolate hillside. Within minutes they were off the ridge and bringing the horses to a walk as they turned down a narrow gorge. Sometime in the distant past, a swiftly flowing river or waterfall must have carved its way downward, forming what was now a steep wooded path that dropped toward the lake below.

Garn whistled a long, low blast, which was quickly answered from among the trees, as they picked their way down the narrow track between dense groves of spiky pines.

The orange-brown bark of the pines was rough and peeling, and the thick beds of needles muffled the horse's hooves as the fresh scent of the trees filled the air. At any other time, she would have thought it beautiful. The sharp scent of the trees in the cold air would have filled her with nostalgia for the pine forests of her childhood. But this felt nothing like her childhood memories. This felt like a trap. Like the end of everything she had ever hoped for.

Bard. She had been so desperate to see Tor again. What a mistake that had been.

She closed her eyes and tried not to think about the look on his face as he accused her of taking his family away. Pale, lined with exhaustion, unshaved from many days on the road. His dark eyes filled with… anger?

Was it anger?

Now, with the long, painful miles between them, it was less obvious. Had he really been enraged, or was he afraid? The intensity of what they'd shared had almost been overwhelming, even for her. And the Bard knew, Tor didn't handle emotions well.

Keely understood—she'd been through it herself. The horror of discovering that the world didn't work in the way you thought it did. That all your plans, your solid foundations, could be ripped away in a moment. It was easier to stay numb and hide behind your walls. Especially for a man like Tor, whose walls had been sky high to start with.

But he'd gone too far. Both times she'd trusted him, he'd hurt her. Badly. She was done with giving him the benefit of the doubt.

And yet…she couldn't forget the hope and joy that had sparked in his eyes when he first realized they were having a baby. Or the desperate sincerity of their reunion. He had followed, not realizing she was pregnant. He had followed *her*. He had chosen *her*. And then, when he was tired and vulnerable, he'd had a shock.

What had he said…? *How could you do this to me?* Do what, exactly? What had he meant? *It's you.* What was her?

Bloody hell. She'd done it again. She'd walked out based on two vague sentences without demanding a proper explanation. Without giving him a chance to process his feelings or to say what he really meant. When she knew that her walking away was exactly what he was afraid of in the first place.

She truly hated this feeling. Confusion, anger, and guilt all warring inside her, underpinned by hurt.

Keely sighed. Did any of it even matter when she was unlikely to survive the rest of the day? She pinched herself, hard. Fuck that. She wasn't going to think like that. She was going to survive, and she was going to make a home for the pea. Just like she'd promised.

It took nearly an hour of bruising riding to reach the marshy bank of the lake and another to pick their way along its shore before she started to sense a new tension flicking through the man in front of her as he watched the camp ahead.

They reached the palisade that formed the front of the encampment and stopped to dismount at the narrow entrance. Keely shivered in the growing cold, painfully aware of the vigilant gaze of the guards in the large wooden towers that protected the gate.

A Verturian guard—distinctive green bicep tattoos revealed by his sleeveless jerkin despite the dropping temperature—stepped back from the gate to allow two large Apollyon soldiers to stride out and stand at the entrance to the camp. Why the hell were Verturians and Apollyons working together?

Both Apollyon soldiers had the characteristic wide shoulders and strong arms, dark hair and eyes, that she knew so well from Tor. But unlike him, these men were cold and hard, their gazes flickering over her captors and settling on her, assessing.

The first turned to sneer at Garn. "You're late."

"Sorry… ah, sir. We had a small problem… but we brought…." Garn gestured toward Keely.

The first of the new guards looked her up and down with narrow eyes. "I know you."

Keely tried to step back, but Garn grabbed her arm and pulled her, shoving her forward. "She was with Princess Peevish."

She narrowed her eyes and glared at Garn. If she had to hear Alanna called Princess Peevish one more time, she was going to punch someone.

The second guard's jaw clenched tightly as he scowled at Garn. "You were supposed to confirm whether the princess was there and assess her guard, then come back and report. Not bring—" He glanced at Keely "—whatever this is."

She rolled her eyes and crossed her arms over her chest, slowly breathing in the cold mountain air. At least she was off the horse and away from her captor's stench. Even if where they'd brought her had turned out to be even worse than she'd imagined.

Garn wiped his hand down his hair, tugging at the long locks. "She… ah… she might have, um…."

She'd seen them, was what had happened. She had gone to the outhouse, planning to pee before going on a very long, very distant walk, far away from Tor. She'd come out of the small outbuilding, looked up the hill, and seen them watching her.

She had opened her mouth to scream as she turned to run, but something had hit the back of her head—a stone, maybe—and knocked her out. And then she'd woken up in the gully.

Garn didn't seem to be about to explain it, so she filled in for him. "Yeah, these super scouts might need to go through their 'how not to be spotted while spying' training once more."

Garn glared at her, his fingers twitching as if he was holding himself back from walloping her, but it was the guard from the camp who spoke. "I do know you. I'd remember that bitchy attitude anywhere. You're the queen's maid."

What the hell? She looked at him more carefully. He did look vaguely familiar. Had he been in Kaerlud? That made sense, if they knew her and Alanna. She had never gotten to know the palace guards. Getting to know them did not end well for women in the court, and they had far less respect for her. She had kept her eyes down and her door locked. "I don't—"

"No," he replied with a dark look. "You wouldn't remember the lowly cavalry surrounding your mighty shrew of a princess. She was a spoiled ice queen for sure, but you… you were the harpy."

She pulled her shoulders back and straightened her spine. Asshole. So typical of Ballanor's court. Any woman who didn't immediately fall over herself trying to serve them was obviously an ice queen, and any woman who refused to let them walk all over her was clearly a harpy.

Well, she hadn't cowered in front of these bullying assholes when they were locked in the palace, and she wasn't about to start now. She lifted her chin. "You bast—"

He stepped in front of her and growled. "Shut up."

"No. I—"

He grabbed her shoulders and shook. Hard. "I said shut the fuck up."

She swallowed the words, settling for a violent litany of cursing and hatred in her mind instead.

The guard's big hand clamped over the back of her neck as he turned her toward the gate. "Andred will want to see you."

Chapter Sixteen

TOR PUSHED THE STALLION HARDER, sweating despite the freezing air as they clattered through mile after mile of bleak, stone-strewn mountain gullies.

What was Keely feeling? Was she terrified? Fuck knew that he was terrified enough for both of them.

Did she know he would come for her? Did she think he didn't care? Gods. They had to move faster.

He and Rafe pushed up the last steep climb and emerged onto a windswept ridge just as Jos landed lightly on the side of the path, gesturing for them to stop. Ahead, the path tracked along the ridge toward the mountains and then split.

One path continued on, rising up toward Verturia. The other turned down into a pine forest that covered the hillside leading sharply down toward a distant, misty lake.

And worst of all, there beside the lake, just visible at the bottom of the hill, past the trees and low-lying fog, lay a huge encampment surrounded by towering cliff walls. Even from a distance, it was clear the camp was formidably well structured with high walls and orderly lines.

It was also, strategically, probably the best military position Tor had ever seen. Only one way in—down a narrow gorge surrounded by trees that were certain to be filled with sentries—plenty of water and firewood, and utterly hidden unless you were right on top of it. The only risk was flooding, but that wasn't a consideration until the snow melted in spring. And in these northern mountains, spring came late.

Who the hell were these people? And what did they want with Keely?

"They took her onto the path down the gorge," Jos said quietly, admitting what they all already knew. "Toward the camp."

"Okay then." Rafe nodded, firming his shoulders.

"No." Tor grabbed his friend's bridle. "They'll kill us all. Probably as soon as we get under those trees."

"Or sooner," Jos agreed. "They must have seen me in the air. My guess is we've got a minute or two before company arrives."

Tor kept his voice low and firm. "You have to go back, warn the others. Send a messenger to the queen."

Both Jos and Rafe shook their heads immediately.

"We can't leave you here alone. They'll rip you apart," Rafe muttered, "and the archangels know that I'll be the one trying to stitch you back together."

Tor reached over to clap Rafe on his shoulder, hearing the true depth of worry underlying Rafe's words. His friend's fear that there would be nothing left to stitch together.

Gods. How had he spent so long wishing for his old life back instead of appreciating what he already had with the

Hawks? How had he wasted so much time he could have spent with Keely?

The Hawks had joined him without hesitating. They would ride into the certain death of that narrow gorge with him. He'd been in mourning when his real family had been right beside him the entire time.

Tor cleared his throat. "Thank you. Both of you. That means—" He tried to find the words but couldn't. "You are my true brothers," he said eventually.

He brought his fist to his heart and bowed his head, honoring his brothers. They were all silent for a long moment as the wind whispered down the gully behind them.

He lifted his head and continued, "I can't leave Keely, but someone has to warn Queen Lucilla that there is a fighting force building on her northern border. A force that, judging from that encampment, has discipline, military experience, and resources."

He did his best to sound confident as he added, "And someone has to be here to meet us when I get her out."

"I don't like it," Jos stated through clenched teeth.

"No one likes it," Rafe said in a rough voice.

Tor nodded, agreeing. No one liked it. But it was all they had.

Jos reached out and shook Tor's hand, his usually open face turned grim. "You are our brother too. Don't forget."

Rafe gripped Tor's shoulder. "Do what you have to do. And stay alive. We'll get help and come back."

He dipped his chin in agreement. "I'll do my best. And if you see the rest of the Hawks before I do—" He hesitated for a second. He was *not* going to admit that he might never see them again. "Tell the others thank you, for everything. And if Keely gets out without me, please look after her." He met Rafe's eyes. "Please look after them both."

"Yes. Of course." His friend nodded, no flicker of surprise in his eyes. "She's our family too. They both are."

Gods. Tor couldn't have this conversation. It was killing him. He whispered a hoarse, "Thank you," and then dug his heels into his stallion's sides and sped away, leaving his brothers, possibly for the last time.

He rode hard over the ridge and then slowed as he reached the trees, walking the horse and raising his hands to show he held no weapons.

"I ask for passage!" he called loudly, praying they would let him get close enough before shooting, from curiosity if nothing else.

No one answered. But no one shot him either.

Within a few minutes, he was on a narrow path between tall, spiky pines, their sharp, sweet scent rising all around him. There was a still, heavy feeling in the wood. No birds sang. No small creatures scampered through the undergrowth. And it wasn't only because of him.

They were watching him, and if he didn't convince them to let him live, he would die within the next few seconds. He fought back the intense urge to pull out his greatsword and raised his voice. "I wish to speak with your leader—I have an offer for him."

A second later, an arrow thudded into the soft carpet of needles two feet from his horse's hooves. The stallion danced back, startled, and Tor fought to bring him back under control.

The arrow was fletched in black and carved with runes. Verturian.

Gods. Had Keely been taken by her own people? People who would love nothing more than to end the life of a man who had been one of the many soldiers who had thrown themselves against their border again and again. A man wearing the Blue of the royal guards. Was this how he would atone for taking so many of her people's lives? By losing his own?

But if this was a Verturian fighting force, why hide on this side of the border? Why lurk down here surrounded by reivers and empty farmhouses when they could stay safely at home on the other side of the mountain passes and sweep down into the now undefended Brythorian moors when they were ready?

Or, if they were ready to leave their Verturian strongholds, why stop here? Why not simply continue the movement south and attack? It didn't make sense.

He lifted his eyes to sweep the heavy gray-green branches of the pines. "I'm no threat to you. All I want is to speak to your leader. I can pay a great deal—although I have nothing with me, if you're thinking you might kill me and take it now—or offer information."

He didn't have any wealth. The vast family holdings he'd been heir to were no longer his to claim. But they didn't know that, and he had to start somewhere.

"What kind of information?" A voice demanded, far closer than he'd expected. Perhaps he'd been sneaking between the trees? "What, exactly, will you pay?"

It was a smooth, glib voice with a northern accent. A Brythorian accent. Had the Verturians in the camp recruited men from the starving northern towns?

Tor shrugged. "Why don't you tell me what you want— that's how negotiating works."

"Why shouldn't we simply kill you?"

Honestly, they should have killed him already. What could he say to convince them? He cast his mind for a sensible lie but couldn't find one. He only had the truth. And a threat of his own. "You have taken someone that belongs to me, and I will pay to get her back. Tell your leader that I can make him extremely wealthy. Or go and tell him you killed the man offering riches for a chance to talk."

There was a muttered conversation from high among the trees, and then a short, spiky-haired Mabin flew down to land a little way further down the path.

Seconds later, a Tarasque with amethyst scales banding his wrists jumped down to join him.

A Mabin and a Tarasque using Verturian arrows? What the fuck was going on?

"Here—" The Mabin held out his hand. "We'll take the crossbow and sword. And all those knives."

He'd known that if he survived for any length of time, he'd have to give up his weapons, but it still burned. These men had Keely, and now they wanted his sword. But he would never get anywhere near her if he refused.

He lifted his crossbow over his head and handed it to the Mabin, followed by the knives, then slowly drew out his greatsword and dumped it into the Tarasque's hand, gratified when the man dipped heavily, struggling with the weight. "Look after that. It was my grandfather's."

Finally convinced that he had handed over everything, they led him silently down the steep gully to the lake, and then along the damp, marsh-like banks.

The Tarasque jogged swiftly beside him as the Mabin flew ahead to confer with someone at the camp, and then returned to fly above him, watching him like a cat watching a rat as the spiked wooden palisades drew nearer.

Every second that passed lay heavily on his soul. What

was happening to Keely while they meandered along the bleak, rocky lakefront?

The sun dipped behind the mountain peaks, throwing them into a deep shadow. Clouds built in the small amount of sky visible above them as icy mists from the lake spread up the shore, cold as the horror seething in his gut. Never in his life had he felt so helpless. Not even when his father threatened to call the guards.

It all took too long. The Tarasque leading the way was too slow. The infernal, never-ending trotting grated against his nerves as his entire being screamed to spur the horse on and gallop as fast as he could. The only thing that held him back was the certainty that he would be shot down within seconds of attempting to storm that lurking encampment.

By the time they reached the gate, he was ready to explode, and he had to force down the violence simmering through him to concentrate.

The orderly rows of tents he'd seen from the ridge were hidden behind a high wooden palisade of sharp stakes embedded into a low rampart. The uniform row of stakes was tall and formidable, broken only by a narrow gate flanked by two wooden guard towers. It would be extraordinarily difficult to breach, whether from the outside or the inside.

It was exactly the kind of encampment he had overseen during the northern campaigns. A Brythorian military encampment. And yet, here were the Verturian guards he'd been expecting since he'd seen that arrow. Men with bare arms and twining green tattoos around their biceps were watching from the towers.

But then two large Apollyon soldiers stepped through the gate, nodding at the sentries that had escorted him and ordering them back to their posts. Not just any Apollyon soldiers. He knew these men. Caius and Usna.

"What the actual fuck?" The words were out of his mouth before he could stop them.

Caius, the leaner of the two, slightly shorter and more likely to smile, leaned back, arms folded over his chest, and raised his brows. "Tor, Grandson of the Bar-Ulf."

Tor slid down from his horse and patted the steaming animal. No longer of the Bar-Ulf, or any ancestral house for that matter. But he wasn't discussing that with these men. Men he hadn't seen in months. Men he had thought were long dead.

Usna stepped forward, his lip twitching up. "Apparently you have riches you want to trade."

Tor folded his arms over his chest, mirroring them as he looked them up and down. They were obviously senior here. But if they had come to the gate to meet him, they weren't who he wanted to see.

He dipped his chin. "I'll trade with whoever's in charge."

Usna took another step forward. "How do you know that I'm not in charge?"

Caius and Usna had come up through the ranks of the Black Guards—the cavalry—making their way into the Wraiths. Highly mobile, famous for their fast horses and their heavy weaponry, they had always been the first in any skirmish. And had been richly rewarded for it by Geraint. Land, power, prestige had poured over them. And then Ballanor had claimed them as his own and elevated them even higher.

The Wraiths had offered him a place in their squad— only extremely well-connected Apollyon were ever considered—and his parents had been ecstatic. Until he'd turned it down.

Even in their last conversation, they had still been reminding him that they had wanted him to take the glory he'd been offered. Reminding him that they had wished he had died with the Wraiths rather than lived with the Hawks.

But he hadn't regretted his choice to stay with Tristan, Mathos, and their squad. Men he respected, admired, and trusted. And he still didn't regret that decision.

Yes, the Wraiths had been rich and powerful. But they were also merciless. Their decisions sometimes questionable. And he'd had no desire to serve under their captain. A man who was fearless, tactically brilliant, and utterly ruthless—the kind of man who would set up this camp. A man Tor had thought had died in the massacre of Ravenstone.

"I'll only speak to Andred," Tor replied.

Caius's eyes narrowed, and Tor knew he was right.

"Andred doesn't want to see you," Usna sneered. "He's busy right now."

Fuck. The coiling, seeping dread that had been snaking through his gut since he'd first realized Keely was gone sharpened into a vicious poison. "He'll see me now, or I'll go."

Usna threw his head back and laughed as the guards in the towers lifted their crossbows and took aim at Tor's heart. "Go where?"

Tor raised his voice, making sure all the guards nearby could hear him as he called out, "Kill me then. I honestly don't care. You all know about my family's wealth—tell Andred he could have named his price and you lost it for him."

"Fuck you," Caius muttered, glaring at the other guards.

Tor shrugged and tugged at his horse, turning to go. His

shoulder blades prickled with the awareness of the crossbows pointed at him as he took a step along the stony path and then another.

"Fine. Fuck. You can see him," Usna grated out from behind him.

Thank the gods. He was in.

Tor turned back and followed Caius and Usna through the palisades and into the camp. It was exactly what he'd expected. Inside the palisades there was a deep trench, an open space and then neat rows of canvas tents flanking a central "street."

He knew this layout like the back of his hand. There would be storage areas, a field hospital, drainage ditches, and most importantly, guard towers at all entrances, catapults along the walls, and almost certainly booby traps in the killing ground between the palisade and the tents.

He was in…. But how the hell were they going to get out?

They reached the center of the camp, where the most senior officers' tents would be, and paused outside the most opulent tent of all. Made of leather rather than canvas, inside it would be warmer and quieter than any of the others. It was slightly smaller than most of the tents he'd passed, but it would sleep only one officer where the others probably slept six, and would still have enough space for a cot and a small desk.

He was about to step closer when he heard it. A woman cursing loudly and creatively, her voice rising in fear and anger. A voice he would know anywhere. Keely. "I told you to get the fuck away from me."

There was a rumble of masculine laughter.

Keely's voice lowered menacingly. "If you touch me, I will kill you."

No. Absolutely not. All the fear and rage he'd been holding tight inside himself for so long roared up and through him in an agonizing tidal wave of fury.

Tor didn't bother to consider the guards escorting him, his lack of weapons, or any kind of strategy. He ignored Usna and Caius's roar of outrage and the scrape of metal as they drew their swords, and ripped open the leather tent flap.

It took a second for his eyes to adjust to the dim light cast by one small lantern; one more second to see Keely standing at the far side of a low camp cot, fists raised, face pale in the flickering light, her cloak hanging off one shoulder, hair loose and disheveled.

A large, familiar Apollyon stood in front of her, face drawn into a black scowl as he spun toward the chaos at the entrance to his tent, sword already half drawn.

Tor was nearly incoherent with the need for violence, but he forced the words out. "If you touch her, she won't have time to kill you. You'll already be dead."

Andred looked at him, back to Keely, and then back to him again. Finally, his gaze settled on Caius and Usna, standing behind Tor with their swords up. "What the fuck did you let him in here for?"

Usna scowled. "He said he had a fortune to trade. If we shot him without offering you the option, you'd have been —" He swallowed whatever he was going to say and added, "We thought you'd prefer the choice, General, sir."

Andred narrowed his eyes at the men, while Keely pulled her cloak back together and took a step away. Gods. That small movement was enough to nearly push him over the edge.

"What do you want?" Andred demanded.

Tor tilted his head in Keely's direction. Wasn't it fucking obvious?

Andred shook his head. "She's about to tell me all about Alanna's plans."

"I'll tell you Princess Alanna's plans," Tor growled. "She plans to get back to the nearest barracks as fast as she can. In fact, she's almost certainly already safely locked behind the walls of the outpost at Staith and deployed additional guards. Reinforcements will be here within the day."

Caius cleared his throat and admitted, "The guards report a Mabin flying overhead. He saw the camp."

"One of the Hawks, traveling with the guards assigned to protect Alanna," Tor agreed. "He's probably already reported to Princess Alanna and briefed a messenger to ride hard for Kaerlud. As soon as Queen Lucilla hears about this encampment, she'll order the troops to mobilize."

Andred grunted roughly, tipping his head to one side as he glared at Tor. "Fuck." He slid his sword back into its sheath with a harsh click. "Fuck it all."

Keely took another slow step back, her eyes wide and shocked as she watched them all warily. Gods. She really had thought he wouldn't follow.

He wished he could reach her. Touch her. Do something, anything, to reassure her. But the tension in the tent was too high to risk her by provoking Andred any further.

Andred looked across to Usna. "Go and get her. I want her to be part of this." Usna stepped back with a quick salute, leaving Tor and Andred staring at each other with open disgust.

Tor couldn't imagine who Andred was sending for, and he didn't care. "There is no *this*. I've told you Alanna's plans. Now let Keely come with me. I'll pay you whatever you want."

Andred laughed, the sound harsh and humorless. "You think that we should reward you for exposing us? That we should let you go so you can add to that report, fill in all the details about our camp? Certainly not." Andred tipped his head toward Keely. "You should have left with your friends, Tor. Trust me, she's not worth it."

Tor clenched his fists, breathing through his nose in a desperate battle not to reach over and throttle the man in front of an entire company of his men. "She's worth it to me."

Andred chuckled darkly. "This woman?" He gave Keely a slow look. "She's the one who betrayed you all at Ravenstone. Everything you lost was because of her."

"No." That didn't make sense. "Ballanor—"

"Ballanor needed a Verturian to recruit soldiers for him. Archers from the north who would gladly destroy Geraint. Keely was his liaison," Andred replied.

Tor shook his head. "Ballanor imprisoned her. He was going to execute—"

Andred cut him off with a bark of mirthless laughter. "Of course he was going to get rid of her. He wasn't going to leave the woman who could tell everyone what he'd done to walk around the palace, now was he?"

Tor's eyes flew to Keely's. To the look of stunned horror on her face.

It was me, she'd said, standing in her shift, glaring hatred at Ballanor, *I hated this kingdom, and I hated this court.*

He took a slow breath and then shook his head once more. No. He didn't believe it. But before he could respond in any way, a soft voice spoke from the opening at the front of the tent. "Truth."

Tor looked up to see a young woman stepping awkwardly inside. She had hair of dark mahogany, lying in soft waves over her pale skin, and the soft violet eyes of the Nephilim. A little taller than Keely, but very slight, fragile almost, with her pale skin and huge eyes.

And the entire left side of her face was a mass of shining, knotted burn scars. Starting over her eyebrow, traveling down her cheek and neck, to disappear beneath the collar of her gray woolen dress. She stepped carefully, favoring her left ankle.

"Daena." Andred dipped his chin as the woman limped further into the tent. "Our truth seeker," he added smugly.

"I did not betray anyone. Ravenstone was nothing to do with me," Keely whispered, her face even paler than it had been, dark red blotches climbing her neck as she took a stumbling step backward.

"She hated Brythoria," Andred said, arrogant certainty threading through his voice. "Hated the court. Blamed us all for the war against her people. Who knows, maybe she thought Ballanor would die in the massacre too, leaving the kingdom weak and ripe for invasion."

"No." Keely shook her head, her hand creeping up to rest over her throat.

"Truth," whispered the truth seeker, as Andred continued, "She was the link to the Verturians. Someone had to know how to get a message through the passes. Someone who knew where to find the men who hated the treaty and would be prepared to travel to Brythoria to end it once and for all. Someone who knew where the treaty would be signed. Look around you, Tor, some of those Verturians report to me now, they've told me all about how they were recruited."

"Truth," said Daena yet again.

"Why would you tell me this? I don't—"

Andred cut him off with a vaguely pitying look. "You need to know the truth about the people you've given your loyalty to. Do yourself a favor and cut whatever false ties you have to this woman. Come and work for me instead, Tor—we need someone with your strategic skill. The kingdom needs you."

Keely looked at Daena, and then at him for a long, slow second. Her hand fell away from her neck and she straightened her shoulders. And then she looked away.

Why? Because she was hiding the truth as Andred had said? Or because she couldn't bear to watch? Because she was certain he would judge her and find her wanting? Because the very last thing he'd said to her was that he didn't trust her and now a truth seeker, the highest authority in the kingdom, was calling her a liar. Gods.

Images of Keely kneeling in the banquet hall flickered through his mind. Much of what Andred had said was true. She had hated Brythoria. Maybe she still did. But he also knew *her*. He knew how much she loved her friend. How hard she worked to protect the people she cared for. She had tried to protect *him*, for gods' sake. One of the veterans of the northern campaign.

Andred was saying Keely had risked Alanna's life on the field of Ravenstone. That she would have destroyed the treaty her friend had sacrificed so much for.

The boy she'd loved had died because of that war. And he knew, in his gut—in his soul—that if Keely said she didn't do it, she didn't. It didn't matter what evidence they had against her, or what the truth seeker said.

Andred would love it if Tor threw his experience—and the Bar-Ulf coffers—behind him. Making him doubt Keely was an excellent way to do that.

Keely was looking away because she expected him to renounce her. Expected him to trust everyone else but not her. To take the side of these men, men he could so easily have been one of. And he couldn't blame her. When had he ever given her any reason to expect his support?

Tor lifted his gaze, looking only at Keely as he spoke. "I trust her. If Keely says she didn't do it, she didn't, I don't care what your truth seeker says."

Keely's head whipped back, her eyes rushing to his, mouth falling open slightly. Gods. That proof of how little she expected from him stung. He repeated himself, pouring sincerity into his words, hoping she could hear all the things he wasn't saying. "I trust her completely."

Keely took a small, unconscious step forward, but Andred crossed his arms over his chest and spoke before she could say anything. "You're making a mistake, Tor. This maid and her peevish mistress are a bad choice. Supporting this new queen we've been foisted with is an error. None of them can give you what we can." Andred continued, "We gave you the chance once before, and I'll give it to you for the last time now. Make your offer of wealth again, bring your strategic skills to support us, and we'll accept you. I'll give you a place among the Wraiths. You can help us win this war, and we'll reward you with power and status like you've never imagined."

Andred didn't know the first thing about what Tor wanted. Power and status meant nothing to him. But one thing stood out. "What war?" Tor asked slowly.

Andred grinned. "The war for Brythoria. The war to remove Ballanor's naïve little sister from the throne she should never have been placed upon and take back our rightful place. Ballanor stole from us and ruined the kingdom. It's time to correct those mistakes."

Fucking hell. That was what these soldiers were doing. Preparing for a war against their own kingdom.

But it didn't explain the depth of hatred dripping from Andred's voice. The Wraiths were Ballanor's personal squad and Andred had been one of Ballanor's favorites. What were they even doing out here, hiding in the mountains and recruiting Verturians?

"It was you." Keely's rough whisper cut into the quiet tent.

Andred didn't even flinch. Not a flicker of surprise crossed his face.

And then, with sudden, horrific clarity, Tor understood. The arrows, the dispossessed men, the war camp, the missing cavalry unit—it all suddenly came together, and the words tore out of him. "Gods. *You* are the traitors of Ravenstone."

Chapter Seventeen

"WHY?" It came out as a whisper. Keely cleared her throat and tried again. "Why did you do it? Why would you kill your king?"

Tor's face was pale despite his olive skin as he answered for Andred. "For money. Ballanor would have promised riches and power. And some men... some men like war."

Bard. Her hands were shaking, and she gripped them tightly together over her belly. Tor had lost his king, his position in the Blues, and his family because of Ravenstone. Val had been tortured without mercy. Alanna had been imprisoned and nearly died. Nim attacked. All because Ballanor wanted to be king and Andred wanted to be rich.

She stepped forward, ignoring Andred's snarl. "That's why you want Alanna, isn't it? You want to prevent the treaty... you want Lucilla isolated when you attack."

Andred shrugged, still looking at Tor. "This is our chance. We can make this kingdom what it should have been."

Tor recoiled. "How the fuck did Ravenstone make our kingdom any better?"

"We couldn't let the treaty go ahead; Ballanor was always right about that. We fought too long and too hard to just walk away. Our kingdom, our wealth, all our resources have been dedicated to the war. Geraint expected us to put down our swords and walk away like it was nothing, but Ballanor promised to cancel the treaty and finally win the war. To finally get us access to the Verturian mines."

Tor wrapped a heavy hand around the back of his neck, his jaw clenching. "Was it worth it, Andred? To see King Geraint, your king, falling in a pool of his own blood. Men you'd fought beside screaming and dying as you shot them down. I lost… fuck…."

"No, it was not bloody worth it," Andred growled, gesturing to the camp outside. "Does it look worth it to you?"

Bard. "Ballanor betrayed you." Keely's words were low, but everyone heard them.

"Ballanor was a useless child who had no understanding of how to be a king," Andred growled. "If he had kept his faith, we would have stood beside him, protected him, and he would still be alive today."

Caius and Usna grunted their agreement as Andred continued, "It no longer matters. Ballanor set us free. Now we'll make our own way."

"With more death. More destruction," Tor said quietly, grief etched in the lines bracketing his mouth and the heavy furrows on his brow.

Despite everything he'd said, despite her hurt and confusion, his pain stabbed at her. She wanted to go to him, stand beside him and show him that he was not alone.

Keely blinked slowly. Tor had been hurt too. And he had still followed her. He was risking his life for her.

Andred looked between them, face set in a formidable frown. "Choose a side, Tor. Us or her. Wealth and power—and the chance to set the kingdom right—or a bunch of useless women we will never allow you to serve."

"That's easy." Tor looked at her, eyes soft, and she knew exactly what he was going to say.

Fear rushed through her in a torrent, her heart thudding heavily in her ears. Tor was going to choose her and Andred would kill him for it.

Hell no. For so many years she'd kept herself safe, never taking the risk of loving anyone else. She had finally taken a chance and found someone she cared for, and she was not about to watch him die.

Tor smiled. "I choose K—"

She stepped forward, frantically interrupting. "There's another option. Please." Andred looked at her, his cold eyes full of contempt as she continued, "You can hold us hostage."

"What?" Andred's scowl darkened.

"You wanted wealth, lands, even power," she explained, speaking fast. "Tor's the most valuable of all of us. Mathos, his best friend, is consort to Queen Lucilla, and Tristan, his captain, is now Supreme Commander of the Blues. They'll pay whatever you ask to get him back. Whatever Ballanor promised, they can give it to you."

Tor blinked, his expression stunned. As if he hadn't even imagined he could be of any value.

Andred nodded slowly, digesting the idea.

"The same is true of Keely," Tor added, his eyes clearing as he focused on her. "Her mother is Moireach's cousin. She was offered a position on Lucilla's council.

Together, we would make excellent hostages. A bargaining chip that you would be insane to waste."

Andred grunted, looking between them, considering.

"Truth," Daena murmured, watching them all warily. Andred looked to Daena, standing quietly as she met his eyes, and then from her to Caius and Usna.

"I don't like it," Caius muttered. "We should execute them both and get out of here, move the camp before the queen's guards come back."

"Let me think." Andred folded his arms over his chest, jaw clenched.

Keely took the chance to look across at Tor. The tent was crowded and oppressive, every word a balancing act. And yet he hadn't once backed down from his support of her. He had looked Andred in the eye and told him that he trusted and chose her, in the face of the truth seeker's pronouncement. Knowing his faith in her would almost certainly get him killed. Strategically, it had been the worst thing he could have done. And yet, he'd done it for her.

He had followed her north. And he had followed her now. Could she let his actions guide her, rather than his hurtful words? The words she hadn't let him explain.

She took a step closer to Tor. She didn't know what to think, but she did know that if they were going to die, she wanted to be standing next to him, facing it together.

"It'll take a few days to get back to Kaerlud," Andred said slowly. "Even if the message is passed from rider to rider. Then another two weeks to gather troops, at least a week to march north. Lucilla is not an immediate problem."

Bard. Where was Andred going with this? She took another step closer to Tor.

"Alanna isn't a threat either," Andred continued. "She'll spend the night in Staith, and then, perhaps, they'll return.

The barracks are almost empty. At best she can send one squad, maybe two, up against our full company. They won't risk the ridge in the dark. My guess is they'll get here mid-morning tomorrow." He looked at his men. "We should take tonight to prepare and march south at first light."

Usna folded his arms over his chest, frowning. "A half-trained company filled with unprepared fighters from different backgrounds and different squads. Gods, Andred, half of them are reivers we've recruited from the mountains and Verturians who've fled their own kingdom. We were meant to spend the winter forging weapons and running drills." He shook his head. "We're not ready."

"It's true," Caius added. "Most of them are still half savage. If we meet Lucilla now in open war, we'll lose."

"Oh, please. What can a woman do?" Andred sneered. "A young girl sitting on the throne, completely untrained, unsuited for war. Trust me, Ballanor was fucking useless. She'll be even worse."

"Lucilla, maybe," Usna agreed, "but not Tristan. He's fought for longer and in worse places than any of us."

Andred leaned back against the small table, nodding slowly. "Which is exactly why we should act now. No one suspects anything. The northern towns are empty and poorly defended. Tristan has been supreme commander for only a few weeks, while we have been preparing for this for half a year."

"Truth," whispered Daena from her place at the side of the tent, so quietly that Keely didn't think anyone else had heard her.

Keely looked up into the other woman's eyes and, unexpectedly, saw her own horror reflected there. Who was this woman who had blithely lied about Keely's involvement in Ravenstone and now looked appalled at this talk of war?

Andred caught their look and stood with a growl. "Take Tor and the women away. We need to plan."

"We should kill them now," Caius repeated.

"No," Andred disagreed. "We might need them— hostages are always useful, especially such politically connected hostages. Take them all to Daena's tent and allocate two extra guards."

Keely wiped her face with her hand, trying not to show the depth of her relief. Thank the Bard. They were leaving the tent alive. Even if they were being stuck with a woman who they absolutely could never trust, at least they were still breathing.

Usna muttered a low string of curses, but he gestured for Daena to lead the way and then grabbed Keely's arm and pulled her out of the tent with Tor beside her.

The sun had set and the clouds were dark and heavy above them as Daena limped slowly ahead, leading them to a small tent on the far side of the camp.

Keely took long, slow breaths of the cold air, tasting the bitter tang of snow and letting the biting wind clear some of her terror. She had been afraid since she'd been captured, but by far the worst had been the fear that Tor was going to be cut down in front of her. She cast a glance toward him, quiet and stern beside her, reassuring herself that he was unharmed. She was still deeply angry with him, but it didn't change the fact that his death would have broken her.

Caius bellowed and within a minute three guards were stationed outside, watching as Keely, Tor and Daena shuffled into a tiny canvas tent. It was threadbare and bleak, holding nothing but a pile of ancient sleeping blankets and an unlit lantern swinging from a hook. The guards took up position arrayed around the front of the tent and pulled the flap closed, leaving them huddled in the darkness.

Goose bumps prickled over Keely's arm as the wind rattled the canvas. Bard, it was freezing. And then, before she could even pull her cloak tighter, Tor was there, running his big hands up her arms, across her back, and pulling her tightly to his chest.

"Gods, Keely," he whispered into her hair. "I thought I'd lost you. I've never been so frightened before in my life."

She leaned back, trying to see his face in the darkness. She wanted him to hold her, wanted to lean on him, but she didn't know if she could. She didn't know if she could bear to have her hope crushed again.

He loosened his grip, letting her go, but at the same time, he spoke softly. "I'm sorry, Keely, so fucking sorry. I do trust you. Completely."

Hope and fear battled each other in her belly, and she held herself still. "Did you mean it, Tor? When you said you believed me?"

His fingers flexed against her back. "Yes. With my life. With the life of our child, I trust you."

Bard. She blinked heavily at the threatening tears. "But then why did you say—"

"Keely." His voice was warm and certain, the same strong anchor that had held her in the churning moat all those weeks before. "When I said, 'it's you,' I meant that you're it for me. You're the only one who makes me crazy. But it's not because you're not enough, it's because I'm fucking terrified you'll leave."

"I make you crazy?" she repeated softly.

"You make me vulnerable. If you go, you'll take the last remaining piece of my heart with you. I'm afraid of saying the wrong thing, and so, sometimes, I don't say anything. Or I try, and the words come out wrong. But it's only because it means so much to me. Because *you* mean so much to me."

"Bard, Tor." She swallowed down the burning tears. It was the longest speech she'd ever heard him make. And it meant the world. "All I wanted was for us to take a chance on each other."

"I'll give anything, do anything, to take that chance. Please forgive me."

His fingers trembled on her back. He held her like she was precious to him, like he never wanted to let her go.

"Can I trust you, soldier?" she whispered.

"Yes." His deep voice rumbled in the darkness. "You can trust me with your life." And then he added, "I trust you too. With my life, and with… everything."

It was all she needed. She trusted him. And she could forgive him. She ran her hands up to find his face, then went up on her toes to set her lips on his. Nothing else mattered, only that they were together. That he was alive.

Tor slanted his mouth over hers, and they both sighed. His fingers threaded through her hair and held her locked against him as if he was terrified she might pull away. But there was nowhere she wanted to be other than in his arms.

A flint struck, and light flared around them, and then a quiet voice whispered, "Oh, damn, sorry. Ah… truth, by the way… if you wanted to know. Never mind."

They pulled apart, her hands still wrapped around Tor's neck, his fingers still entwined in her hair, and Tor rested his forehead down on hers. They stayed like that for a moment, not speaking. There was too much to say. And this was not the time.

Keely turned her head to take in the woman currently carefully looking away. Now that they were closer, she could see Daena wasn't quite as young as she'd first suspected. Fine lines wrinkled the sides of her eyes, and she had a steady, quiet presence that spoke to some maturity.

Daena pulled out a water skin and offered it to them. Keely glared at it, and the woman holding it, shaking her head. Certainly not.

Daena took a long series of swallows herself before offering it again. "It's safe."

Keely took the water skin and drank deeply before passing it to Tor, but she never took her eyes off the Nephilim.

Eventually, Daena lifted her arm and turned to show a small hole in her dress, stained dark red. "Usna had his dagger in my ribs. I didn't have any choice but to confirm whatever Andred said."

Keely leaned against Tor, so grateful he was there, and glared at Daena. "Why should we trust you?"

"I'm a prisoner, like you," Daena said softly.

Keely couldn't help her disbelieving snort.

Daena smiled sadly, the flickering light playing over the burns on her face. "I was living in the temple a couple of miles outside Staith. There was a great herbalist there, and I wanted to learn. I'm not a healer, but I thought one day I might.... Anyway, we were attacked by reivers. It was after the war and people were hungry. They burned the temple, and I got trapped inside. Andred himself lifted the beam that set me free."

Daena shrugged, a wealth of pain glimmering in her eyes. "The Wraiths took me back to their camp and looked after me. Shared their food and water. Changed my bandages. When they asked me to help, I felt I owed them. I didn't understand that Andred would never let me leave."

"But surely this isn't safe for you?" Tor rumbled from behind her. "This camp full of reivers and soldiers who abandoned their posts."

"It's not," Daena agreed, "but I told Andred that if one

of his men so much as touches me I will never read truth for
him again. Turns out having your own truth seeker is pretty
valuable… more valuable than the life of a rough, half-
savage reiver. The men understand that touching me earns
a death penalty."

"So why lie about me?" Keely demanded.

"The men can't touch me. That doesn't mean I'm safe
from Andred. I read the truth for him, but I also confirm his
truth to others when he demands it." Daena gestured
toward the tent flap. "You've seen the guards. They keep the
men out and me in. Not that I'd get far on this ankle."

Damn it. Keely almost felt sorry for the woman. Almost.
Not enough to trust her though.

"You have to get out of here," Daena said. "Caius wants
you dead, and Andred will listen to him eventually."

"What was their original plan, Daena? What were they
intending to do in the spring, once the men were better
trained?" Tor asked quietly.

The Nephilim woman sighed. "They planned to sweep
south, taking the poorly defended northern cities, emptying
the barracks, and recruiting men. By the time they reached
Kaerlud they expected to have amassed a huge fighting
force: enough men to easily overwhelm the city guards…
and then the palace." Daena closed her eyes for a long
moment, and when she opened them again, they were
bleak. "Andred wants to be king."

Bard. "On what grounds?" Keely asked.

"His grandfather was a marquess—one of the original
councilors. Andred claims the title and the noble Apollyon
bloodline that goes with it. And he believes he'll have an
army behind him."

Damn. "What about Lucilla?" Keely asked. "Surely he
recognizes her as the true queen?"

Daena rubbed her fingers slowly down her scar. "He hates Lucilla as much as he hated her brother."

"Because Ballanor reneged," Tor muttered.

"Yes," Daena agreed. "They were supposed to get lands and a huge payment after Ravenstone. Instead, Ballanor sent a message to say they were discharged, and if he ever saw them again their lives were forfeit."

"So, they planned to take it for themselves," Keely said quietly, her heart thudding heavily in her chest. "And they've just moved up their schedule by six months.... Now the war starts tomorrow."

Chapter Eighteen

TOR WAS SO sick of war. Sick of all of it. He had never questioned his family's belief that he should be a soldier, but now he did. Now he wondered what else he could have done with his life. How would he feel knowing his child was going to war? Or Keely?

Deep in Keely's belly was a tiny spark that would one day grow to be a person. A little girl with her mother's green eyes and fiery spirit, or a boy with black hair and a cheeky grin. And one day that child would grow up and choose what to do with their life.

The thought rocked through him. *Please gods, please, not a soldier.*

This was why Keely had left. Why she had fought against giving her heart to a soldier. Not because she didn't believe in him. But because she understood the agony of losing someone to war. She had been trying to protect herself. Protect their child. And yet she had still been prepared to take a chance on him.

Gods, she was strong. After all she had borne, she was

still standing. Still fighting. By some miracle, she was still with him. She had let him hold her when he had been half certain that she would push him away.

She hadn't said that she forgave him, but she had kissed him, her arms had wrapped around him and held him close. It was a start.

When she'd put herself between him and Andred, he'd thought his heart was going to stop. And now she was caught up in this nightmare war that the fucking Wraiths were determined to start.

They had to get away from Andred and his insanity. They had to warn the others. Prepare Lucilla for what was coming. Most importantly, Tor had to get his family—Keely and their child—to safety.

He closed his eyes and visualized their position. For the first time in months, he felt confident in his abilities. He hadn't failed Geraint; they had all been betrayed, again and again.

He could come up with a strategy to get them out; it was what he was good at. And then, once Keely was safe, they would plan their future.

They were inside a tent, with no weapons, guarded by three soldiers and possibly Daena. The tent was surrounded by many more tents all filled with soldiers, many of them undisciplined, little more than the reivers they'd been. Beyond that were the ramparts topped with palisades, sheer mountain walls, and one narrow gully leading to an exposed ridge. All bordered by a huge mountain lake.

His eyes snapped open. That was the weak point. The lake. The huge, mist-covered, icy lake that led who the fuck knew where.

"Where are the boats?" he asked.

Daena frowned. "What boats?"

"This position is strategically extremely defensible, but it wouldn't last in a protracted siege. Andred will have a way out, and his way out will be by boat."

The Nephilim woman considered for a moment. "There is a guarded area behind the stores, right on the lakeshore. It has its own palisade and a low canvas roof strung over the top. I've seen tree trunks taken in there. Maybe they used the wood for boats."

"How do we get there?" Keely asked.

"It's not far," Daena replied. "Two rows along from here. But how will you get past the guards?"

"We all need to get past the guards," Tor replied firmly.

Daena's eyebrows raised. "We?"

"Yes. You're coming with us. If you're a prisoner, this is your chance." And if she wasn't a prisoner, then he had her where he could see her.

Daena met his eyes. "Okay. Thank you. But we still have to get past the guards."

Tor considered the ancient canvas of the tent. "We'll go out the back." He grabbed the mildewed fabric in his hands and ran a finger along the seam until he found what he was looking for, a small notch, made from years of use, rubbing against the stony ground. He worked it between his hands, twisting and pulling in opposite directions until it started to tear.

He looked up at Keely. "You'll have to distract the guards."

"Let me." Daena pushed herself heavily to her feet and limped to the front flap. She took a deep breath and then let herself out.

"Do you think we can trust her?" Keely whispered.

"I don't know," he admitted. "I don't think we have a choice."

"What do you mean 'no'?" Daena's voice rose sharply outside the tent. "We have to eat."

There was a rough murmur of male voices, then Daena again. "If you won't let me go, then one of you has to."

"Our orders don't—"

Tor stopped listening to the words as he gripped the rough canvas, and then, as soon as Daena started loudly complaining about being hungry, he gave a sharp tug.

The canvas split upward in a long, ragged rip.

He and Keely both froze, listening carefully, but the guards were still arguing loudly with Daena.

He risked another series of small tugs and managed to rip a hole halfway up the back of the tent before Daena gave a last exasperated complaint and let herself back into the tent.

They all stared silently at the hole, it would be tight, and he couldn't predict what they would find outside, but this was their best chance. Who knew how long Andred and the others would be distracted, or when the guards might decide to check on them?

Daena pulled a brown cloak from a bundle beside her bedroll and tugged it on, then slung a small leather satchel over her neck, across her chest. "I'm ready."

Tor nodded, looking at Keely. "I'll go first."

Keely narrowed her eyes, but she didn't disagree. She laid her hand on his arm, gripping tightly. "Be careful."

Gods. He leaned down and kissed her, quick and hard, pressing his lips against hers. As if that one second would be enough to tell her everything. To let her know that he would be careful. That he had every intention of getting them all out. That as soon as they were safe, he would make a plan for their future together. But that if it came to it, she was his priority.

She must have realized his thoughts, because her fingers clenched on his arm as he moved back, and for a moment he wondered if she would hold him there. But then she slowly released him and stepped away, his arm tingling where she'd touched him.

Tor ducked down through the hole; it was a tight squeeze, but he twisted to the side and pushed his shoulders through, emerging into the dark space behind the tent.

Lanterns shone, glowing on the tent fronts and casting long shadows back onto the foggy water of the dark lake behind them. The air was heavy and damp, the stars and moon completely blocked by thick clouds.

Tor crouched low, keeping his body in the shadows as he made his way carefully through the tent's ropes before turning to offer his hand to Keely and then Daena. The Nephilim woman moved agonizingly slowly on the muddy ground, gripping his hand as she avoided the guy ropes and the wooden pegs they attached to, protecting her ankle.

Long, tense moments passed until they were through the gap and almost to the water. A glance at the shore showed it was heavily pebbled, guaranteed to crunch underfoot, and they stuck to the frozen mud at its rim, following Daena as she limped ahead.

She led them past the backs of two more tents, passing quickly through the narrow, lamplit channels between them and back into the dark shadows each time. Thank the gods the tents were set close to each other.

Daena raised her hand and they stopped behind her, huddling in the gloom as soldiers shouted commands and called orders nearby. Ahead, Tor could just make out a blocked-off area surrounded by a shoulder-high palisade and covered by a high canvas ceiling.

"There's a back gate that opens toward the lake, but it's

always barred," Daena whispered. "The guards rotate, one at the front where the main entrance is, one at the back. I don't know how often they change."

Tor glanced at Keely, who gave him a small nod. They had no choice—they had to try.

The two women hunched down deeper into the shadows and he stepped silently over to the shore and picked up a flat pebble, weighing it in his hand. He pulled his arm back and then snapped it forward parallel to the water, flicking his wrist and letting the pebble fly so that it skimmed across the lake, bouncing four times before it finally sank.

"What was that?" called a rough voice. "Anyone there?"

They stayed silent.

"Problem?" called a voice faintly from the distant front of the fenced-off area.

The guard stepped out from the back gate and stared at the water. After a long moment, he shouted back, "No, something in the lake."

Tor waited, hoping that these men were as poorly trained as Usna had suggested, and no one would arrive to do a sweep of the lakeshore.

The guard took another long look at the dark lake. Then he turned to look away, down the narrow beach. It was Tor's chance. He jogged silently along the muddy path up to the guard and hit him with a brutal downward strike on the back of his head, connecting with the sensitive area behind the guard's ear.

Tor caught the guard as he crumpled into an unconscious heap and dragged him up into the shadows, laying him down on his side. He felt briefly on the side of the guard's neck and found a pulse. Damn, he couldn't decide if that was a good thing, or a bad thing—the last time he'd knocked a man out and left him alive, it had been Dornar.

Gods, he was sick of fighting.

A second later, Keely joined him, and without even blinking, simply helped with using the soldier's belt and laces to tie him up, and then ripped up his threadbare shirt and stuffed it into his mouth as a gag.

Tor took the man's sword and only knife, and Keely took the crossbow and bolts. The sword was lighter than Tor was used to, nothing like his own sword—the Bar-Ulf sword—but there was nothing he could do about that. The Wraiths had his grandfather's sword, and there was no way he would risk Keely by trying to get it back.

As soon as they were done, they turned and rushed up to where Daena had lifted out the wooden bar and started to push open the gate. They slipped inside and stopped as their eyes adjusted to the darker area under the canvas.

Thank the gods. Dugout canoes lay in a row, carefully shaped from pine trunks, all with their own paddles. Daena ran her eyes along the row of ten canoes and then growled softly. "That asshole. He only made plans for the Wraiths to escape. I mean, I knew he was a bastard, but this…." Her voice trailed off.

Tor grunted. That was Andred all over. Tactically, it made much more sense to leave the bulk of your army fighting on the shore while you made your escape. But you had to be fucking ruthless to do it.

"Can we scuttle them somehow?" Keely murmured.

He wished they could. "I don't think so. We don't have enough time and we can't do anything noisy. If we set fire to them, the smoke will alert the guards. Our best option is to get away and warn Lucilla."

Keely nodded grimly. "Okay, let's do it."

They worked together to lift a canoe and carry it out while Daena quickly barred the gates behind them.

A soldier whistled loudly somewhere within the camp, and they all froze. Gods. If they were caught now, it was over.

Another whistle sounded and voices called. The wind gusted in icy drafts, ruffling his hair and carrying the fresh scent of cold water, so near to them, and still so distant.

Slowly the voices faded. No one appeared through the gloom, demanding to know what they were doing. Tor looked at Keely and tried to smile. They had to move.

They had no choice but to cross the narrow shore. The crunching of the pebbles underfoot seemed to echo loudly, reverberating around them with every step, but within a few minutes, they had the canoe on the beach.

Keely helped Daena into the canoe and then quickly followed her, holding the oars safely. Tor gripped the wood and heaved. It stuck for a long moment, but then slid roughly into the water, and he leaped into the narrow dugout. It wobbled for a moment, heavy in the water, but he quickly sat, and the canoe stabilized.

There was just enough space for the three of them, thank the gods. The two women shuffled around, making room for him to take the oars, and then with a long pull, they were away.

Tor rowed hard, sculling them swiftly toward the middle of the lake. Carefully listening for any sign that their escape had been detected.

Long minutes passed with no noise except the oar splashing quietly as it sliced through the water.

Somehow, they had made it out of the camp without being caught, but they were still far from safety. They couldn't stop anywhere on the same side of the lake as the camp, and they had no fucking idea what they would find on the other side. And with the darkness, the swirling, changing mists, and the feel of a storm coming, Tor had no idea how they were even going to find the other side in the first place.

Chapter Nineteen

KEELY CONCENTRATED on breathing slowly as the oars dipped again and again in Tor's firm grip. The blade splashed softly in the lake, and the canoe pulled quickly through the water carrying them away from Andred and the Wraiths' camp. They'd been on the water for what felt like days but was probably closer to half an hour.

Thunder rumbled ominously in the distance and the wind whipped up across the lake, plucking at her hair and drenching her with icy spray as the oars raised and dipped. The cold breeze brought with it the frozen tang of snow from the high mountains and the scent of pine trees from the shore. But beneath those clean, clear scents, she could swear she smelled fish.

Perhaps the boat had been used for fishing in the past and the wood had absorbed the putrid odor of scales and bones and blood. Or perhaps there was a fishiness to the water itself or the mud on the distant shore. Or perhaps it was all in her mind. A memory jogged by the sensation of being back on the water, swaying and rolling and cold.

Bard. She was so tired, her body heavy and lethargic; drained by hours of fear. Her stomach clenched on itself, finding only bile after a day without food. The hours of staying strong and keeping herself together were hitting her. And her morning sickness was back with a vengeance.

She swallowed heavily, closing her eyes. And then immediately opened them again. Even the swirling misty darkness was better than having all her senses focused on the rocking heave of the canoe and the rising scent of decaying fish.

Keely swallowed again, trying to breathe as they crashed heavily down the side of a swell, the canoe pitching and rolling unsteadily on the churning whitecaps. The wind blew harder, carrying the storm closer.

Damn. Breathing was a mistake. A lungful of fishy air slid down the back of her throat. She couldn't…. Keely twisted onto her knees and leaned against the side of the canoe, trying to move slowly enough not to tip them into the lake, but fast enough that she could get her head over the side of the boat in time, and then retched out over the water.

Her stomach cramped around nothing, her eyes watering as her body spasmed, and she fought to hold herself still enough that the boat didn't rock. Keely wiped a shaking hand across her eyes and stared down at the dark, seething water, trying to get herself under control.

There was a clatter behind her, perhaps the oars being stowed, but she didn't dare turn to look. And then Tor was there. His big hands swept her hair out of her face and held it safely at the back of her neck. Bard, what a relief to have those damp strands out of her face.

"Here, take my handkerchief," Daena said softly from behind her. "I'll row."

Tor twisted to take it, mumbling a soft thank you, and then dipped the cotton square in the glacial water with his free hand and used it to gently wipe her face, clearing the clammy sweat from over her brow.

He dipped it again and then moved it to dab around the back of her neck. A shiver racked through her body, half hot and half cold, and then Tor gently pressed the handkerchief into her hand, reached down, and brought up a handful of fresh water.

She stared at it in confusion for a moment until he murmured, "Drink." She carefully leaned down and took a sip. Bard. The ice-cold mountain water soothed her tight throat and somehow settled the churning acid in her belly. Enough that she could take a proper breath.

She hated to imagine what she must look like, hunched over the side of the boat, sweating and gulping water. And yet his hand still gently cradled the back of her head while his body stayed reassuringly close. The warm scent of his skin was soothing and safe and she leaned into him.

Tor dried his hand on his breeches and then tipped her chin up to look her in the eyes, his face dark and serious. "Is this what it was like for you? On *The Star*?"

No. On *The Star*, she had been alone and terrified, just starting to suspect that she was pregnant. Sick and exhausted and desperately uncertain of herself. She had wanted to go to him but didn't know how. Now they were lost and running from the Wraiths in the darkness—but he was with her.

The words caught in her throat, and she shook her head instead. Somehow, he must have read the thoughts in her eyes because he lowered his forehead to hers. "I should have been with you."

That was true. But maybe he would have been if she'd

dared to ask. Maybe all their misunderstandings could have been avoided if either of them had been less afraid. If he had thought she would stay—and she hadn't kept proving him right by leaving.

She looked up into his worried face; his care and concern written in the deep lines on his forehead, the depth of his dark eyes, even the gentle grip of his fingers on her chin, and tried to smile. "You're here now."

Tor took the handkerchief and dipped it into the water again to press against her neck. Somehow the cool cotton on her skin combined with the warmth of Tor's arm around her shoulders soothed her enough that her stomach settled and she was able to sit back into the boat. "Thank you."

He pressed a soft kiss onto her forehead and then helped her to sit curled in front of him, his legs bracketing her, surrounding her in his warmth.

"Rest for a bit. I'm happy to keep rowing," Daena murmured, and Tor grunted his thanks.

Keely leaned back against Tor's chest and let herself drift as he gently stroked her hair. Daena pulled the oars, and they skimmed through the darkness. Somehow, out in the middle of the dark lake, far from their friends, hunted by the men responsible for Ravenstone, she felt safe.

"Do you hear that?" Daena stowed the oars, and they all stopped to listen. A trumpet blared out across the water and whistles blew in the distance.

Tor stiffened, his big arm locking across her chest as if he could hold her safe against him.

"They know we've gone," Keely whispered.

"Yes, but that's not our biggest problem," he replied. "We've turned around somehow. Listen."

They all froze, heads tilted, listening. And then she

realized. The sounds of alarm from Andred's camp were coming from away to their side—not behind them.

Now that they were silent, unmoving on the water, they could hear the crash of wavelets on the shingle. Damn. The beach was right in front of them.

A loud, answering whistle pierced the darkness ahead of them and they all flinched, the boat rocking unsteadily on the rising water.

And then, as if in competition with the Wraiths and their battle calls, another deep roll of thunder grumbled through the air. Followed a few seconds later by a sharp flash of lightning that split the sky and lit up their surroundings in a moment of stark white light.

An image of dark trees and steep mountainsides imprinted on her eyelids and with a sickening lurch, Keely realized exactly where they were.

"Gods and angels," Daena whispered. "We're at the gorge."

"Fuck." Tor's voice grated harshly beside her ear. It was exactly where they didn't want to be. "Unless..." Tor rumbled. "Maybe this works better for us. I don't know what we would find on the other side—if we can even find our way across the lake—this way, at least, we have a chance of getting back to the Hawks."

Keely turned her head to look at Tor, at the muscles bunching in his jaw. "Yes. They'll expect us to go across the lake.... They're distracted, and it's dark. If we can get up the gorge, we can get back to the others." She turned to Daena. "Are there any other paths? Maybe a way up the horses don't use?"

Daena grunted in the darkness. "There's no way up except through the gorge. The sides are very steep and covered in stones and rocks that easily give way into dangerous slides. We would have to follow the path. And the path is guarded." Daena left the rest unsaid, but they all knew just how difficult the path would be for her on her weak ankle.

"How many sentries are there?" Keely asked softly.

"Usually, four. Two at the top, two at the bottom. At least one Mabin in each pair," Daena replied.

"I don't think we have a choice," Tor said quietly. "We have to get off the water. If that lightning strikes the lake——" He didn't need to say anything more.

Damn. What was worse, facing the guards in the dark or death on the water?

They were silent for a long moment. Weighing their options.

"I think we have to try the shore," Keely admitted slowly.

"Yes," Tor agreed, while Daena merely nodded.

Tor picked up the oars and sculled them swiftly to the shore, beaching their small boat among the shingles, and then turned to help her and Daena.

Keely couldn't see ahead of her, or even a few feet to either side, but Tor was still holding her hand, and she gripped it gratefully.

Beside her, she heard Daena muttering unhappily, and she reached out a hand to help support the other woman over the shingle. They all stumbled blindly up the narrow beach and under the trees to the small protection the branches offered, and huddled there, surrounded by darkness.

Keely shivered helplessly in the cold. It was too dark to see, but she knew from the rasp of fabric and the low groan that Daena had pushed herself back until she could lean against the tree, no doubt resting her ankle.

Tor closed in beside her, wrapping his arms around her in a comforting blanket of warmth and safety. Bard, it felt good. To have that quiet reassurance. To finally have him with her. This was what she'd wanted all along, just this. Damn. Her eyes prickled, and she turned into Tor's wide chest, letting his scent, leather and salt and man, surround her.

She blinked away the stinging in her eyes. They had another chance. A chance she was going to take. But first, they had to get away from the Wraiths.

The temperature was falling rapidly, the storm was almost on them, and the guards might have already heard them—they had to get moving. But how was Daena ever going to make it up the gorge in the dark?

Another roll of thunder rumbled overhead. The sharp flash of lightning threw the forest into stark shades of black and white before fading.

"Can we distract the guards?" Keely asked.

Tor was very still beside her. It was as if she could feel his entire body focusing on working through the options. Sifting through strategies. "We could light a fire," he suggested. "Their training is poor. With luck, they'll choose to send one person to check it out while the other stays in position, and we can pick them off more easily. Then we can make our way up the path."

Yes. That made sense. "I'll do the shooting," she said softly.

"Keely—" Tor's deep voice rumbled from behind her.

"No." She cut him off, knowing what he would say. He would want to protect her, keep her from having to take a life, keep her hidden away where she would be safe. But she knew she could do this. And she knew it was the best option for all of them. "I can shoot, nearly as well as you, but I can't swing the sword. You have to be ready in case there are two of them."

There was a moment's loaded silence and then Tor grunted heavily. "Fine. but——"

She shook her head against his chest. "No buts. I can do this."

His grip tightened on her, and he pressed a kiss onto the top of her head. After a long moment, he whispered in a rough voice, "You're right."

Bard. His quiet confidence in her settled into her heart. They could do this. Escape, and everything that came after.

"I have a flint," Daena offered from beside them. A soft rustling suggested that she was looking in her satchel.

Tor moved away, and a minute later whispered, "I have an old pine branch here." He grunted, and there were a series of muffled scrapes before he added, "I've managed to split it and force in a pinecone and some needles. That should do."

"Here's the flint," Daena murmured.

Tor struck the flint with a shower of sparks. And then a second time. On the third, one of the tiny glowing sparks settled on the bunch of pine needles and they quickly caught. More needles caught and then the pinecone itself. Soon they had a small torch, and for the first time since they'd left Daena's tent, they could see each other clearly.

But if they could see each other, so could the sentries.

Tor jammed the torch into the branch of the nearest tree and then turned to Keely. "Ready?"

She shrugged and pulled the stolen crossbow off her shoulder. She was as ready as she was going to get.

Chapter Twenty

TOR TOOK the lead as they made their way. Hands outstretched, feeling for low branches, and trying not to wince at their horrendously loud footsteps as they hid themselves among the trees.

Less than a minute passed before he heard the first whistle from within the gully. The guards had seen their fire.

They froze as, seconds later, a Mabin landed heavily in the woods nearby. They heard him rustling around, cursing, and then saw the light flickering among the trees as if the torch they'd left was being held up, the guard spinning slowly as he searched the darkness.

The guard's soft footsteps receded slightly and Tor lifted his sword, ready. Keely stepped out from beside the tree. There was a creak as she pulled back the crossbow string, took aim, sighted, and then with a soft thwap, released the bolt.

The Mabin guard lurched forward with a rough gargle. She had taken him at the back of his neck, a perfect shot. The guard stumbled, clutching at his throat, and then fell on top of the torch, plunging them all into darkness.

Keely loaded another bolt and they waited for long moments while nothing happened.

"Keely?" he whispered, stepping up beside her. Gods. She had just killed a man. "Are you okay?"

"I...." She swallowed heavily. "Yes. I think so."

He ran his hand down her hair, feeling the slight tremble in her frame. Wishing he could have protected her better. "I —" His words cut off as the first tickle scratched across his throat. Smoke.

He spun away, jogging to where the guard had fallen and rolled him over. The former Wraith had fallen onto the torch, which had lit the carpet of pine needles beneath him.

Tor stamped and kicked at the sparks, and in seconds Keely was beside him, soon followed by Daena, as they worked to put out the fire. He was about to let out a breath of relief when Keely grabbed his arm and pointed behind him. Then he heard the first crackle. The soft snapping. Gods. Sparks had leaped into a fallen pine log and the sap had caught—a thick oily smoke was already forming.

Pine sap could burn for hours, viciously hot and sending flames to all the nearby trees. Fighting it would mean running back to the lake and trying to fetch enough water before the fire spread. But what would they carry the water in? And, even if they could carry the water, they would be instant targets for Andred's men.

Keely's hand still rested on his arm, and he held it there, needing the contact while he frantically considered their options.

They couldn't fight the fire. Running was their best choice... but which way? Run down, back to the lake and the lightning storm; caught between the fire and the camp?

Or run up, toward the Hawks and freedom, but have to pass the remaining guards.

The branch popped ominously as a flame licked its way higher, brightening the small glade. The autumn woods were an inferno waiting to happen. They had to make a decision.

Keely met his eyes in the dim red glow, her face pale and drawn as another vicious arc of blue lightning lit up the sky. And that decided him. Even if they made it across the lake and found some kind of beach, all in the middle of a lightning storm, she would be exhausted, wet, and very cold. Without food or any way to contact their friends. How long until she became seriously unwell, with no way back, and no way to help her? Not forgetting that they would have abandoned their people to Andred and his plans.

"I think we should run up," he said softly. "What do you think?"

"Agreed," Keely replied. "We don't know which way to go on the lake and we need to get back to the Hawks."

Keely helped herself to the dead guard's sword and slid it into her belt, then gestured toward Daena. "Can you carry her?"

He could, but…. "What about you?"

She grinned tiredly. "I'll go ahead. You just have to keep up." She patted him on the bicep. "I've been wanting to see some of that famous Apollyon strength in action."

He snorted. "We'll be behind you."

"Eh." She shrugged, eyes gleaming in the growing light. "I can picture it."

Gods. She was magnificent.

Tor looked across at Daena, her hunched shoulders and uncertain eyes. But when he raised an eyebrow, she nodded.

He turned and waited, and, after a brief pause, she climbed onto his back without complaining.

A whistle blew across the woods. The dead guard's partner. Checking on his missing comrade. Bollocks. "Time to go."

"Yes," Keely agreed as the flames licked along the log. They had to reach the top of the gorge before the fire took hold and swept upward.

Tor settled his grip around Daena's thighs, holding her securely. Keely started to run and he followed.

They joined the narrow path of the gorge a few feet up from the beach to find a guard already running fast toward them. He stumbled to a surprised stop as Keely lifted the crossbow and shot him without hesitating.

Keely slung the crossbow over her shoulder, and they ran past the downed guard, not stopping. Another death. Gods.

The path rose ahead. It was dark with the fire behind them, the footing treacherous and unstable as they fled up the twisting path of the gorge.

The scent of pine trees hung heavy in the air, but below it, at the back of his throat, Tor could still feel the rasping tickle of smoke. He heard Keely panting ahead of him, bent forward as she pushed herself up the slope. On and on. Their footsteps thudding on the soft ground.

How much farther? He tried to remember the journey down, to reverse it in his mind.

Daena clutched him tightly, but she still bounced uncomfortably, her weight dragging him backward, upsetting his balance, and he sweated as he pushed himself harder. Faster. Always following Keely. Keeping as close as he could. She was carrying another person. He could do the same.

They were somewhere close to halfway up when he heard a flurry of heavy wings and a black shadow landed heavily on the path ahead. A Mabin guard, lifting a crossbow of his own.

Tor pulled to a hard stop behind Keely, Daena clinging to his back like a monkey. Keely lifted her crossbow and two soft thwaps broke the silence as they both fired.

The Mabin grunted heavily, and then there was a loud crash as he fell, tumbling away to the side. But it wasn't loud enough to cover Keely's soft curse. "What the fuck have they all got against my bloody arm?"

Tor lowered Daena to the ground and ran to Keely. Gods. She was holding her hand over her arm, her breath shuddering as she gritted her teeth.

She was hurt. Again. He wanted to howl and roar and pull down the world. Instead, he forced himself to stay calm, to keep himself under control, as he asked, "How bad is it?"

"A scrape," she said tersely.

A scrape? Gods. He'd seen what she was like the last time she was shot. If Keely said it was a scrape, she was lucky to still have an arm.

"Tell me the truth," he demanded.

Keely groaned. "It sliced through the muscle. Hurts like hell, but I'll live."

"Here." Daena pulled a small knife out of her satchel, sliced away a strip from the hem of her dress, and quickly helped Keely to wrap her arm. Keely flexed it a few times and grunted. "It'll do."

The rough scent of fire rasped more heavily at the back of his throat, and he turned to look down the path.

A dark red glow flickered below them in the distance.

The trees were catching. Fuck. The gorge would soon become a chimney; the wind that howled up its length pulling the flames up faster than they could ever dream of running.

Keely caught his gaze and then spun back to the path. "Let's go."

He lifted Daena onto his back once more and followed Keely. Up they ran, panting and sweating. The orange glow of the fire behind them lit the path, and they ran faster, leaping over roots and scrabbling over stones. Their breath rasping and panting. His lungs burning.

Tor could hear the fire now. A low, crackling roar in the distance. Daena whimpered as she gripped him more tightly, her breath huffing in short, panicked gasps. Gods, what horrific memories was she reliving?

The path flattened a little and they ran faster. Keely widened the distance between them as she sped ahead.

He pushed past the screaming tension in his shoulders and hips where Daena's weight bore him down. Pushed past the acrid burn in his ragged throat where he tasted blood. They were almost to the top. Almost to the ridge, and from there, the safety of the bare gully with its stone-strewn path and steep rock sides.

Just a few more—

A crossbow bolt whistled past his ear, coming from above and thudding heavily somewhere behind him.

He reacted on instinct, flinging himself behind a tree, hauling Daena with him, and roaring out a warning to Keely up ahead.

Fuck. The final guard was in the trees.

Keely leaped behind a huge pine just as another bolt thudded into the trunk where she'd been standing only seconds before.

Tor crouched low, frantically trying to see where the last guard was among the branches.

"Save yourself," Keely called out toward the guard over the distant crackle. "You can't stay here."

A dark voice chuckled from the canopy on the other side of the path. "Neither can you. And the difference is… I can fly."

Another Mabin. Damn. How was it possible that they could have been so unlucky?

The last guard dropped down from the trees, farther along the path, close to Keely.

The guard's face was heavily bearded, his ancient uniform torn and mended in multiple places, trinkets—spoils—sewn onto the sleeves glimmering in the dim light. A reiver. And, by the look of him, a Brythorian deserter.

"The fire will pass. And then I can be the one to give Andred your heads," the reiver observed in a low voice as he raised his crossbow and took a step toward Keely's hiding place. "Maybe I'll even be promoted. Get one of the cushy camp jobs."

God of the Abyss. Why hadn't Keely fired and ended this already?

Tor pulled out the knife he'd taken from the guard at the camp and spun it in his palm. It was poor quality, unevenly weighted. And the only one he had.

He sidled slowly around the tree, looking for a good shot. The reiver was too far away to guarantee hitting him, and he didn't want to lose his only knife.

Keely flittered out, a pale wraith in the darkness as she lifted her crossbow and fired. But the bolt thudded heavily into a tree, passing the reiver far too wide.

She dashed back behind the trunk, but not before he

saw how unevenly she was standing. Gods. Her arm. She was struggling to hold the crossbow.

The reiver flapped his heavy wings, launching himself toward Keely's hiding place, and Tor pulled back his arm to throw. But Keely leaped out. Right into the space between Tor and the reiver.

Tor spun, still gripping the knife he couldn't risk releasing.

Fuck. What was he going to do? He started to run.

Keely beat the reiver's crossbow to the side with her own, and then threw it down to pull out the sword she'd taken earlier.

The reiver mimicked her, flinging his crossbow down and drawing his sword to circle Keely menacingly.

Tor ran up the path toward them, forcing himself to run faster than ever in his life before, not daring to throw the unbalanced knife in case he missed and caught Keely.

The reiver stabbed and swore, but Keely danced back, screaming out her rage and swinging her sword desperately. Her movements were stilted, but she was fighting with everything she had.

The roar of the flames rose like a rabid beast below them. The wind whipped up the gully carrying sparks and choking smoke as Tor leaped over the yards between them.

The reiver chuckled as he belted Keely hard across the face with his free hand, then lifted his sword for the final blow as she stumbled. There was no chance to get closer, use a better weapon, or even pray. He had no choice. Tor threw the knife.

It caught the reiver high in his belly, and the Mabin doubled over with an agonized grunt, collapsing to the ground where he curled into a ball just as Tor reached him.

Tor pulled out his sword and lifted it high as the reiver

reached down and slowly pulled out the knife. It was the wrong thing to do. The blade had caught an artery, and as soon as it was out, the blood flowed freely. The reiver gasped out a broken cough and then lay still as Tor slowly lowered his sword, panting hard.

Tor spun toward Keely just as she stumbled a last step toward him. She started to fold and he flung his arms out, catching her as she slid down to her knees, collapsing into the leaves and detritus of the path.

The reiver had cost them vital time. And the battle had cost Keely even more. Her arm was slick with blood, her face almost gray it was so pale. She trembled, leaning heavily against his chest. Gods. Had she been bleeding this whole time?

"I'm sorry," she whispered brokenly against his chest. "I can't—"

Gods. No. He pulled her into his lap, wrapping his arms around her. She was so small compared to him. So vulnerable in his arms.

She dropped heavily against him, her head falling back, and he realized she was unconscious.

He tightened his arms, holding her safely gripped against him, and fought to keep from screaming.

What was he going to do? Nothing, not even a thousand demons rising from the Abyss, would induce him to leave Keely. But he couldn't carry two women. Not if they were going to reach the top in time.

Daena stumbled closer, gave him a long, slow look, and then started to half-jog, half-drag herself, limping up the path.

He rose, cradling Keely in his arms, and followed.

They staggered together, Daena leading upward, as ash began to fall around them. The fire was a living, breathing monster now. Hot enough that Tor could feel sweat running in rivers down the inside of his jerkin.

Daena turned to look past him down the gorge and screamed for him to run, forcing herself into a shambling gallop that must have been pure agony. His eyes and throat burned with the smoke and he coughed relentlessly as he pushed himself forward.

And then another Mabin landed heavily on the path ahead, wings spread wide in the hellish glow.

He almost went to his knees. They were so close. So godsdamn close. He lowered his head, breathing hard, taking in Keely's face one last time. Saying goodbye.

"Give her to me."

His head whipped back up. What the hell?

"Tor, for fuck's sake. Give her to me."

It was Jos. Gods.

He handed Keely to Jos, lifting his head to see Val grabbing Daena and then launching back into the air.

The Mabin were there to help. There were Hawks and Blues in the woods.

Jos pushed off a second later, carrying Keely. Tor stood, stunned, watching him leave. Almost unable to wrap his mind around what was happening. Until Rafe grabbed his shoulder and shouted in his face. "Fucking run!"

He didn't need to be told again. He fucking ran.

Chapter Twenty-One

THE FIRST THING Keely was aware of was the smell of soap, and then the fresh feel of clean sheets. Thick and rough, not palace sheets, but clean. Then she heard the rain, a steady drumming as it fell heavily outside.

She opened her eyes and looked around. She was in a screened-off area of a bigger room. A fire burned low in the hearth opposite her, and a muted light filtered through the rain-drenched window. The bed was basic, but far more comfortable than the bedroll she'd been sleeping in, and someone had dressed her in Tor's old shirt from her satchel.

She immediately dropped her hands to her belly. It felt the same. *She* felt the same, mostly. Heavy breasts. Slight morning queasiness. Dry throat. But otherwise, nothing different.

Was the pea okay? She hadn't felt any movement yet; all she had was a stubborn belief that her baby was growing safely in her womb. And now... how could she tell? Had her baby been hurt by their frantic escape? By the fire?

Bard. Not only hers, *theirs*.

Where was Tor? The last thing she knew, they were in the woods about to be overtaken by the fire. Was he safe? Was he even alive? If he was hurt…. She swallowed against the ache in her throat. He couldn't be. They'd come through too much.

She prodded the bandages on her arm, bound tight and tucked in neatly. Bard, she was lucky to still have an arm. Half an inch to the side, and the reiver would have shattered the bone. She snorted; half an inch to the side and he would have shredded the artery, and she wouldn't have been alive to worry about it.

She pushed herself up with a groan. Damn, she felt terrible—weak and shaking. Her stomach twisted on itself. When last had she eaten anything? She needed to find food. Nim's ginger tea. Something to settle her stomach.

There was a cup of water beside the bed, and she drank it in long swallows. Then she swung her legs over the side of the bed and pushed herself to her feet.

A shower of bright stars exploded across her vision, and she breathed heavily, leaning over to support herself with her good arm just as Rafe appeared around the screen.

"Keely. Sit down, for gods' sake." He strode forward and firmly guided her back down as she wiped a shaky hand over her face.

It was terrifying to be so weak. Not knowing what had happened. "Rafe… is the baby okay?"

He smiled warmly, the corners of his purple-blue eyes crinkling. "Baby's fine."

Good. That was good. She slowly met his eyes. "And Tor?"

He nodded. "Also fine."

"Thank you." It came out as a hoarse whisper as she sagged down, pressing her palms to her eyes. Trying not to cry but failing. They were safe. They were all safe. Bard. The sudden relief was almost too much.

She took long breaths as Rafe patted her arm. Eventually, she was able to ask, "Where are we?"

Rafe rested his hand gently on her forehead and then moved his fingers to the pulse at her throat while he talked. "The barracks at Staith."

"How did we get here?"

"After we left Tor to go down to the camp, I rode back, and Jos flew. He caught up to Alanna and Val just as they reached Staith and warned them. Alanna went on to the barracks with one squad of Blues, and we came back with the other squad. We were planning to spend the night in the gully at the top of the mountain path, but then we saw the flames and knew we'd better take a look."

Rafe filled the cup again and passed it to her. "Jos and Val carried you and Daena out while the rest of us ran. The horses were only a couple of minutes away."

"Daena's okay?" Keely asked softly.

"Yes." The answer was clipped, irritated even.

She frowned up at him, about to ask why Rafe— probably the nicest, least judgmental person she'd ever met —would sound so annoyed about someone he hardly knew, when she heard a sharp bugle call from outside, followed by the tramping of boots splashing through puddles. Many boots. It was the sound of soldiers leaving.

She immediately pushed herself off the bed, swaying as the blood rushed from her head. Damn. She didn't have time for that. She needed to move.

She shook herself, trying to clear her vision, and used the bed as a support as she took a step and then another. She had to get to him. See him, before he left.

"Whoa, let's get you back down." Rafe took her arm and tried to guide her back to sitting, but she shook him off.

He ignored her muttered curse and stood, blocking her way as he folded his arms. "You've been unconscious for more than a day, and you're not in any shape to go rushing off."

"I have to—"

"No. What if you have a fall? What about the baby then?"

She narrowed her eyes and gave him her best death glare, reevaluating her earlier opinion of how kind Rafe was. "I have to get to Tor."

"I told you, Tor's safe. If you just sit down for a moment—"

"Yes, but what's that noise?" she interrupted, pointing to the window.

Rafe pinched the top of his nose and sighed. "That's what I'm trying to tell you. Those are the squads going back to assess Andred's encampment. The scouts reported back that the heavy rain and sleet over the last day has put the fire out and it's safe to try the path."

That was exactly what she was worried about. Commands were called in the distance. She heard a sharp whistle and then marching feet; they were leaving. She had to convince Rafe to let her go. She had to see Tor.

"Please, Rafe. I have to talk to him before he goes."

Rafe chuckled, still blocking her way. "He's not going with the squads, Keely. He's not going anywhere."

She spun to glare at him. "What do you mean? I thought you said he was safe!"

Rafe gestured toward the bed. "Sit down, and I'll tell you."

She wrinkled her nose at him. "I think I hate you."

Rafe laughed. "You're not my first patient to feel that way."

Grumbling loudly, she lowered herself to the bed and waited, fidgeting impatiently as he moved to the side of her bed and quietly folded away the screen to reveal the rest of the room.

She was in a clinic. A large cabinet against the wall held rolls of bandages and labeled bottles in an array of glass and clay. The room was large enough to hold three beds. The farthest was neatly made and empty, but the closest, just on the other side of where the screen had been, held Tor.

He was fast asleep, his face relaxed, still unshaven, his body covered in a woolen blanket except for one heavy, tattooed arm which he'd flung over the top of the covers.

"Why the screen?" she asked in a whisper.

"Alanna was worried you'd wake up, see him lying beside you in a clinic, and immediately assume the worst."

Well. Yes. That was almost certainly what she would have done. Assuming the worst had kept her safe for years.

She looked over at Tor, lying so still and silent. "What's wrong with him?"

"Nothing that a good sleep won't fix. He refused to rest, refused to eat, alternating between sitting with you and pacing around the clinic, interfering with your care, and driving the rest of us insane."

"So how did you convince him to sleep in the end?"

"Well…." Rafe's lips twitched up.

Why did he look so smugly guilty? She raised an eyebrow. "What did you do, Rafe?"

"It's possible that Tor may have taken quite a strong sleeping draught."

"And he was happy to do that?" she asked, already suspecting the answer.

Rafe's grin broadened. "It's also possible that he couldn't taste it in the tea I gave him."

Damn. She shook her head at the healer. "He's going to be all kinds of pissed off when he wakes up. Especially when he discovers you took off his clothes."

Rafe chuckled. "Nah, I'm not worried."

"Why not?"

"When he wakes up, the first thing he'll see will be you, and he's going to forget all about me." Rafe gave her a long, considering look. "The first thing he'll see will be you, Keely, won't it?"

"Yes." She wasn't leaving him again. Standing beside him in the burning woods, wondering if that was the end, had made it abundantly clear for her. She had to stop running and start fighting. For him. For herself. For the future they could have.

"Tor's a good man," Rafe said quietly. "I know he's not the best at dealing with his feelings, but he would do anything for you. And the baby."

"I know." The truth settled through her. She did know.

He smiled warmly. "Back in bed then, and I'll send someone up with some food."

She clambered back into the bed, letting herself drift in the pleasant warmth, watching Tor sleep, until a noise at the door woke her.

Alanna came in, carrying a tray with a small cup, a bowl of soup, and a plate of fresh bread. The rich scent of vegetables and mutton filled the room, and Keely's stomach growled ravenously. She hadn't felt so hungry in months.

"Ah, you're an angel. Thank you."

Alanna chuckled as she set the tray over Keely's lap.

"Not an angel, but I'm happy to play nurse. Here—Rafe said you should start with some ginger tea, then if your stomach can handle it, you can try some soup."

She sipped the warm tea gratefully, and then when her stomach growled loudly once more, quickly turned to the food. Nothing had ever tasted so delicious.

Alanna settled on the bottom of the bed. "Looks like you're starting to get your appetite back. Rafe said he'd spent some time settling your morning sickness after he finished working on your arm. Hopefully, that'll really help."

Damn. Why hadn't she asked him for help before? All this time she'd suffered alone when Nim and Rafe could have helped her from the beginning.

Keely took another huge bite of soft bread, heavy with butter. It was delicious. Bard. Rafe was a magician.

Alanna gave her a long look. "We were so worried about you. And Tor… none of the Hawks have ever seen him look so devastated."

Keely looked down at her bowl as she mopped up the last of the soup with her bread. "I'm sorry you were worried, Alanna."

"What was that?" Alanna leaned forward cupping her ear. "Did you just apologize? And admit that someone might be worried about you! I don't think I've ever heard such a thing before."

Keely stuck her tongue out at her friend, who giggled cheerfully as she moved the tray away.

Alanna's face grew serious as she came back to her seat on the bed. "I'm glad you're safe, Keely. I've missed you these last weeks."

"I've been with you all this time," Keely replied quietly.

"Yes, but not the real you. You haven't sung. You haven't wanted to talk." Alanna's green eyes grew somber.

"Honestly, Keely, I've felt as if you were preparing to leave even before everything happened with Tor."

Bard. She had been preparing to leave. "I didn't think you needed me anymore," she admitted quietly.

"Keely, you're my best friend. Why would I not need you?" Alanna asked carefully.

"You have Val—" Keely saw the look on Alanna's face and left the rest of the sentence unfinished. It had all made so much sense before. But now? Now she wasn't so sure.

Alanna sighed. "I love Val, it's true. But Keely, you must know that I love you too. We've been friends for so many years—why would I ever not want you to stay? And when you knew... didn't you think I might have wanted to be part of your baby's life?"

Keely looked down at the sheet, twisting it between her fingers, not knowing what to say.

"I think," Alanna said quietly, "that you were already planning to go off and live alone long before Tor hurt your feelings. You might have told yourself that it was because we didn't need you anymore, but the truth was that you were starting to realize that *you* needed us. And you didn't stop to think that walking away might be painful for the people you left behind." Alanna's voice lowered. "Might be painful for me."

Keely looked up, met Alanna's eyes, and saw the truth. As much as she had loved her friend and dedicated herself to Alanna, she had always kept a distance between them. She had been happy to give care and support but had been too terrified to take affection in return. Terrified that she might grow to need it.

How many years had she spent relying entirely on herself? Telling herself that she was perfectly capable of walking away at any moment. Without ever really thinking about what it meant to the people she left behind.

Bard. She had hurt her friend as much as she had hurt herself.

She needed her friends in her life. And she urgently needed to tell them they were important. "Alanna, you're my best friend, and I love you too. I'm sorry I hurt you."

Alanna leaned forward and took her hand, softening her words with a sympathetic smile. "I know. But our friendship has lasted for many years, through all kinds of difficulties. We understand each other. Does Tor?"

Keely blinked.

"Keely," Alanna asked quietly, "did you tell him that you were leaving?"

She didn't want to admit it, but she had to. "I told him I was thinking about going back to Verturia. Before anything happened between us." She bit her lip and then confessed the rest. "It was what started all the trouble…. Tor thought I was leaving, expected me to go after we…. And then he said… he said…."

But he hadn't really said anything. She had.

Damn. He'd handled everything badly… but so had she. She had decided to take a risk, but then never actually took it. She was going to have to make it clear she wanted to stay. And then stay.

Alanna squeezed her fingers, acknowledging her unspoken words. "Take it from someone who had to learn the hard way: you need to tell him how you feel."

Keely couldn't help her sad snort. "Bard, Alanna, what makes you think that any of this was easy?"

Chapter Twenty-Two

TOR CAME BACK to consciousness slowly, trying to figure out where he was and why his body felt so heavy. Why was he lying on his side? He never slept on his side. There was something pressed up against his back, stopping him from rolling. Gods, he was hot.

Fucking Rafe. The last thing he could remember was his friend bringing him some kind of pungent herbal tea and promising it would make him feel better. Rafe had definitely drugged him. Which also explained the weird buzzing in his ears.

Tor opened his eyes, blinking to clear his hazy vision, then lifted his head to look behind him, and understood.

Keely had crawled into the clinic bed with him, fitting herself tightly against him, her chest against his back, her bandaged arm cradled between them. And she was snoring softly. It was the most beautiful noise he'd ever heard.

He rolled over carefully, pulled her close, and wrapped his free arm over her waist, pinning her safely against him. Then let himself drift back to sleep.

The next time he woke, the room was almost dark, while the gentle sound of soft rain pattered against the windows. And Keely was trying to sneak out from under his arm.

She wiggled, huffing out a breath as she silently slid down his body.

He grunted and closed his fingers over her hip, holding her tighter. "Stay, please." His voice sounded rough in the calm quiet of the clinic.

She froze for a moment and then softened into him. "The baby needs to pee."

He snorted. "The baby?"

She huffed louder. "Yes. Apparently, it's one of the things that babies do. Make their mamas pee. Which makes the name I gave her even more fitting."

"What name?" he asked softly.

"The pea."

"You call her 'the pea'?"

"Yup. Small. Helpless, and kinda sweet." Keely shrugged slightly. "And, it turns out, doing something terrible to my bladder."

He chuckled, a strange warmth growing in his heart. The pea. "Okay then."

She looked pointedly at his hand on her hip. "I still need to go."

He forced himself to lift his arm and give her space, but she must have sensed his reluctance, because she leaned over and kissed him on the forehead. "I'm coming back. I promise."

She slid from the bed, wrapped a blanket around her shoulders, and tiptoed from the room.

He let her words repeat in his head. *I'm coming back.* Reminding himself that she had chosen to sleep beside him.

She could have left while he was unconscious if that had been her intention.

Tor pushed himself up and leaned back against the wall, one knee bent, letting the blanket pool in his lap as he watched the rain trickle down the window in glistening paths.

Gods. He had come so very close to losing her. To losing *them*.

First his awful words. Then Andred's camp. The desperate escape. The fire. The reivers. And then watching Keely lie completely unresponsive as Rafe stitched her up—again. Alanna crying as she dressed her friend in his old shirt. It had almost been too much.

The door clicked open, and Keely let herself in, hovering for a moment before shutting the door behind her.

Her hair gleamed gold and red in the low firelight, spread in an unruly mass over the gray blanket around her shoulders. She stepped closer and his heartbeat thudded heavily in his ears as he fought not to crack his knuckles.

She had climbed into his bed. And she had come back as she promised. But maybe now she was remembering the rest of what had happened between them? Maybe now she was realizing he was not the kind of man she wanted around their baby. A soldier. One who hadn't even been enough for his own parents. The kind of man Andred wanted to claim as his own. The kind of man who hurt her with his words. Maybe now she had decided to take their child and walk away?

Keely crossed the room and sat on the bed beside him, turning so her body faced his, her hands held together in her lap. She took in a long, slow breath. Then let it out, equally slowly.

Her eyes were on his, but her body was far away—too

far—her teeth worrying that swollen bottom lip. It was so much like that first time, he couldn't help repeating himself. He dragged his thumb down her lip, tugging gently until she released it, and then he leaned forward and kissed it better.

She sighed into his mouth and wrapped her good arm around his neck, holding him closer. He tasted her mouth, pressing gentle kisses onto her soft lips. Not hurrying, not demanding, simply feeling her with him. Alive and safe. But then she pulled away and pressed her forehead against his. "We have to talk."

They did. He knew it and dreaded it in equal measure. "Okay," he agreed. "If you'll sit closer."

She arched a delicate eyebrow, but she slid closer. He watched her for a second and then reached over to pull her higher so that she was curled up with her back resting against his bent leg. He settled one of his hands on her thigh, leaving the other free to tangle in her loose hair. Now they could talk.

"Why do I feel as if you're getting ready to hold me here?" she asked.

He shrugged. "I've learned my lesson. This time when I say something stupid and fuck everything up, I'll have a good grip on you. That way you can't go anywhere until I've fixed it."

She chuckled. "Fair enough. But first I should tell you that I'm not planning to go anywhere."

"Really?" He wanted to believe her. Desperately.

She lifted her small hand to settle it against his jaw, looking into his eyes. "I was hurt, Tor. And afraid. But I've started to realize that you were afraid too. You said all the wrong things… but maybe, if you hadn't thought I was leaving, you would have handled everything differently. Can we, maybe, try again? Start over from the beginning?"

Gods. He wanted that to be true… but he still wasn't convinced. The very last thing he wanted was to chase her away, but there was one thing still standing between them. Something he didn't know how to solve. "You didn't want to be with another soldier, Keely, but that's all I've ever been."

Her fingers twitched on his cheek. "That's simply not true. You're so much more than just a soldier. You're the best, most honorable man I've ever known."

He let the warmth of her fingers settle into his skin, gently filtering down inside him, and tried to explain. "Keely, I don't have anything to offer you. You want a home and security, and—"

"Tor." She kissed him gently, a soft press of her lips to his, interrupting him. And then again, another fleeting pressure. "I don't have a home either. You don't count that against me, do you? Isn't this something we could figure out together?"

He swallowed, trying to think. He had been so focused on his failures. His losses. Why had he been so unable to get past them? Why had he spent so many months wrapped in such helpless misery, convinced he could never move forward? Why had he assumed that she couldn't possibly want him?

Keely bit her lip, eyes soft and shining suspiciously. "It's true that I was afraid of caring for a soldier. But I was prepared to risk it for you. I still am, Tor. I'm prepared to take the risk if that's what you want. Whatever the cost might be in the end, you're worth it to me. And if the last days have reminded us of anything, it's that our lives are so very fragile. We should take this chance at happiness."

You're worth it to me.

Gods.

Whatever the cost.

When had he ever been worth anything? The roaring in his ears was back. Along with a burning in his eyes and an ache in his throat.

Her fingers pressed into his cheeks, tilting his head up to meet her eyes. "Did you hear me, Tor? You are worth the risk."

Her words broke something inside him—some tightly coiled leash that had been holding him together—and he started to cry.

He had carried so much loss with him for so long and never mourned it—the king, his family, his place in the palace, his understanding of the world. And so much fear; that he was not and never would be good enough, that Keely would leave, that she could never genuinely want a man like him.

Now, with her hands on his face, her soft, jade-green eyes looking into his, full of acceptance, full of the belief that he was worth taking a risk on, all that buried emotion came pouring out.

His father would have been horrified. Men didn't cry. They didn't show feelings, didn't experience fear or grief. But he couldn't find it in him to care about whether tears would make him seem weak. The torrent of emotion inundating him was too overwhelming to try and hold back.

He had never allowed himself to grieve, but now he did. Now, with her holding him gently, he allowed himself to let it go, and the tears rolling in hot waves down his face purged the darkness that had been festering inside him, scoured it away, and made space for the light she let in.

"Oh, Bard." She wiped away the tears with her fingers as she murmured helplessly. "I'm sorry. I'm sorry. Bard."

"No." He forced the word up through his aching throat as he ran his hands up her back, one between her shoulder blades, the other behind her head, and pulled her into his chest. "This is a gift—you've given me a gift. This... I've just never felt...."

She kissed him again, understanding what he couldn't say—that he'd never allowed himself to feel at all until her.

She lifted her eyes to his and smiled. "We're going to make a family."

Gods. "We already are a family," he whispered. His dream of what a family should be.

Keely sighed softly. And then, almost too quietly to hear, she murmured, "You're going to be a wonderful father."

He didn't know about that. He would have to learn everything from scratch, learn how to be the kind of father he had wished for. The kind of father that was worthy of Keely and the pea. But he did know that nothing would ever hurt them. He would never let her go again. And he would tear down the world to keep them safe.

She lifted her face and kissed him again. He tasted salt, and warmth, and Keely. Could feel her body, alive and soft and vibrant in his arms. The light in his heart grew, warming and spreading through him, reverberating around the woman he hadn't imagined he could possibly deserve.

Their kiss deepened until he was pouring himself into her and she was responding just as urgently. She kissed him with a desperation that he felt all the way down his spine, a desperation that matched his. He needed to be inside her. To feel her around him, holding him inside her body.

Tor rolled, carefully guarding Keely's hurt arm as he spun her under him. The thin shirt between them did nothing to dampen the heat of her body against his, but he wanted it gone, wanted his skin touching hers. He tugged it up, loving how she arched her back to help him as he pulled it over her head.

He knelt between her legs, settling back onto his heels, and paused, looking down at her, letting the knowledge that she was truly his filter into his heart. Letting his eyes run slowly over her heavy breasts, pale belly, the red patch of hair at the junction of her thighs.

She bit her lip, the blush on her cheeks darkening as she sucked in a shaky breath and he rested his hands on her thighs. "Bend your legs."

Keely let out her breath in a whoosh, her eyelids fluttering closed, but she bent her legs. Gods, she was so beautiful. Soft and pink and glorious. He could smell her arousal, and he wanted to push his tongue inside her and taste. But he wanted this first.

He ran the back of his knuckles up the inside of Keely's thigh to her groin and then skated over her mound, so lightly he knew she would only just feel him pass. He tugged gently on the tight curls before gliding his other hand up the inside of the opposite leg, scraping gently with his nails. He continued the motion; warm fingers on one thigh, nails on the other, alternating sensations, with light teasing touches over her clit.

Her breathing deepened and her nipples pebbled into tight buds. "Bard.... Tor."

He was so hard that he ached. The desire to take himself in his fist was almost overwhelming, but he controlled it. Instead, he leaned forward to breathe against her center, letting his hands settle over her hip bones, his thumbs in the hollows of her groin.

She whimpered, her hips twitching up, but he wanted to take his time. To feel the smooth softness of her skin, the heat of her body, to see her pulse jumping in her neck as her breath shuddered.

"Tor... I don't. I've never—"

"You've never what?"

She shivered. "I've never been so…." Her voice dropped to a husky whisper. "You're looking at me."

Ah. He understood. She'd been young, and so had her lover. They would have been hurried and inexperienced. He liked that he could give her this. Gods. He liked it a lot.

"I am looking at you. I like seeing you all laid out for me. And you will let me take a bite, won't you, Keely?"

She nodded, her teeth sinking into her lip.

"Say the words then."

"Yes, Tor. Please."

"Put your hands on the headboard and keep them there."

She lifted her hands behind her to press against the wood, lifting her breasts like an offering. And he couldn't help but take it.

He leaned over her, resting a hand beside her for balance, and then took a nipple in his mouth, sucking and teasing at the same time as skating his other hand down, parting her folds with his fingers and finding her clit. She was so wet and swollen, her breath coming in rough pants.

She shuddered but didn't move her hands, even as he bit down gently on her nipple and tugged, and then ran soothing kisses over her breast to the other side.

He used her wetness to slide over her folds, spreading her, exploring the sensitive inner skin and swirling back up to her clit. Keely whimpered, shifting beneath him restlessly, and he let his fingers dip inside her, not moving, hardly more than fingertips inside her entrance as he ran a string of stinging nips over her breasts and collarbones to finally find her neck.

He sucked the delicate flesh of her throat into his

mouth, sinking his fingers inside her at the same time in one long, slow movement. Then slowly out.

She shuddered, lifting her hips as he dragged his mouth up her throat and kissed her. He slid his tongue into her mouth as he curled his fingers and found that rough, swollen area on her front wall, and stroked.

She spasmed up, gasping into his mouth, and he rubbed her again, fucking her with his fingers until she was panting, hovering right on the edge. Then he dragged his fingers out to wrap them around his aching cock, bringing it to her entrance and paused. Waiting for her.

Her eyes opened, pupils blown wide, her hands leaving the headboard to rest on his shoulders. "I want… Bard, I want you. Please, Tor."

He pushed inside her desperately slowly. So slowly that he could feel her inner muscles stretching to take him, gripping him. Her chest rose and fell below him while her pulse shuddered above the reddening mark he'd left on her neck.

He held himself over her, not moving. Absorbing every detail that was Keely. Feeling her twitching under him, the way she groaned as she wrapped her legs around him. Long slow moments of heat and pleasure as her body rippled around his.

"Please move. Tor. I—" Her voice broke.

"Anything, Keely," he whispered. "You must know that now, I'll give you anything. Tell me you understand."

She whimpered. "I understand."

And then it was too much. He couldn't hold back anymore. He wanted to lose himself in a way he never had before.

He shifted back up onto his knees, hauling her with him

until she straddled him, open on his lap. "Take us over, Keely love. You do it."

Her eyes opened. So close to his. "Are you sure?"

"Yes." He was. He didn't have to be in total control. Not all the time. Not with her.

She raised herself slowly and then slid back down his length, finding her rhythm as he steadied her. Finding the angle that ground her clit down over the base of his cock, seating herself on him again and again.

All he did was hold her, one hand on her hip, the other supporting her back, using his strength to balance them both so she could soar.

Her movements faltered, her breath panting in rough gasps beside his ear as her hips rolled frantically and his spine tingled in pulsing waves, his balls pulling up, tight against his body.

Gods. Any second now.

He ran his hand up her back to her hair, threading his fingers in the strands, bringing her face down so he could kiss her, open-mouthed, panting heavily as their tongues danced and writhed together, sharing each other's air.

He slid his other hand between them, using his thumb to add a constant pressure on her clit, following her movements. Keely shuddered, her body grinding in his lap as she gasped out his name. Her inner walls clamped down, and her hips jerked forward helplessly as she buried her face in his neck and came, quivering and writhing on his lap.

Tor followed right behind, letting himself go, thrusting up into her clenching heat in a wave of ecstasy unlike anything he'd ever experienced in his life before.

Chapter Twenty-Three

KEELY SAT on the side of the bed pulling on her clothes while Tor leaned back against the wall and watched her. He had his arm bent behind his head, bunching his biceps, and her eyes lingered for a moment on the sharp ink of his tattoos over his arms, the rough hair on his chest trailing away beneath the blanket gathered in his lap.

Damn. She hauled her eyes back up his body, determined not to give in and rip her clothes back off and get back into bed. "We have to get up," she said as she pulled on her boots.

"Yes, we do," he agreed, not moving an inch.

She grinned and then leaned over and kissed him gently, feeling the muscles in his abdomen bunching under her hand. He wrapped his fingers around her neck and held her closer.

She broke the kiss and ran her fingers through his dark hair. It had grown since she first met him, and now it was sleep-mussed and standing in different directions. Not that they'd had a huge amount of sleep. They'd spent the night slowly exploring each other's bodies, whispering to each other in the warm darkness, coming together again and again. Sometimes he took her so slowly she thought she would explode if he didn't move. Sometimes hard and fast. But every time felt like a promise.

"If we don't get up, we'll miss the report on the Wraiths' camp," she reminded him.

Tor groaned and pressed one last kiss against her lips before letting her go and then swinging his legs out the opposite side of the bed. He stood, dropping the blanket, and she lost track of her thoughts as she watched his ass muscles bunching as he pulled on his breeches.

He must have heard her stifled groan, because he turned to grin at her over his shoulder. "I'm not the one who wanted to get out of bed."

Had she ever seen him look so relaxed? So disheveled and playful. And so insanely attractive?

She stuck out her tongue, and then quickly closed her mouth when his eyes dropped to her lips and he took a step closer. Almost close enough to reach across and pull her back down to the bed.

"No, not again." She shook her head, as much at herself as at him. "The pea needs breakfast."

He chuckled as he pulled on his shirt. "Then the pea must have breakfast."

They were still smiling when they walked into the mess hall, but within a second of walking through the door, she knew something was wrong.

The Hawks and Daena were in the hall, the other guards conspicuously absent, and the room was silent. Val was sitting with an arm curled protectively over the back of Alanna's chair, while Alanna leaned back with her arms crossed over her chest. Rafe and Jos were frowning heavily.

All of them were glaring at Daena, who was self-consciously rubbing her face.

Keely and Tor paused for a moment in the entrance, their relaxed banter fading in the heavy atmosphere. Tor reached down to take her hand, lacing his fingers through hers. It had been a bloody long time since she'd held hands with someone. Strangely, this felt almost as intimate as everything else they'd done. And a great deal more on display. She pushed down the shiver of nerves; she was a grown woman, and he was the father of her child.

She glanced up at him to see a strangely uncertain look on his face, a furrow deepening across his forehead. His fingers tightened in hers and then slowly released. As if he had to force them apart.

Bard, he'd felt her tension and he was giving her space. Despite everything they'd shared, he still expected her to push him away.

Keely gently pulled her hand out of Tor's, feeling his body stiffen beside hers and then slump with a resigned sigh.

He was about to step away, but she grabbed his arms and pulled him to face her. "Tor."

His body turned toward her, but his eyes didn't meet hers.

"Tor, I want to tell you something."

He finally raised his dark eyes to hers. "What?"

"This." She went up on her toes, still gripping his arms, and pressed her lips against his.

His breath released in a groan and she pushed herself closer, sliding her arms around his neck. A long moment passed, and then his hands tightened on her waist, pulling her up his body, and he kissed her back.

All she knew was his scent, his warmth, the way he sipped and tasted at her mouth, and she almost forgot his friends were watching until Rafe commented wryly, "I wish Mathos was here. He'd know exactly what to say."

The Hawks chuckled, and Tor and Keely broke apart but stayed holding each other for a moment, looking at each other, his hands firm on her back. "Thank you," he whispered, too softly for his friends to hear.

She smiled up at him and threaded her fingers back through his as they made their way to two open seats at the long table.

Tor pulled a couple of plates in front of them, and they grabbed freshly baked scones, slathering them with pats of yellow butter and big dollops of gleaming blackberry jam and fresh cream.

The food was delicious, but the atmosphere in the room slowly returned to the frosty hostility they'd walked into.

Keely looked between Daena and the others, remembering Rafe's curt tone when he mentioned the Nephilim the day before. "What's going on?"

Val scowled at Daena. "Jos and I went down to check on the Wraiths' camp yesterday. We flew over a couple of times, saw that the camp had been badly decimated by the fire before the rain started but that there were still men living there. Eventually one of them approached the squad at the top of the ridge, carrying a white flag. The whole camp surrendered."

Jos took over the story. "They had been abandoned by Andred and the Wraiths, who took the few boats they had prepared and left them all to die in the fire."

"Fucking Andred," Tor muttered beside her.

"Yes," Rafe agreed. "There wasn't time to douse the flames or make a firebreak. They survived by standing in the lake. It was icy cold, far too cold to stand in. At least half of them died, and the rest were suffering from severe exposure.

The few supplies that Andred left were destroyed. They had nowhere to live, nothing to eat, all of them badly weakened, so they surrendered."

"They're all here?" Keely asked, casting a worried glance toward Alanna. An entire barracks full of men taught to hate the Verturian princess was hardly reassuring.

"Yes and no," Val replied. "We called in extra forces from nearby barracks to help—the reivers have been taken to the local magistrat, the soldiers who abandoned their posts have been sent back to their regiments, whether Verturian or Brythorian, and in the end, only a handful were from Staith."

"But how did you know where to send them?" she asked.

Val tipped his head toward Daena. "Truth seeker."

"If we can trust her," Rafe muttered.

Val snorted rudely. "We can't."

"Didn't you just say that she's been helping?" Tor asked. "And she helped us get free, too."

"Did she though? Or did she use you to get out?" Rafe asked in a voice heavy with suspicion.

Keely frowned. Despite her own initial concerns, Daena had seemed genuinely desperate to get away. "Why would she want help to escape unless she was a prisoner?"

Rafe shook his head. "This is Ramiel's niece. Her family thought she'd died in a fire, but she never bothered to let them know she was still alive. More importantly, she is also Andred's wife—the remaining soldiers were only too glad to tell us all about how she lived with him and helped him set up the camp."

Bard. Keely spun to stare at Daena, taking in her pale face, her wide, fearful eyes and the red flush creeping up her neck.

"I told you already that I am not Andred's wife." Daena let out an aggrieved huff. "If you have to know, he was extremely clear that he would never marry me."

"But you were still working for him," Keely said slowly, remembering the dark moments in Andred's tent. "You tried to convince Tor that I was responsible for Ravenstone."

"And you were rowing when we lost our way on the lake," Tor added in a low voice.

"Gods and Angels." Daena glared at them all. "I already explained that Usna had his dagger in my ribs. And I'm sorry that we got lost on the lake. I assure you that I had even less desire to climb the bloody gorge than you did."

"But how can you explain that Andred's men think you're married to him?" Val demanded.

Daena wiped her hand down her face tiredly. Eventually, she looked up and met their eyes one at a time. "Andred was my lover. He was with me when the reivers attacked the temple, and he pulled me to safety when the beam fell on me. He had his people look after me when I was recovering. And I did live with him, in his tent, for some time. I helped him build his army...." Her voice faded away in misery.

"And then what happened?" Alanna asked more gently.

Daena shook her head, and Keely would have sworn she wasn't going to answer. Finally, she admitted, "I found out that he had no intention of any kind of real relationship with me. I was a truth seeker and a warm body to him. Nothing more. That was when I realized exactly what he was planning. But by then it was too late."

"Surely, if that was the case, you would have left?" Rafe demanded.

Daena gave a rough laugh. "Do you think Andred would have let me wander out, knowing what I knew? Let me send a letter to my family? It was never going to happen."

"No." Rafe shook his head angrily. "You're a truth seeker. You would have known if he lied, right from the beginning."

"I thought so too," Daena agreed sadly, "which is why I never questioned anything." She gave Rafe a pointed look. "The arrogance of the Nephilim."

Daena closed her eyes for a long moment before opening them to look at the Hawks once more. "Andred did tell me the truth…. He just never told me all of it. It's a hard day when you have to look at your reflection in the mirror and admit how badly you misread everything." Her fingers lingered on her scar before she dropped her hands to her lap. "Just how badly you've messed everything up."

Damn. That must have hurt. Even Rafe's gaze softened slightly.

Keely pushed herself closer to Tor, feeling his reassuring warmth against her arm. Despite everything that had happened between them, he had only ever tried to help and protect her. Bard, she was lucky.

Tor scowled down at his plate, a bleak look on his face, full lips turned down, and she knew he would be thinking about Andred. The captain of the Wraiths, general of his own little army, a man with no morals or honor whatsoever, who killed and used people without hesitating. And now he was loose somewhere in Brythoria, with a vendetta against the queen.

There was only one thing they could do. "We have to go back," Keely said softly. "We have to warn Lucilla."

Alanna wrinkled her nose. "Val and I must keep going north. We have to get this treaty signed. We're lucky that the snows have held off this long; if we wait any longer, the passes could close."

"Yes," Keely agreed. "You take Val and the men, and Tor and I will go back to Kaerlud."

Tor wrapped a hand around the back of his neck, slowly shaking his head. "No."

Keely turned to glare at him. "What do you mean, no?"

He met her glare with his own narrowed eyes. "I mean, no. First of all, it's too dangerous for you and the baby to be on the road without any guards—"

Her spine snapped straight. "I can look after myself."

He ignored her and kept speaking. "And secondly, you wanted to go home. You wanted to see mountains and spend time with your mam. If we go back, I don't know when there'll be another chance."

Her whole body softened. "But what about you? I don't—"

"I'll come with you, of course," he stated, as if it was all decided. "Messengers will warn Lucilla."

"That would be a mistake," Val countered. "They need you, Tor. You're the best strategist of all of us. And Andred is a ruthless, intelligent enemy. You should go back."

"I'm not leaving Keely," Tor said firmly.

Keely stared at him for a long moment. He meant it all. He would go with her because it was what she had said she wanted. And because he didn't understand just how valuable he was.

But she did.

She took both his hands, holding them tightly, and looked into his eyes. "I want to go to Kaerlud with you. I know it's the right thing to do. We can visit Verturia another time. We'll take the baby and show her around when she's older."

Tor shook his head, dark eyes filled with uncertainty.

Keely leaned forward, lowering her voice to a murmur only for him. "You're needed at the palace, and I need to be with you. That is where we should make our home."

He bent forward, resting his forehead on hers. "Are you certain, Keely? I know you wanted to go north."

"Yes." She was certain. If he was in Kaerlud, it was the right place for her to be. She would rather be where he was than anywhere else in the world.

Damn. She blinked, realizing the truth—she loved him.

She had never expected to feel love again. And this was nothing like her first love—that had been all excitement and hope and youthful romance. This was deeper. Stronger. Built on mutual respect and admiration as well as insane levels of attraction. The understanding that came from having lived, and lost, and learned what was important.

And Tor was important. Especially to her.

Chapter Twenty-Four

GODS. She *was* certain. He could see the stubborn look in her eye. The spark that told him she'd made up her mind and they would be traveling back to Kaerlud and staying there. Together.

She'd told him she was prepared to take a risk on him. That they were going to be a family. And then she had immediately acted on it, confirming the truth of everything she'd promised. She had kissed him proudly, publicly. Claimed him, for everyone to see, in a way that no one in his life ever had before.

And she wasn't just anyone. She was Keely.

He grinned down at her, wondering whether it would be acceptable to scoop her up and carry her back to their room. She was wearing far too many clothes, and their audience was already annoying. He wanted her back in his bed where he could show her, very, very slowly, exactly how much she meant to him. Just because he *could* let go of his control occasionally, didn't mean he had to.

Her eyes gleamed up at him, the sides crinkling with

amusement. She knew exactly what he was thinking... and she liked it.

He was about to excuse them from the conversation and drag her from the room, when a Mabin guard carrying a rolled parchment tapped at the door.

Alanna waved him inside. "Thank you, Tomas, you can put it here." She gestured to the table next to them. "Were you able to get to the other side of the lake?"

"Yes, Your Highness." Tomas strode forward and unrolled a large map as they all stood to take a closer look.

Tomas pointed to the large blue body on the map. "It would have been difficult to see from this side because of the fog as the rain came in, but the lake is L-shaped. The fire burned the forest that led up to the camp, and the other side is formed from sheer, mountainous walls. We followed the bottom dog-leg and eventually reached a sandy shore with a path out over the hills."

Tor ran his eyes over the map, reluctantly impressed. The spot Andred had chosen for the camp was even better than it had first seemed. Easy access to the Great North Road, close to the passes into Verturia, almost impenetrable, but with a tiny, hard to find, built-in escape hatch. Thank the gods they'd chosen to run up the gorge when they escaped the camp. What were the odds of them finding that one small beach in the storm?

And, even more terrifying, if they hadn't realized Keely was missing as quickly as they did; if he had sat in her farmhouse bedroom like an asshole for even half an hour more, she would have disappeared. They might never have found her. Certainly not in time.

He kissed the top of her head. She was safe, thank the gods.

Tor brought his attention back to the map, running his

finger along the detailed images. The mountain ranges of Verturia spread out to the north of Staith, thin silver lines highlighting the few passes leading into the northern kingdom.

Wide grassy plains lay to the east. A relatively easy couple of weeks' ride to the Asherahn Sea and across to the Continent of Sasania. To the south, the Great North Road —or the longer, winding roads and tracks through the villages and market towns—leading back to Kaerlud.

Andred's camp was destroyed, and the bulk of his army was lost. Which way would he turn? North or west to disappear into the mountains to rebuild his army, east to start a new life in a foreign land, or south?

Val grunted, watching Tor. "Will he hide or fight?"

Tor ran his eyes over the map once more, but he already knew the answer. He settled his finger on a market town a day's march southeast from the lake. "He'll start here, pick up horses and buy supplies. And then, from there… he'll head south toward Kaerlud."

Tor could feel it in his bones. Andred hated Lucilla, and he would have a backup plan for his backup plan. He wouldn't let the loss of a bunch of half-trained reivers and dishonorably discharged former soldiers stop him.

"I agree," Keely said, a reassuring warmth beside him. "Andred wouldn't let his feud go just because he had to change his strategy."

"He genuinely believes that he has the right to be king," Daena chimed in softly, her pale face throwing her burn scar into stark relief. "He honestly thinks that his noble Apollyon heritage puts him in line for the throne and that he would be doing the right thing for the kingdom if he takes control. It is the truth as he sees it."

Rafe glared at Daena as if he still wasn't convinced, but

Tor knew Andred and his arrogance. The man probably did sincerely believe he should be the king. And Ballanor had betrayed him; that would color everything he did.

Andred would go south. But then what? And what did they need to do to stop him?

Tor wrapped a hand around the back of his neck, thinking, while Daena fidgeted across from him. Daena. Andred's former lover. Gods. That was the answer.

"He'll have a woman," he said, working through his thoughts. "Someone in, or close to, the palace. Someone who can give him access to the queen."

Daena looked as if she'd been punched in the gut, but she didn't disagree. She merely nodded sadly. "Probably."

Tor looked at Val. "When the palace guards were questioned by Tristan and Jeremiel, did anyone check the staff?"

"Yes, after Dornar got in, all the staff were spoken to," Val said, frowning. "But—"

"But we didn't know to ask them about Andred," Tor finished for him.

There was a moment of silence as everyone digested the thought. The queen was at risk from yet another threat.

Alanna folded her arms over her chest. "We need to let Lucilla and Tristan know about Andred's plans. And we need to take another urgent look at the people in the palace. How long do you think we have?"

Tor looked down at the map. "It took me three days to get here, riding hard through the day and long into the night. It'll take them longer—they've been forced east, and they won't be in a position to keep changing horses. They'll have to take the back roads. Maybe a week? Then I expect they'll take some time forming a base when they get to Kaerlud."

"What kind of base?" Alanna asked.

Tor considered it for a moment. "If it were me, I'd find a manor home on the outskirts of the city, much like the one Reece found for us. And I'd start building support. Looking for people with power, people who are unhappy with Lucilla."

It was what Andred would do too, he was sure of it. And he knew exactly where a privileged Apollyon from a noble family would start. He would start with the people who had lost the most when Lucilla took the throne. And since she'd cleaned out the palace, there was a large pool to choose from.

"Gods," Val muttered, following his thought. "You're right. He'll look for support among the former councilors. He'll promise them their positions back."

Tor grunted in agreement. "Andred won't rush in. He knows we'll be expecting him; open war was ruled out when he lost his army. He'll aim for a far more subtle approach, and he'll make sure to build his resources carefully, in secret, before he reveals himself. He's almost certainly already been cultivating those relationships—he was remarkably well-informed for a man hiding in the wilds."

"But if we can find his contact in the palace, we can remove them immediately. That'll give us time to hunt Andred down," Alanna said hopefully.

"He'll just find someone else. Assuming he doesn't already have more than one person ready to help him," Daena replied in a low voice. "He's very… persuasive."

Daena was right, Andred was guaranteed to have more than one person already prepared to help him, both living in the palace and outside it—especially after Lucilla's massive purge. He had been a captain in the cavalry, leader of the Wraiths, and one of the most highly regarded of the king's soldiers. He had wealth, charisma and a handsome face. He would have had palace women seducing him and men desperate to join him.

Simply removing Andred's contacts in the palace wouldn't be enough. And, worse, it would warn the Wraiths that they were looking for them within Kaerlud.

"I've got a better idea," Tor said slowly. "Andred believes that Lucilla is too naïve and unprepared to expect him. We need to let him continue to think that. We should act as if she has sent a squad to look for him in the north, while ignoring the danger at home; then use this opportunity to infiltrate his conspiracy."

He resisted the urge to crack his knuckles as he continued. "We need to get someone close to Andred so we can find out what he's planning and identify everyone working with him. That way we can remove them all in one go. But if this is going to work, it must be someone he knows. Someone he trusts."

"Who exactly did you have in mind?" Daena asked suspiciously.

He looked at her silently. She already knew.

"No." Daena barked out an angry laugh. "No way. He'll never let me back in, not after I helped you escape. He hardly trusted me before; now he definitely won't."

Keely patted Daena on her shoulder. "But you didn't help us to escape, we forced you to help us, and then arrested you. And if you arrive back in Kaerlud as a prisoner, filled with hatred toward the people who treated you so badly…." Keely let the sentence fade.

Everyone else was nodding, but Daena was still shaking her head. "It's far too dangerous. Do you have any idea what he'll do to me if he discovers I'm spying on him?" She shuddered.

It was a fair point. He couldn't expect her to go to Andred on her own. "We'll send someone in with you."

Daena glared at him. "Who?"

Gods. That was the question. "I don't know. But I promise I'll find someone suitable, someone who can protect you."

Daena closed her eyes for a moment, and when she opened them, they were shining suspiciously. "What about the soldiers here? They know the truth."

"Do they?" Rafe retorted. "All they know is that you were pretending to be on our side, but we heard the full story when the men from the camp were questioned. As soon as we learned the truth, we arrested you. If they see you riding out under guard, they'll believe it."

Daena's shoulders hunched as she stared down at the table. "You're not going to give me a choice, are you?"

Tor blinked. Gods, what kind of person did she think he was? She'd spent too much time with Andred. "We *are* giving you a choice. There's absolutely no way you can do this if you're not completely committed. If you want to go back to the Temple at Eshcol, we'll arrange for you to go. But you should know that you are likely our best chance at finally creating stability in our kingdom."

"And that's what you want, isn't it?" Keely added softly, looking at Daena. "That's what Andred told you he was working for all along." Keely laid her hand on Daena's arm. "The truth is that you did commit these crimes. You did actively support a revolution. This is your chance to make it right."

"Gods and Angels." Daena let out a long breath. "Can I think about it?"

"Absolutely," Tor agreed. "But think quickly; we need to

leave within the hour. And you'll have to go back to your room under guard for now."

He glanced over to Keely, raising his eyebrow, and she nodded back. This was their best plan. And she was with him—that was the most important thing.

The next hour passed in a frenzy of final arrangements. Tor and Keely would ride together, guarded by a small squad, leaving the carriage to continue north. Alanna had offered it to Keely, who had immediately turned slightly green and promised that she didn't want it.

Keely's trunks full of her belongings would be sent south after them. She would only be taking a few items that could fit behind her saddle and then borrow what she needed from Nim and Lucilla for the first few days when they got back to Kaerlud. Speed was their priority.

It didn't take long before they were standing in the frozen barracks courtyard, the wind plucking at the dry leaves and rattling across the icy cobbles as they checked saddles and lengthened stirrups.

Everyone was there except Daena. Tor still thought she was their best hope for infiltrating Andred's conspiracy, but he had meant what he'd said—he certainly wasn't going to force her. He would use the long journey back to the palace to think of a different solution if that's what it came to.

Alanna stood beside Keely, speaking softly, and Tor hesitated, wondering if he could join them or if they wanted privacy.

Keely chuckled at something Alanna said and then turned to glance over her shoulder, smiling when she saw him, and he made his way toward her. Gods. All he wanted was to have her close to him. She had kissed him in front of the others. He could touch her, couldn't he?

He wrapped an arm around her shoulders, pulling her

to his side, and she immediately softened against him. A stupid grin spread over his face, but there was nothing he could do to stop it. She was the only woman he had ever held in public.

Alanna passed Keely a bundle wrapped in waxed cotton and tied with string. "The kitchens made this for you. Oat and ginger cookies." She gave Tor a stern look. "Please make sure she eats one when she wakes up."

Keely huffed a disgruntled breath as he nodded his agreement, but her eyes shone as she took the parcel from Alanna. "Thank you, my friend, for everything. Please say hello to my mama for me. Tell her the news; she'll be excited about the baby."

Alanna smiled gently. "I will. And you look after yourself on the road, and especially in Kaerlud. We'll be back when the passes clear."

Keely folded her arms and gave Alanna a stern look. "You'd better not leave me there surrounded by Brythorians."

Alanna laughed and winked at Tor. "Oh, I think you'll manage being… ah… surrounded."

Keely choked out a laugh, a deep blush spreading up her cheeks, and Tor couldn't help laughing too. He had never imagined anything that could unsettle Keely.

She nudged him, hard, with her elbow, which just made him laugh harder.

The women said their final goodbyes, and he boosted Keely into her saddle, about to take his own, when Daena emerged from the barracks, led by a Blue guard, arms tied behind her. Her face was pale, but her chin was up, and the guard carried a small roll of provisions from the barracks for her. Tor dipped his chin, silently recognizing her decision and her courage.

He turned to the guard. "Thank you, we'll take her from here." The guard saluted and stepped back as Tor undid the ropes that had held Daena's arms. He lifted his voice to carry to the group of guards preparing to join them on the road. "Daena, you are now in my custody pending your trial in Kaerlud. You stand accused of conspiring with the Wraiths and aiding them in their plot to overthrow Queen Lucilla."

Daena's face grew even paler, but she stood her ground. He turned to look at the soldiers who would be accompanying them and commanded sternly, "This woman is my prisoner. While she's in my custody, I consider her my responsibility. Until she has been tried for her crimes and her fate decided, she is to be treated with all respect. I will take it as a personal insult if she is not." He gave them a slow look. "I would also remind you that Ramiel, the Supreme Justice of the Nephilim, is her uncle."

A few of the men threw worried glances at Daena, hopefully fully understanding the depth of trouble they would find themselves in if they didn't treat her well, and he thought he saw her relax slightly.

Keely stepped closer to Daena, lowering her voice so only the three of them could hear. "You're doing the right thing. Tor will find a way to keep you safe, I promise. You can trust him."

Gods. Such a small sentence, and yet it meant the world to him that Keely had such faith in him. It filled him with warmth. And a difficult to name emotion... gratitude, maybe? Hope? Or something else?

He looked down at her, slowly realizing the truth. It wasn't only gratitude and hope he felt when he looked at her. It was love.

Chapter Twenty-Five

KEELY CRAWLED onto the bed and collapsed face down onto the blankets, leaving her feet hanging over the bottom of the bed and enough space for Tor to lie down at her side.

The sun was low in the sky, just about to dip behind the battlements, and the room was pleasantly dark and quiet. Bard, she was exhausted, and her arm ached relentlessly. Four and a half days of hard traveling—through rain and mud, staying in dingy taverns and spartan barracks—had tired out even the toughest among them. And she felt like she'd fallen down a mountain.

But now, finally, they were back. Back in the palace, but in a new room. One with a sitting area, a screened-off bathing area, and a much bigger bed. Thank the Bard. A beautiful, huge, soft bed. Covered in pillows and cozy blankets. A bed for both of them. Heaven.

They had rushed straight into Lucilla's council room the moment they'd arrived. Thankfully, Lucilla had already received the messages about Andred—as much as they could risk committing to paper, anyway—and she'd taken one look at them and ordered them to go and rest. There was time to take a bath. Time for clean clothes. Maybe even a short nap.

Keely had pulled off her cloak, washed her face in the warm water left in a large basin for them, and then while Tor washed his face and loosened his jerkin, she'd collapsed.

She groaned, and then whimpered with relief as Tor pulled her boots off, one after the other, releasing her aching feet. He crawled up beside her and tugged her onto her side so he could lie behind her, cuddled up against her, his knees slotted into hers, his big arm lying across her hips so his hand could spread out to cradle her belly.

It was the position that they had gone to sleep in every night, no matter how small the bed. And just like each of those nights, his breath blew out gently against her hair as he sighed; the soft sound filled with contented relief, as if he could finally relax.

"We should get changed," she said without opening her eyes. "Don't want to get mud on the sheets."

"Yes, we should," he agreed, not moving.

"Just one more minute."

"M'kay." His voice was deep and soothing, rumbling behind her as she drifted in a tired haze.

Someone knocked heavily on the door, and she flinched. Tor tightened his arm around her and growled.

"Ignore them, and they'll go away," she whispered.

Tor grunted in agreement.

The person in the corridor knocked heavily again. "I want to see you both. Right. Now." It was not a question.

Bollocks. Keely opened her eyes as Tor pushed himself up to sitting. "Was that Ramiel?"

"Think so," Tor muttered, dragging his hand through his hair and leaving it standing in spikes.

"I guess we have to answer."

Ramiel knocked again. "Tor!"

Tor pushed himself up and stalked over to open the door while Keely dragged herself off the bed. Couldn't they have had five bloody minutes?

Ramiel strode in, his purple eyes flashing as a muscle jumped in his jaw. "Tell me you didn't arrest my niece and throw her into the Constable's Tower."

"Bard." She closed the door gently behind him and lowered her voice. "We didn't—"

Ramiel's eyes narrowed, and he turned his glare on Tor. "The palace staff are buzzing with the news that a Nephilim truth seeker called Daena was dragged through the gates by Tor and thrown into the cells. I heard them whispering to each other. It. Was. The. Truth."

Tor shook his head slowly. "Yes. But not the whole truth." He waved toward the pair of armchairs beneath the window. "Have a seat."

Ramiel folded his arms over his chest, raising himself to his full, formidable height, and glared at them both with all the authority of a man who carried the mantle of Supreme Justice. "I'd rather stand."

"Fine," Tor muttered as Keely took his suggestion and lowered her aching body into one of the comfortable chairs.

Tor watched her with concern and then glared at Ramiel, folding his own arms as he answered, "Daena was being held captive in Andred's camp and helped us to escape. But before she was his prisoner, she was his—" He shrugged, looking to her for help.

"Lover," Keely supplied. "Daena was Andred's lover. And she helped him set up the army he planned to attack Kaerlud with."

"Gods," Ramiel muttered. "Surely, she wouldn't. Her

family, my sister.... We've all mourned her, all this time. And to help with...." He scrubbed a hand down his face tiredly.

Damn. Poor Ramiel. His face was strained, and his hair seemed to have gone grayer since she'd seen him last. He lowered himself slowly into the opposite chair.

"Andred lied to her," she said softly, trying to explain.

"That's not possible," Ramiel insisted. "She's a truth seeker."

"I think that's what hurt her the most," Keely admitted. "She was arrogant, thinking no one could lie to her, which made it easier for him. And he was careful. He only told her the things he really believed. He was the one who saved her from the reiver attack, pulled her out of the fire, and organized for her to be nursed back to health. You can understand why she fell for it."

Ramiel pinched the top of his nose with a sigh. "She's going to be tried as a traitor?"

"No." Tor sat heavily on the end of the bed. "For now, Daena's safely ensconced as the only prisoner in the Constable's Tower. She's been given plenty of comforts; blankets, lamps, even books to read, and Jeremiel and Garet are taking personal responsibility for her security and well-being."

Ramiel leaned backward, his frown fading slightly.

But then Tor continued, "There's more."

Ramiel narrowed his eyes. "More?"

"We believe that Andred is going to come back here, to Kaerlud," Tor explained. "He hates Lucilla and believes he should be king. He has the military experience and political connections to make him a genuine threat. Daena is going to infiltrate his conspiracy and report back to us on their plans."

Ramiel thrust himself up and stalked aggressively toward Tor. "You can't be serious."

Tor stared at the Supreme Justice, eyes narrowed, not flinching, but not replying either as long seconds passed in weighted silence.

"Aren't you going to say anything?" Ramiel demanded.

Tor shrugged but didn't reply.

Damn. That was what it looked like. Keely finally understood that this was how Tor dealt with high levels of stress—by going silent. He didn't know what to say, so he said nothing. But it wasn't because he didn't care. She knew just how concerned he was about Daena and how many hours he'd spent worrying about how to keep her safe.

But Ramiel didn't know Tor like she did, and he was a powerful man, used to getting answers when he demanded them. He would enjoy the silent stand-off about as much as she had.

She heaved herself out of her chair and pushed herself between the two men. "Daena wants to do this. She was given the choice, and she decided for herself. I understand that you want her safe—we all do—but we also want the queen and the kingdom safe, and this is the best way. Daena wants this chance to make things right, and you have to give it to her."

A heavy moment passed as Ramiel scowled at Tor and Tor glared back, and then Ramiel took a step back, growling out a frustrated, "Truth."

"She won't be going in alone," Tor added, glancing at Keely. "I've been thinking of someone to go in with her, and I have an idea of someone who'll be perfect. If he agrees."

"Who?" Ramiel demanded.

Tor shook his head. "I haven't had a chance to discuss this with Keely yet."

Ramiel's scowl darkened. "Discuss it now."

"No, I—"

Damn. With Tor's face looking so stoically grim and shut down, she had a suspicion she wasn't going to like his suggestion. But she also knew Tor would have a good reason for his recommendation. And she trusted him.

She laid her hand on his arm. "It's okay; tell me now."

Tor glared at Ramiel for a moment, and then stood and wrapped an arm around her waist as he said quietly, "I think we should send Reece."

She blinked. Bloody Reece. The man who had deeply insulted Alanna, who had sunk himself into a drunken tantrum that lasted weeks, and who had now dropped out of the Hawks to feel sorry for himself.

A man who had been severely beaten by Dornar and his thugs and never given up his squad. Who had apologized to Alanna.

She dipped her chin slowly. "Yes. I see why you chose him. He's believable—he's already out of the Hawks—and he'll never give her up, or Lucilla. But do you honestly think you can convince him to stop wallowing and come back into the squad?"

"I don't know," Tor admitted. "But Mathos has seen him a few times recently and seems to think he might be starting to turn the corner."

Ramiel grunted. "I met with him at Eschol… I can see why you chose him. And I agree, underneath all that angry misery, he has honor."

"Good." Tor nodded tiredly, looking relieved. "If Lucilla approves, then I'll go and see him."

"When are you meeting the queen?" Ramiel asked.

Tor flicked a glance toward the clock on the mantelpiece. "Soon."

Bard. That was all their time gone. If they washed and changed quickly, they could get downstairs in time for dinner. But there would be no nap.

Ramiel looked them up and down, seeming to take in their lack of boots, dirty, rumpled clothes, and weary faces for the first time. "Sorry for interrupting," he said in a gruff voice.

Tor pulled her closer and she leaned into him. "We understand. You needed to know. We'll clean up and meet you down there."

"I am genuinely sorry for disturbing you both." Ramiel tilted his head to the side as he watched her. "You do look exhausted."

Keely tried to give him a reassuring smile, but she was so tired that it came out as more of a grimace. Tor's arm tightened, his hand circling round to settle protectively on the side of her belly.

Ramiel glanced down, and then immediately looked back up, his eyes flashing speculatively. He looked between them for a moment, and then, for the first time since he'd come into their room, he almost smiled. "Well. You need some time to rest. And… ah… if there's any happy news, or you want someone to officiate at any ceremonies, of any kind, I'd be honored."

Beside her, Keely felt Tor go completely stiff, his voice strained and tense as he replied, "Thank you, that is… uh… kind of you."

Not *yes please*, or *I haven't talked to Keely yet*. Not *we'll let you know* or *maybe one day*. Just a deeply uncomfortable thank-you. Damn.

She hardly heard the final words as Tor said goodbye to Ramiel and let him out of their room, quietly locking the door behind him.

Why had Ramiel's offer made Tor so uncomfortable? He was always with her, touching her, delighted to be a family. Excited about the baby. Protective of them both. She knew that. So why had a casual offer made him so uneasy? She could still feel the tension shivering through him.

Old instincts suggested she walk away and get some space to shake off this sudden stab of hurt. Get some fresh air and maybe some perspective. If Tor still didn't trust her, what hope was there for them?

But she had learned her lesson the painful way. She knew that walking out of their room would be the worst mistake she could make. Instead, she let out the breath she was holding and sank into her armchair. She didn't run, not anymore.

Tor took one look at her and strode across the room to her side. Without saying a word, he bent down to lift her into his arms and then carried her to the bed. He lowered her gently onto the blankets and then climbed beside her, bending his elbow to prop his head on his palm while he looked down at her. Then, with slow deliberation, he laid his heavy leg over her thighs, pinning her down.

"What are you doing?" she asked quietly.

"I told you," he stated firmly, "this is how we are going to have all our discussions. I need to know you can't run, and you need to know I want you here. This works the best for everyone."

"I wasn't running," she whispered.

"But part of you wanted to," he replied. "Tell me why."

She ran her hand over her burning eyes. Damn baby-tears. "I felt you get all uncomfortable when Ramiel suggested a ceremony, and I wanted... I mean, not immediately. Bard." She swallowed. "Maybe, one day, eventually, I guess I thought...." She let her sentence fade away.

He smiled down at her. "I want that too. One day. Eventually."

"Want what?"

"Marriage. Oaths. Binding our lives together formally, forever."

"Okay...." That was intense. And didn't make any sense. "Then why...?"

His smile slowly faded. "In Apollyon culture, before a couple marries, they create a symbol together based on the tattoos on their arms. It's an important ceremony that joins the heritage of their two families and adds what they've built themselves. That new tattoo is something unique, special, to them. It's the basis for the markings each of their children will take when they reach sixteen." He leaned down to press a kiss to her forehead. "On the night before the wedding, the symbol is tattooed on the bride and groom, just above their hearts."

He looked down at her, his eyes dark and sad. "You probably already know that when an Apollyon brings their fist to their heart, they're recognizing the person they're saluting as their family, as deeply important to them.... Every time a married person brings their fist up to their chest, they're acknowledging their chosen life partner. Testifying to their shared connection, to the new family that they've created together."

She blinked away the moisture in her eyes. "That's beautiful."

"It is." His voice softened as his lips turned down sadly. "But I no longer have a family. I can't claim any heritage. I literally have nothing to offer you—not even my half of the symbol."

Oh Bard. She reached up to smooth away the lines between his brows. "Tor, you're enough exactly as you are. Just you, that's all I want." She looked into his dark eyes and told him the rest. "I love you."

His breath caught, and his fingers stilled on her cheek as he watched her. "You love me?"

"I love you, Tor," she repeated. "And I want you exactly as you are. We can create our own symbol together, something different, for our family." She smiled. "Maybe even use a little Verturian green."

His fingers trembled against her skin as he leaned down to whisper, "I love you too." His face grew even more serious. "No one else has ever said those words to me before."

"Not anyone? Ever?" She didn't want to believe it, but with what she knew of his parents, it was sadly not even surprising.

"No one. And I've never said them either."

Bard. She wrapped her arms around his neck and lifted her face to kiss him. Hoping he could feel just how much she loved him.

He pulled away, his lips hovering so close she could feel his warm breath on hers. "Tell me again."

"I love you, Tor."

"Gods." He threaded his fingers through her hair and tilted her head up toward his. "I love you too." And then he kissed her again.

Chapter Twenty-Six

REECE SAT in his usual corner of *The Cup*, nursing his third ale and wondering whether yeast, malt and water could be considered food. The roasting pork that had been cooking over a spit for the last several hours smelled divine, and his mouth watered at the idea of salty meat and rich gravy. But he was down to his last few groats, and he'd had to choose —food or ale—and ale had won.

How else was he going to make his fucking beast shut the hell up?

Reece lowered his head to the table and let out a low belch. It wasn't as if anyone else gave a shit what he was doing. He should have taken the purse Mathos had offered. But at the time he'd been filled with righteous indignation mixed with just enough self-hatred that he'd told Mathos to stuff it.

He couldn't quite decide if the fact that Mathos hadn't come back since then was a good thing or a bad thing.

He was so tired of what his life had become. A dismal room within smelling distance of the Fish Street Dock. Only a few dirty streets from the flower market where his mother had eked out a miserable existence for them both... until she'd died and he'd learned was real misery was all about.

And here he was again. The full fucking circle. Gods, it was pathetic. At least his savings were enough for a room. And ale. But arguably not for much longer. Ten years in the king's army didn't amount to much in the end. Especially if you started as an infantry sapper.

Still, he'd made it all the way to the Hawks. Handpicked by Tristan himself on the northern battlefields. And then a Blue Guard. That was something. Wasn't it?

A throat cleared beside him, and he opened one eye to see Visker, the tavern keeper, lowering a heavily loaded platter to his table. Juicy pork with thick slices of bread slathered in butter, roasted carrots, cabbage, and a large ladleful of rich gravy steaming gently over it all. Gods, it smelled amazing.

He pushed himself up and gave Visker a suspicious look. He'd spent enough time in the tavern to know the innkeeper by name, sure, but he also knew Visker didn't do handouts. "What's this?"

"Lad from the market came in, paid for the food, told me to give it to you—with this." He passed over a small, folded note. It was heavily sealed—not that a seal would make all that much difference to anyone who really wanted to read it.

"What lad?" Reece asked, ignoring the note.

Visker wiped his hands down his apron before shrugging. "Dunno."

"Why would he give this to me?"

Visker rolled his eyes, not bothering to answer.

Reece looked down at the food even more suspiciously than he'd looked at the innkeeper.

The older man shrugged again. "I served it myself not one minute ago, same as all the other food in here. Might as well eat it."

Reece nodded slowly and then picked up a slice of bread and took a bite. It was warm, slightly chewy and everything he'd imagined. Gods.

"You going to read that?" Visker asked, nodding toward the paper.

"No."

Visker huffed and walked away, and Reece tucked the offensive note into his pocket to think about later.

By the time he'd finished his meal, sobriety was rearing its head, and the irritating rumble of his beast had returned.

Fuck it all. He had fully intended to drink enough to keep it quiet—at least long enough to stumble back to his dirty little room—and for the love of everything holy, try to finally get some sleep.

His beast twisted in displeasure, flicking an irate shiver of deep indigo scales up his wrist. *Can't sleep with no one to watch our backs.*

Reece growled back. Trying to silence the beast's constant demands and running commentary had landed him in at least half of his current troubles, and the last thing he needed was another fuckup.

Then stop drinking, his beast replied smugly. Reece didn't bother to credit that with a response.

He left the tavern and wandered down a narrow alley to take a long piss against a wall before making his way slowly through the city. He took a random, circuitous route, watching carefully behind him. But no one was remotely interested in one more rough-looking former soldier, and he finally made his way into his lodgings and up the stairs to his room, grumbling about the waste of his time.

He lit the lamp and opened the note. It was only six words. *Usual dock. The Kennel. Usual time.*

Fuck. Only a handful of people knew he had grown up near Fish Street Docks. And only one would send this kind of vague passive-aggressive note. Mathos, the bloody busybody who always knew everything about everyone. Mathos who, like all the Hawks, would remember their two o'clock in the morning operations using their Tarasque night vision to guide the squad deep into enemy territory to steal supplies and disrupt encampments.

Not their enemy anymore. Gods. Had they ever been? Or was that all just another lie?

He lay down on the narrow bed, still wearing his clothes. He was far too tall for the bed, and his feet hung over the bottom whatever he did, but he couldn't be assed with taking off his boots. Or even his coat. Why bother when it was rumpled anyway? The room was cold, and it was an effort to take it off just to put it back on again.

You used to care. Used to take pride in how we looked.

"Yeah, well, it didn't do us any favors, did it?" he muttered back. How many hours had he spent working on his accent, spending his wages on the right clothes, the right boots, always being the most charming member of the squad? How many hours had he spent making certain that no one would ever look at him and see the half-feral street boy he'd been? Making certain that everyone loved him. Wanted him. And in the end, none of it had meant anything at all.

Helaine was always a bitch. I told you not to touch her. Even Tor told you.

Reece sighed. That much was true. But she was beautiful and refined and everything he'd wanted. He'd loved having her beside him at palace functions, loved having her in his bed, and he'd genuinely thought she'd help the Hawks. That the time they'd spent together, the plans they'd shared, would have counted for something. He hadn't imagined that she'd smile to his face and then turn around and stab him in the back. Just like his fucking mother.

Mama did the best she—

Shut. The. Fuck. Up.

His beast subsided into an annoying string of low mutterings while Reece lay staring at the ceiling ignoring its complaints, and the bells in the distant Nephilim temple rang out the hours.

Finally, it was time. Reece pushed himself off the bed and let himself out of the lodgings. Somewhere more salubrious might have been bothered by the hours he kept, but in this part of Kaerlud, nobody cared.

He didn't know exactly where he was going, but with Mathos's sense of humor, it had something to do with dogs.

The docks were still busy—the tides didn't care what time it was—but the crowd was decidedly disreputable, even by the usual standards of sailors off fishing boats. The stink of decaying fish guts mixed with mud and ancient refuse made his eyes water and burned the back of his throat, despite the thick woolen scarf covering his nose and mouth.

He passed a dingy tavern and then stopped. Went back. Looked at the sign swinging outside again and groaned. *The Dog House.* Fucking Hilarious.

He pushed his way into the busy taproom. Even a few streets over, the doors would have already been closed for the night, but not here where sailors came and went at all hours.

He glanced around the tavern, raking his eyes over the patrons, and quickly settling on a dark shadow in the corner. The shape was cloaked, face hidden inside a hood, the man barely visible in the dim edges of the room. But Reece would know a member of his squad anywhere, and he knew this man.

It was not, however, Mathos.

He made his way to the table and sat down opposite Tor, who pushed a mug of ale across to him.

He took a sip. Bitter and heavily watered. Not nearly good enough to compensate for dragging him out in the fucking cold. Reece crossed his arms over his chest and raised an eyebrow. "You think you're bloody amusing."

"What?" Tor asked, frowning.

"*The Dog House*? Really?"

Tor chuckled. "Not my idea."

"Mathos is a bastard," Reece grumbled as Tor shrugged. They each took a sip. Gods, it was even worse the second time. Tor wrinkled his nose and pushed his ale away.

"I wouldn't have thought all this sneaking around was your style," Reece pointed out. He needed to get whatever this was over with so he could go home and lie awake in the discomfort of his own bed.

Tor watched him for a long moment—assessing—before nodding slightly. "I need your help."

Reece narrowed his eyes. None of this was remotely reassuring. Not the location, not the time, not the secrecy. And definitely not the concerned look on Tor's face.

"Help with what exactly?" Reece asked as his beast turned over uncomfortably.

Tor leaned forward and dropped his voice even lower. "Did you ever wonder what happened to the traitors of Ravenstone?"

A ripple of scales slithered up his arms. In the aftermath of the massacre, they had been certain the traitors were Verturian. They had blamed Alanna and Val.

Later they'd learned the truth: Ballanor had arranged the whole thing and Alanna and Val were innocent. But in all the frantic days of trying to survive, no one had questioned exactly who could have carried out the massacre. Honestly, given the brutality of King Geraint's death and the rune-covered arrows left behind, Reece had still suspected the Verturians.

But that wouldn't explain the grim look on Tor's face. "You know who it was," Reece said slowly.

A muscle ticked in Tor's jaw. "It was the Wraiths, under Andred."

"What!" His voice came out as a hoarse whisper. "That's not possible." Reece had known some of those men. He'd been friends with them. He'd grieved them, believing them killed in the massacre. Believing they'd been slaughtered by the Verturians working with Ballanor.

Tor looked around as if checking no one could hear their whispered conversation. "They've been living up north ever since Ravenstone. Ballanor promised them gold and power, but then betrayed them and cut them off after the massacre. They've been building an army ever since."

Shit. His scales were all the way up his neck, the heavy stench of the tavern suddenly cloying and stifling. Reece shook his head. "I don't—"

Tor cut him off, his eyes dark. "They kidnapped Keely."

Fuck. Reece didn't even know what to say. What would Andred do with Keely? Gods, the man had zero concerns about anyone except his own squad, and even they came a distant second to his own skin. How could Tor be sitting there so calmly?

"I got her back," Tor added. Well, that made more sense. "And we came straight back to Kaerlud to warn Lucilla. We think the Wraiths are on their way here."

Thank the gods, Keely is safe.

Reece and Keely did not have a good history. Just thinking about her and Alanna made his beast writhe in shame, but he actually liked her. Liked her fiery spirit and the way she kept Tor on his toes. He was genuinely glad she was okay.

But if Keely was safe, then why was Tor meeting him in secret in this dingy pub? Gods. There was only one possible reason why the team strategist would set up a clandestine meeting with a former member of the squad while a power-hungry Apollyon with an ax to grind was running around Kaerlud.

"Fuck no." Reece shook his head, getting ready to push away from the table. "You're insane," he hissed, glaring at Tor.

Yes, his beast offered. *This is exactly what we should do. Make things right. Earn our way back to the squad.*

Tor reached up to wrap a hand behind his neck, and it knocked his hood enough that Reece could see just how exhausted his former friend was. Dark rings under his eyes. Unshaved. Gods. Whatever happened, it had been bad. And then he must have ridden back day and night.

And then Tor had come directly to find him. Reece honestly had no idea how he felt about that.

"We expect the Wraiths to arrive in Kaerlud in the next few days and immediately start working to overthrow Lucilla," Tor said, almost too quietly to hear. "Knowing Andred, there's probably already a plan in place. We need to know what they're going to do. And we need the names of everyone who supports him." Tor dragged a heavy hand down his face. "We expect he'll approach former councilors first, so keep that in mind. None of them are above suspicion. Frankly, you should probably start with my family first. My former family."

"Just like that?" Reece couldn't keep the sarcasm from his voice. "I'll just drop in for tea, shall I?"

Tor pierced him with a dark look. "No one else can do this, Reece. We need you."

Reece forced himself to stay in his seat as Tor's words echoed between them. There had to be a better way. Spying on Andred was a certain ticket to the Abyss, and the road would be as painful as any demon could imagine. "Surely Lucilla can just pay whatever Ballanor owed them. Add in some compensation for the time they've spent in hiding, and be done?"

"It's not that easy. Andred is responsible for the murder of Geraint and the massacre of Ravenstone, as well as the death of half the army he started to build in the north. And he hates Lucilla; he blames her alongside Ballanor and thinks she's useless and naïve. He's utterly convinced himself that he should be the king, through his grandfather's line. Believes it enough that he was able to convince a truth seeker to help him."

"What kind of idiot truth seeker would work with the Wraiths?" Reece grumbled.

For the first time, Tor looked uncertain. "Well… that's part of why we need you."

"Why?" Reece demanded, already knowing he was going to hate the answer.

"The truth seeker's name is Daena. We need you to work with her, protect her," Tor admitted.

"Daena! Ramiel's niece Daena, who the entire city is busy gossiping about being locked in the Constable's Tower for treason… that Daena?" His beast growled, low and menacing—whether at Tor or him, he couldn't tell.

Tor nodded. "Yes."

"Absolutely not."

"Daena's already agreed. She can get close to him. But I can't send her in there alone."

"This is a suicide mission. A suicide mission made even less palatable by having to babysit an idiotic, lying woman who is guaranteed to get us killed even faster."

"Daena got us out of Andred's camp, Reece. She helped save Keely."

"By betraying her lover." His beast's rumbling growl was loud enough that Tor could probably hear it.

"He wasn't her lover anymore, he—"

"Yeah," Reece interrupted, rolling his eyes, "that makes it so much better."

Tor winced. "Fuck. You know what I mean. Andred is a bastard who used her badly. She's on our side."

Reece scowled. "How do you know that? How do you know she won't turn on you next?"

Tor sighed heavily. "I don't know. No one knows for sure. But this is our best chance. If you have another idea, by all means, let me know."

They stared at each other in silence for a long, painful moment, the mugs of ale abandoned between them.

We should do this, his beast suggested. *We can watch Andred as well as Daena. The Hawks need us.*

"Please, Reece," Tor said eventually.

Fuck it to hell. Did he have to say please?

Please, his beast added. *Anyway, why do you care if it's a suicide mission… what exactly were we doing that was a better use of our life?*

Reece ignored his beast's insulting commentary and took a sip of the ale, grimacing at the watery bitterness.

Obviously, there were no better options to suggest. Tor

would have thought of this in every possible direction already. He would have come up with something else if he could. Something that didn't involve the squad's biggest loser.

Fucking bollocking damnation… He was going to have to do it.

He pushed away the mug of foul ale, already regretting his decision. "Okay, fine. Tell me what you need."

Epilogue

TOR HEARD Keely before he saw her. Her voice was raised, singing into the wind on the freezing battlements. Her heavy coat was lifted by the swirling drafts, her hair tugged loose from its braid, whipping wildly behind her.

He hardly felt the icy wind or noticed the heavy clouds and threatening rain. Keely was singing, and all was right with the world.

Her gloved hands were pressed against the rough stone as she leaned out, facing the dirty gray waters of the Tamasa. If they could see past that wide river, through the woods and past the miles of fields, lying fallow now for winter, past the moors and dales, and eventually follow the land as it rose up the distant escarpment, they would see the tall mountains of her homeland.

Was that what she thought of when she stood here, facing north?

She looked over her shoulder and saw him walking toward her, and she stopped singing, a wide smile spreading over her face.

Gods. That smile. That vibrant spark that was entirely Keely. Its warmth filled his dark places, gave him everything he had ever needed.

He came to stand behind her, wrapping his arms around her waist so that his hands could settle on her belly. It was softly rounded now, still small, but he knew their child was growing there.

It still stunned him that he had the right to hold her. To touch her. To wake up beside her. Gods, he was lucky.

"I thought I'd find you here," he admitted.

She nestled back, resting her head on his shoulder, relaxing into his embrace. "I like it," she agreed.

"Missing home?" he asked gently.

"Not exactly." She huffed out a breath. "I miss the mountains sometimes, but mostly I like the space. I like the quiet, the break from all the chaos inside. I like the cold and the fresh air." She twisted so she could look up at him. "Would it help if I told you that when I lived in Castle Duneidyn, I used to stand on the battlements and look south?"

He smiled down at her. It did help. He wanted her to be happy, to have what she needed.

"How's the pea?"

She rolled her eyes. "Apparently she likes apple pie for breakfast."

"Then apple pie she shall have," he agreed seriously.

Keely laughed, settling her hands over his and holding him against her belly as she turned back toward the river. "You came in late," she said softly.

Tor dipped his head so he could speak softly beside her

ear, even though they were far from any guards. "He was able to get away for half an hour."

Her body tensed in his arms. "And?"

"He's in."

"Good." She softened slowly. "And he's working with… her."

"Mm-hmm. He's still not pleased."

"Do you think it'll be okay? The two of them working together?" she asked.

Gods, he hoped so. "I think she'll be good for him—the first woman he's ever spent time with who can hear a lie—or maybe they'll kill each other. One of the two."

Keely chuckled in agreement, and then grew more somber. "I wish this was over."

"Me too." He wished it was over more than he could begin to express. Sneaking around and spying was not his way, and he was so tired of violence. But this was his mission. He had the best insight into Andred, the best chance of predicting what the Wraiths would do next. And someone had to liaise with Reece and Daena.

He let his cheek rest on the top of Keely's head, the silk of her hair soft against his skin. Reminding himself of why he needed to do this. Exactly who he had to keep safe. And remembering why he'd come to find her.

"Would you mind looking at something with me?" he asked. "In our room."

Keely let out an inelegant snort. "Don't tell me… it's your great… big… sword."

He chuckled. "Something like that."

They walked, hand in hand, along the battlements and back into the castle, down the stairs and along the corridor to their suite.

It was the longest walk he'd ever taken. Each step felt

like a thousand miles, the seconds counted out in the heavy thuds of his heart. His palms were damp, but he didn't dare to let go of her hand to wipe them. Instead, he forced himself to relax, to keep his shoulders down.

She loved him. She chose him. It was going to be fine. Gods.

He desperately wanted the relief of cracking his knuckles, but that would be even worse than wiping his palms.

They made it to their door, and he opened it for her, swallowing heavily. She stepped through, her eyes on him as he locked up and turned to face her.

Keely arched a fiery brow. "What did you really want to show me? And why do you look like you want to puke?"

Gods, this woman. He gestured across the room. "It's on the bed."

"Yeah, that's what they all—" Her words faded away as she turned and saw the large wooden box.

It was about the length of his arm, carved from oak and stained jade green. The color of her eyes and the knotwork around her biceps. Mathos had helped him find the best woodcarver in Kaerlud, and the talented Mabin artist had captured the towering mountains and rolling northern forests as if he'd flown over them himself. Perhaps he had.

She ran her fingers softly over the delicate image. "What's this?"

Tor's voice was gruff as he replied, "Look inside."

Keely gently opened the lid, gasping when she saw what was nestled in the box. A brand-new crossbow in polished yew and gleaming steel. The bolts' shafts were carved with Verturian runes, and the fletching was black.

She looked up at him, her eyes gleaming as she bit her lip.

Tor sank down on the bed beside her. "No one should have ever taken your weapons away, Keely. I can't think of a warrior that I would rather have at my side than you."

She blinked, her smile wobbling as she watched him, and he leaned closer, wanting to be near her. Needing to touch her. "You can take it out."

She lifted the crossbow from its case and then paused, noticing the folded parchment that had been hidden beneath it. The parchment with her name scrawled across the top in his heavy hand.

She carefully moved the crossbow and its box to the table, and then sat down beside him on the bed, holding the parchment. She shot him a confused look and then lowered her head to concentrate as she opened the note.

This was his chance. He slipped off the bed, going down on one knee in front of her.

His movement distracted her, and she looked up, her eyes widening as they flew to his. He could see the parchment trembling in her fingers.

"What's this?" Her voice was a whisper.

It seemed safest to start with the drawing in her hand. "It's a cuirass—named after the armor that covers your heart." He looked down on the sketch he had spent so many hours working on; on the stylized crossbow interlaced with a heavy greatsword, the sword's blade pointing down, weaving between the limbs and the strings of the bow. Twining over both was a vibrant whorl of fuchsia heather flowers. The heather that covered the slopes of the far northern mountains.

He cleared his throat. "It could be part, if you like it, of the cuirass that we share. The tattoo over our hearts."

"Over our hearts?" she repeated slowly, the parchment

shaking so badly that he took it gently and laid it down beside her so he could take her hands in his.

"Keely, I love you. I want to stand with you and beside you. I want to be the sword to your crossbow. I want to protect you, as I know you'll protect me. I want to be together, to share the future, whatever we decide that should be."

He took a deep breath and tried to smile. "Keely, will you marry me?"

She stared at him in silence as a tear squeezed out from the corner of her eye and tracked slowly down her face. Gods. It still stabbed him in the heart every time she cried. And for a moment, a long, terrifying moment, he thought she might say no.

But then she leaned forward to rest her forehead against his. "Yes. I would be honored to be your wife. I will stand at your side. I will spend all my days and all my nights loving you, trusting that you will always come back to me, as I will always come back to you. And at the end of our time in this world, I will be grateful for every moment we've had together."

Gods.

He let go of her hand to run his thumb over that beautiful, puffy, bottom lip. And then he kissed her, tasting salt and sweetness and Keely.

She wrapped her arms around his neck and pulled him closer, until all he could feel was her, warm and soft and strong; all he could smell was her, wild heather and fresh air; and all he knew was their love, deep and true and right, surrounding them both.

Thank you!

Thank you for reading *Tor*! I hope you enjoyed his and Keely's story. I love them both and they've been an important part of the story since the beginning. It has been wonderful to finally give them the happy ending they deserve (especially after all the pain they've been through).

Next up, Reece is going to be looking for redemption. Daena is going to make him work for it—and his beast has a few things to say about it all too. I can't wait.

If you'd love to spend some more time in Brythoria (and possibly find out a little more about where the Mabin and the Tarasque came from (hint!)) please join my mailing list at www.jennielynnroberts.com.

I promise first looks, all the news, and bonus content including a **free Hawks novella:**

Kaden
He has to leave. He can't take her with him. And he needs to go *now*.

Kaden has always kept his true feelings for Ava hidden—he couldn't give her hope when he knew there was none. He must walk away even if it breaks her heart and destroys him *and* his beast.

Ava can't let losing Kaden stop her; she has patients to care for and a secret of her own hiding in the icy northern mountains. But there's danger on those lonely slopes—danger that could cost them far more than broken hearts.

Will Kaden walk away like he's always planned? Or will he risk everything for a happily ever after with Ava—and trust her to save him back when the time comes?

Kaden is a prequel novella set six generations before the events in The Hawks series. It's a hundred page (fully resolved!) sexy, steamy, adult fantasy romance with a guaranteed happy ever after.

Sign up for my newsletter and download for free:

Get Kaden now!

Finish the series with Reece and Daena

Reece

She's everything he doesn't want.

Honorable. Beautiful. Strong... wait, what?

Reece lost everything. Twice. Now, he finally has a chance to earn back his place with the Hawks. There's only one problem: he has to work with Daena. He doesn't trust her. He doesn't even like her. And if his beast would just shut up about how perfect she is, that would really help.

If there's one kind of man Daena's learned to stay well away from, it's a handsome liar. But the more Reece reveals—the more she glimpses the vulnerable soul he's hidden for so long—the closer she wants to get.

But now is not a good time to get close to anyone. Reece and Daena are undercover on a dangerous mission. They're surrounded by enemies and one wrong move could mean catastrophe.

Can they let go of the past and find a future, standing strong together? Or will they fall, and take the kingdom down with them?

Reece, the final book in The Hawks series, is a sexy, enemies to lovers, adult fantasy romance full of swords, shifters (kind of), and tons of action.

The Hawks

Sexy adult fantasy romance series (now complete!) full of swords, shifters (kind of), and tons of action. For lovers of fast-paced adventure, soul mates, and found family.

Tristan

His redemption might be* her *downfall…

Val

He'll do anything to save her. And then he'll say goodbye…

Mathos

All he has to do is find the princess, help her claim the throne, and not fall in love with her. Easy…right?

Tor

What is it about her that makes him lose his mind? Every. Damn. Time.

Reece

She's everything he doesn't want.

Honorable. Beautiful. Strong… wait, what?

About the Author

Jennie Lynn Roberts believes that every kickass heroine should have control of her own story, a swoony hero to fight beside her, and a guaranteed happily ever after. Because that doesn't always happen in real life, she began creating her own worlds that work just the way they should. And she hasn't looked back since.

Jennie would rather be writing than doing anything else—except for spending time with her gorgeous family, of course. But when she isn't building vibrant new worlds to get lost in, she can be found nattering with friends, baking up a storm, or strolling in the woods around her home in England.

If you want to talk books, romance or reluctant heroes with Jennie, feel free to contact her.

Printed in Great Britain
by Amazon